Ember's End

Books by S. D. Smith

Publication Order:

The Green Ember
The Black Star of Kingston (The Tales of Old Natalia Book I)
Ember Falls: The Green Ember Book II
The Last Archer: Green Ember Archer I
Ember Rising: The Green Ember Book III
The Wreck and Rise of Whitson Mariner (The Tales of Old Natalia Book II)
The First Fowler: Green Ember Archer II
Ember's End: The Green Ember Book IV
The Archer's Cup: Green Ember Archer III

Best read in publication order, but in general,
simply be sure to begin with The Green Ember.

The Green Ember: Book IV

Ember's End

S. D. Smith
Illustrated by Zach Franzen

Story Warren Books

Ember's End

Trade Paperback edition ISBN: 978-1-951305-03-1
Hardcover Edition ISBN: 978-1-951305-04-8
Also available in eBook and Audiobook.

Story Warren Books
www.storywarren.com

Cover and interior illustrations by Zach Franzen.
Photo with Author's Note by Graeme Pitman.
Art on final page by Chris Koelle.

Maps created by Will Smith and Zach Franzen.

Printed in the United States of America.
21 22 23 24 25 03 04 05 06 07

Story Warren Books
www.storywarren.com

For Josiah Clair Preston Smith

Melius ergo est duos simul esse quam unum
habent enim emolumentum societatis suae.
Si unus ceciderit ab altero fulcietur vae soli
quia cum ruerit non habet sublevantem.

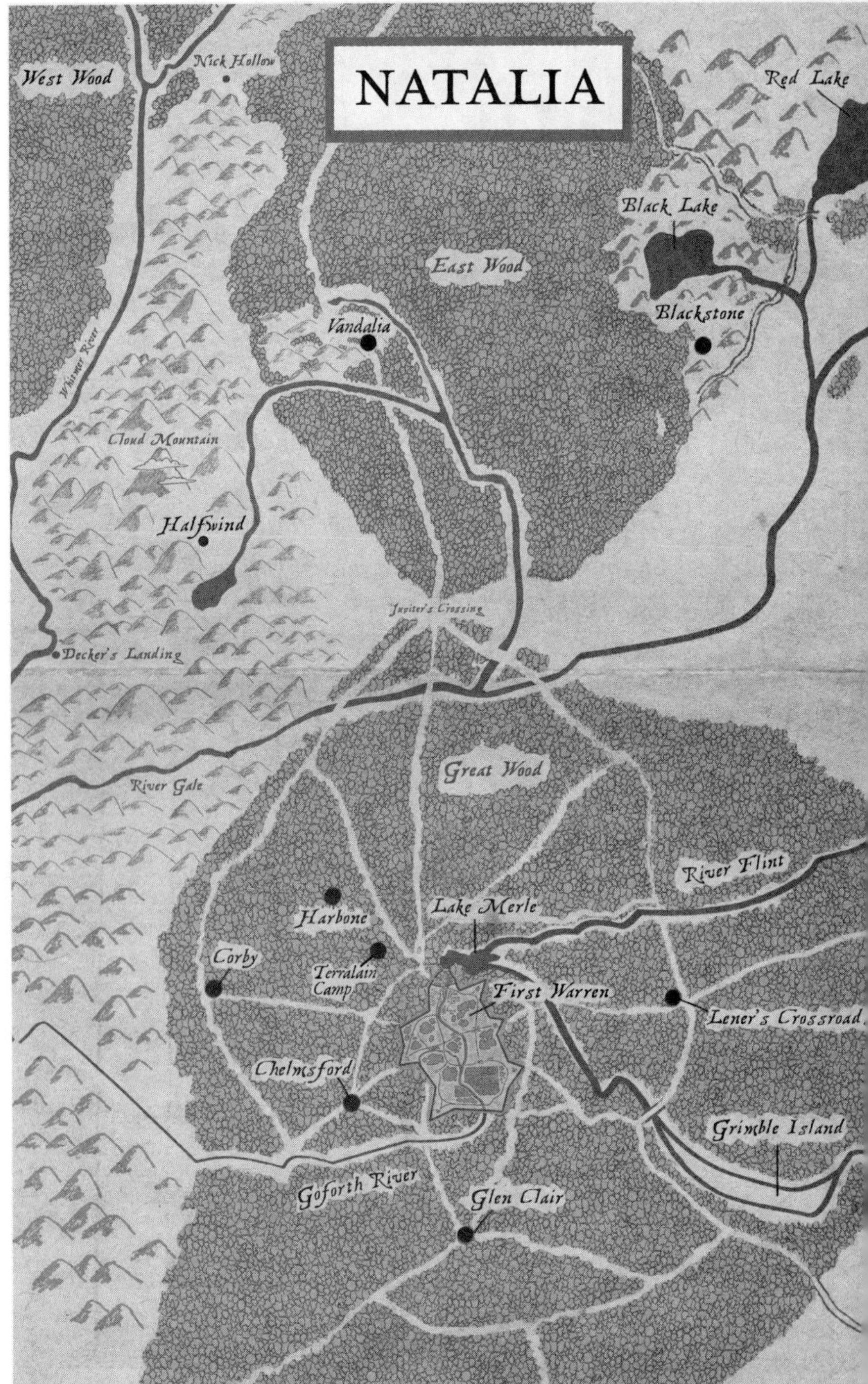

NATALIA
West Wood
Nick Hollow
Red Lake
Black Lake
East Wood
Blackstone
Vandalia
Whisper River
Cloud Mountain
Halfwind
Jupiter's Crossing
Decker's Landing
Great Wood
River Gale
River Flint
Harbone
Lake Merle
Corby
Terralain Camp
First Warren
Lener's Crossroad
Chelmsford
Grimble Island
Goforth River
Glen Clair

Red Valley

Deserted Camp

Bog of the Bleaks

High Bleaks

Morbin's Lair

Akolan

The Waste

Grey Grove

Faraway Forest

Low Bleaks

Krebb's Stand

Hammertop

Kingston

River Fay

Seddleton

Ayman Lake

Massie

Halfmoore Hills

Akolan

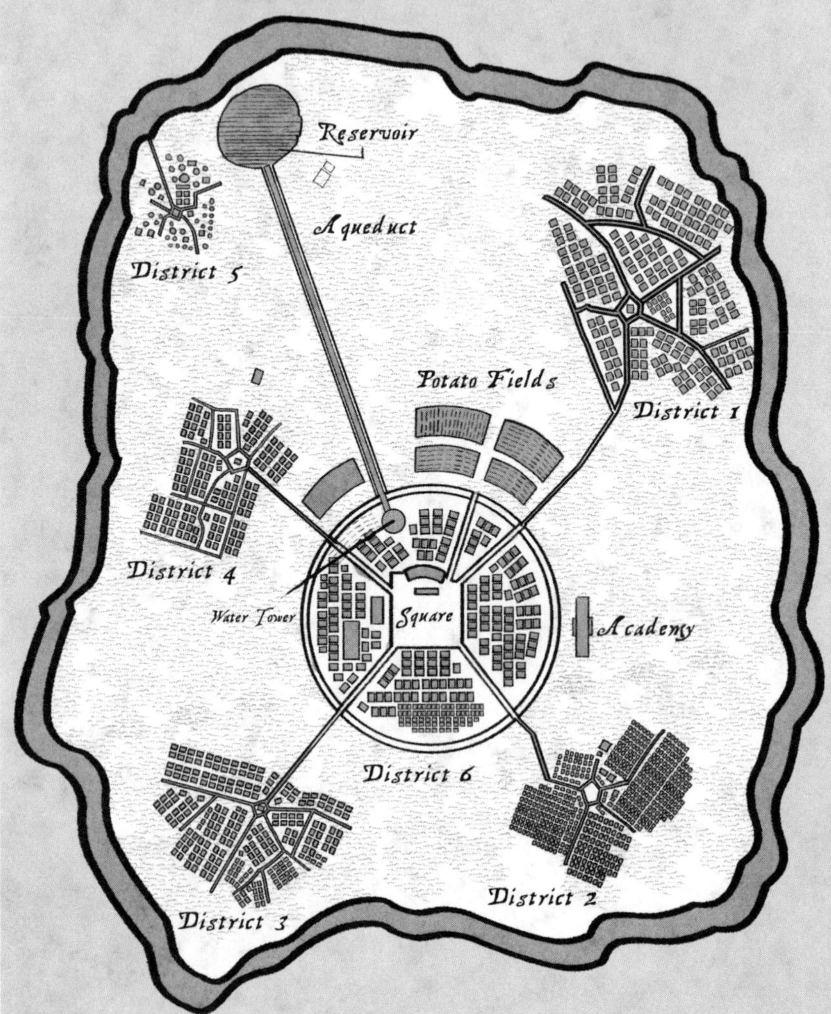
Reservoir
Aqueduct
District 5
Potato Fields
District 1
District 4
Water Tower
Square
Academy
District 6
District 2
District 3

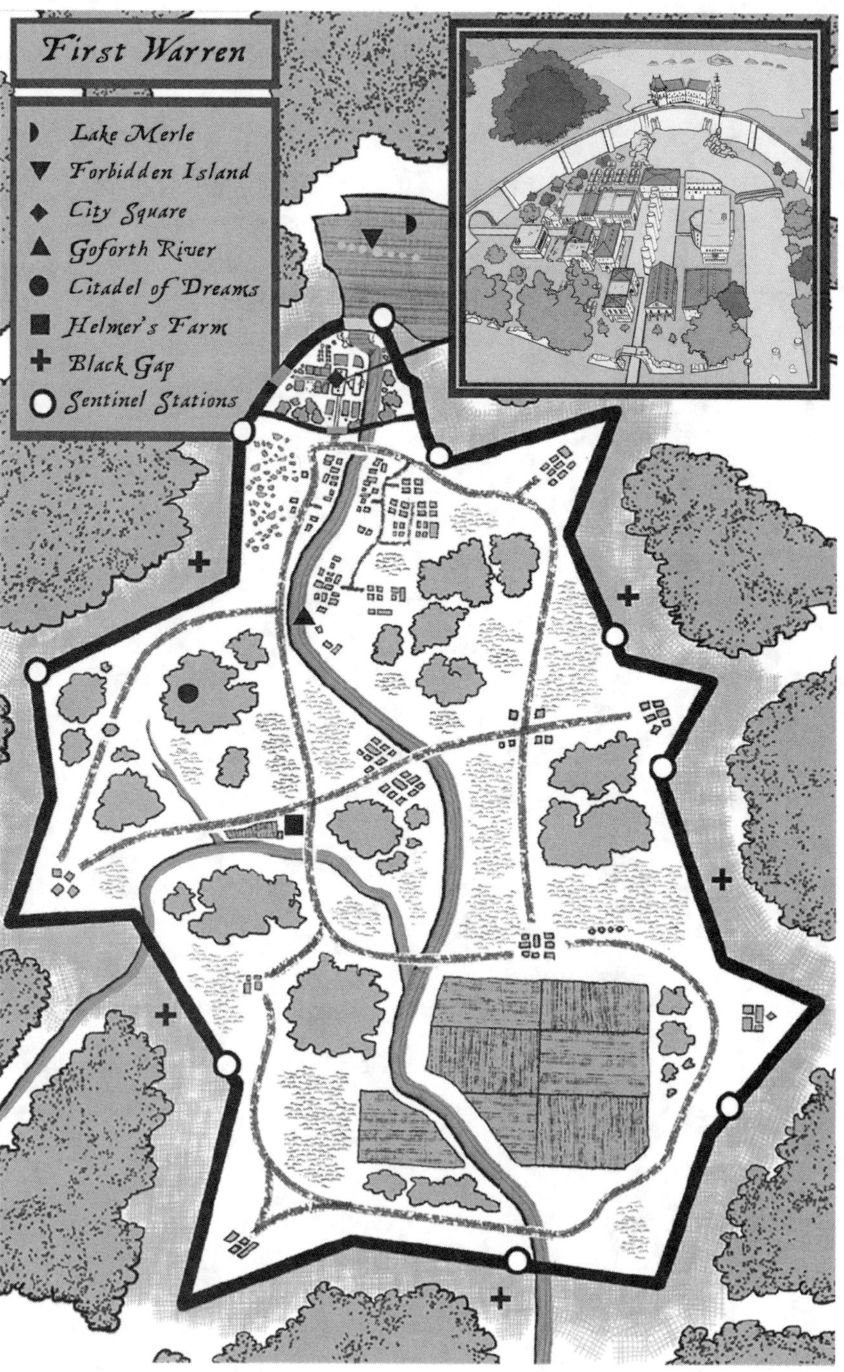

First Warren
Lake Merle
Forbidden Island
City Square
Goforth River
Citadel of Dreams
Helmer's Farm
Black Gap
Sentinel Stations

Prologue

Massie hurried to the top of the central mountain, where Prince Lander stood amid a ruin of smoking rocks. The stench of death hung in the fetid air.

"Your Highness," Massie said, dropping to one knee. "The lords await your decision."

Prince Lander's strange faraway gaze traced the river below; the forest extended from each bank into an incomprehensible distance. "Captain Massie, this wood . . . it is great, I think. I look at it and seem to see our kind thriving here."

Massie rose and turned to take in the spreading forest. "Yes, sir. The wood is vast and uncultivated. It would require tremendous work."

"It will be my life's work," Lander said, unblinking eyes gazing off to the horizon.

Massie passed his hand over his eyes. "Sir, the decision?"

Lander turned to Massie, but his eyes kept their peculiar look. "We must bury the threat and our best weapon against it together."

"What will we do, Your Highness?" Massie asked, eyes closing tight. "It will be too easy to find."

"We'll dam the river, build up our warren, and make this mountain forbidden. We will try to forget."

"But sir, what if the worst happens?"

"Then one from my line will remember. And when the time comes, he will rise."

From *Prince Lander and the Dragon War*

Chapter One

Jo, Cole, and Heyna

Jo Shanks crept through a tangle of trees on the edge of the Terralain camp. Looking back, he saw that Cole and Heyna Blackstar were still behind him. The jet-black twins seemed at ease, despite the unsettling odds of being only three among thousands of enemies. Jo wasn't so calm. He absent-mindedly patted his quiver, locked down and fastened tight on his right side, and pressed ahead. He had to be careful of these new arrowheads with their tiny flint-and-fire mechanisms. *I don't need to blow myself up here.* He smirked and adjusted his pack, with its ramrod staves crossed in an X pattern poking out behind him.

He paused at the edge of a clearing. Bright blazes from successive sentry fires dotted the way to the camp's center, splashing dashes of light along a path clotted with guards. Jo frowned.

It will be better if we don't have to kill any rabbits to get what we came for.

Jo eased past a momentarily distracted sentry and disappeared again into a black patch of shadow, closer now to

the elusive center of the camp. He peered ahead, trying to make out—among the shadows shaking in the flickering firelight—which of those tents might hold the answers he sought.

I wonder if Cole and Heyna made it past the last guard yet. Glancing back, he nearly cried out. Cole's face was inches from his own.

Behind her smirking brother, Heyna smiled. "You seem tense, Jo," she whispered.

Jo sighed, shaking his head. "I'm prepared to die by getting caught," he whispered, "but not by heart attack because of you two idiots creeping up on me like that."

"Which tent is our target, Jo?" Cole asked, peering into

the darkness. Jo turned back to the camp.

Heyna quietly swept aside a knot of braided branches to get a closer look. "Where's a tent that looks like it belongs to a scary old maniac?"

"He doesn't scare me," Jo said, unable even to convince himself.

"Not as much as we do, anyway," Heyna said.

"Shhh," Cole hissed, as two guards broke off from the nearest fire and walked straight toward them. Jo eased onto the ground, eyes wide. He held his breath.

The guards' faces were masked in shadow, but their forms, dark against a blaze of fire behind, were distinct. One seemed average size for the Terralains—still quite tall and strong by Jo's reckoning. The second was, even by Terralain's outsized standards, truly massive. Their words, too distant and quiet to be heard at first, grew distinct as they came closer.

"...always understood. And anyway, we won't get a chance to even prepare for the festival." This was the larger soldier. "We'll never get home on time."

"I know why you want to get back for the festival, Tunk." The shorter guard was speaking. "Just you focus on the battle coming. We knock these betraying bucks on the head; then we head home to the revels."

They stopped ten paces from Jo, Cole, and Heyna.

"I'm focused, Dooker," the giant Tunk said. Jo saw now that the rabbit had grey fur with a white ring around his right eye.

"Stay sharp. See you at next shift," Dooker said. Tunk saluted, and Dooker hurried on past them, peering into the woods as he worked his way up to the next sentry fire.

Jo didn't move. Tunk turned, his back to the forest, and gazed around, back and forth. Seeing none of his comrades, he took off his helmet and scratched his head. "Itch all day..." he muttered. Tunk replaced his helmet, cocking it more comfortably on his head as he pivoted, his eyes thinning to slits, and peered into the forest. Jo closed his eyes, hoping the hulking buck's vision wasn't sharp. After an agonizing minute, Jo opened his eyes and saw that Tunk was turned away again and seemed to be gazing at the distant fires and the moon, alternately. Jo glanced over at Cole, then Heyna. Both twins nodded. *It's time to move on.* Jo rose to his knees, then carefully found his feet.

Tunk began humming, and Jo froze. Then the great buck's hips began to shift, and the humming grew louder. Jo exchanged a worried glance with Cole and Heyna. Then all three looked over at Tunk, whose hips were now moving back and forth while his foot began tapping.

"Come, ye fine..." Tunk began, mumbling at first. Then, finding his melody, he sang softly as his dancing grew more assured.

"Come, ye fine does,
And look upon me!
For I move like a moonbeam,
On the swaying trees.

Come, ye fine does,
And look upon me.
My limbs are all nimble,
My heart is all free!
Come, ye fine does,
And look upon me!
If you like my dancing,
Why, then I'll dance with thee!"

He danced as he sang, leaping and sliding, with such swelling energy that Jo's mouth dropped open and he had to be pulled away by Heyna, who followed her brother along the edge of the forest, closer still to the center of the camp.

Jo glanced back, fearful that they had been heard, but Tunk's song continued, along with his dance, until a noise from the sentry station further back caused him to stop, stiffen, and set his helmet straight again.

They were much closer now, and Cole pointed to a large pavilion just outside the big central fire around which rested many soldiers. Jo followed his gaze and nodded. Then Cole pointed past the pavilion to a section of readied catapults surrounded by blastpowder barrels.

"Okay," Jo whispered, and the Blackstar twins nodded.

Cole shifted forward, and Heyna squeezed Jo's arm. He smiled and saluted, and his friends disappeared into the shadows.

Jo, alone now, turned to the pavilion, scanning for a way in. Five Terralain soldiers were stationed outside the entrance to the large tent, each with a red shoulder shield. These bucks were a different breed than Tunk and Dooker. He remembered them from their days at Halfwind Citadel. An elite guard for Prince Kylen. They never spoke, only peered about them intently, their bodies calm but alive to every motion.

How am I supposed to get past them?

The central fire burst with an explosion.

Jo knew at once what had happened. *Well done, Blackstars!*

In the smoke, the red-shouldered guards darted ahead, drawing swords and arcing out in a practiced advance toward the direction of danger.

Jo saw his chance. While the guards moved toward the fire, Jo sprinted across the clearing and dove at the tent's bottom. He hit the ground and tried to slip under the edge but found it was sewn closed. He drew his knife and sliced across the seam, splitting it in time to slither between the wall and floor. Inside, he lay still. He could hear the waning noise outside. It was quiet in the tent.

The space was ample, but not vast. It was a leader's tent, provisioned with arms mounted along its canvas wall and a desk strewn with papers. Maps lay stacked on the desk's edge, and a wooden throne stood on a slight platform raised midway before a long solid curtain that hid the other half of the inside area. Around the room the banners of Terralain—a black field dotted with silver stars—were displayed on modest mounts hung with lanterns.

Jo listened a moment longer, then rose slowly. He was creeping toward the desk when he heard loud voices just outside.

"Stand aside!" a confident buck cried.

Jo dove behind a banner, then rose to peer around it as two figures entered. One, a stout young buck with a worried expression, had his sword drawn. The other was a lanky old buck with beads and jewels braided into his fur.

Tameth Seer.

"Your Highness," Tameth Seer said, his voice at a strange high and grating pitch, "I sense no danger to your brother's life from assassins."

Your Highness? Brother? Who can this be? Jo looked on, fretful.

"But what about Captain Vulm?" the stout buck asked quietly, gently dividing the inner curtain to gaze inside. Satisfied with what he saw, he stepped back.

"Of course, yes," Tameth said. "That was very sad indeed. But he had not the protection Prince Kylen has. Please, my dear Prince Naylen, trust me—as your father, King Bleston, did. As your brother does even amid his affliction."

Jo's eyes widened. *So Kylen's brother is here.*

"Father is dead, Master Seer." Naylen gripped the armrest of the wooden throne. "My brother seems near death."

"Do not worry, my prince." Tameth stroked the young buck's shoulder. "Picket Kingslayer and the Red Witch will pay for what they have done. They will pay for it soon."

"Ought we attack them?"

"Yes, of course," Tameth replied. "With the forces you have brought with you, we will crush them and seal our pact with Morbin. We shall rule the rabbit lands, and Morbin shall rule those of the raptors. It is settled."

"You believe, honored seer," Naylen began, "that Morbin would honor a pact?"

"I do, yes," Tameth Seer said. "Has he not honored it with his ambassador? Garten Longtreader stood before us and swore it on the bloody edge of his blade. On his own niece's blood."

"He killed his own niece." Naylen grimaced.

"Ambassador Garten killed their Scribe of the Cause. He cut down one of their leaders. This is war. He did what he had to do in service of his lord. The important thing is that Heather Longtreader is dead."

Chapter Two

A Familiar Stranger

Jo's heart sank. *It can't be! Not Heather.*

"I wish Kylen were well," Naylen said, gazing back with concern at the thick curtain, behind which rested Kylen.

"Trust me with this diplomacy, my prince, and prepare yourself to reap the revenge you so justly deserve! Avenge your father's betrayal and murder by Picket Longtreader."

Jo focused in. This was what he had come for, specific intelligence, and to gauge the will of the Terralains.

"I should very much like to meet Picket on the field," Naylen spat. "But the rest... they are rabbits, like us."

"Do not think of it as attacking fellow rabbits who simply oppose Morbin," Tameth said, guiding Naylen to sit on the wooden throne, "but as avenging your father and establishing your brother's rule. It is what your father wanted—to establish Kylen's throne." Tameth Seer hunched at Naylen's elbow. "Of course, my prince," he said, quieter and with a significant tone, "your brother may fall, and the throne may come to you."

Naylen closed his eyes a moment, lost in worried thought. Then he leapt up, shaking his head. "Forbid it."

"Do not worry, Prince Naylen. We will see to your brother's curing. I have seen his coming in battle. I have seen a flood sweeping his enemies away. I have seen it." The old buck's eyes seemed to glaze over, and he tottered.

Jo scowled from his hiding place. Tameth shook his head and then refocused on the young prince at his side. "But know this. One must either sacrifice for great accomplishment or sacrifice great accomplishment. It does not come cheap. There is death for heroes in all tales and history, and they buy the glory that follows with blood. This war will be no different; so be steadfast and shrink not away from your destiny."

"Can you ever see me in your futures?" Naylen asked. "Or is it still hidden?"

"What I may see, I may see, but what I have not seen, I cannot say."

"Your riddles used to amuse me."

"Your future is an untold tale," Tameth said, and Jo thought the old soothsayer was angry at his blindness concerning the young buck, "so you must be bold to write it yourself."

"I just want Kylen to rise and lead us to glory."

"Come now," Tameth said, motioning toward the slit in the tent through which they had come. "Let's away. We must speak to our captains. We must finalize the attack plan."

Naylen nodded, then stepped to the curtain to take another look at Kylen. The young buck frowned, his expression soft with sadness. Then his face hardened to anger and he strode out of the tent alongside the tottering seer.

Jo leapt from his hiding spot and hurried to the desk. He scanned the papers and snagged those he deemed useful, stuffing them into his pockets. Finally, he took fresh paper and pen. Dipping the pen in ink, he wrote a note, blew on it, folded it, and raced across to the throne. Jo reached beneath it, then sprang over to the curtain and parted it to look within. There, sickly and thin, slept Kyle. Jo wanted to drive his fist into the wretch's face, but he settled for a mumbled curse as he spun to rush out.

Jo tripped as he turned back, tumbling roughly off the platform and into a mounted lantern, which spilled and broke on the floor beside him. He quickly smothered the flames, but a groan sounded from the other side of the tent and he heard cries from outside. Jo scrambled to his feet and darted for the side of the tent—the opposite side from where he had cut his way in—and dove for the edge. The noise grew louder as he reached for his knife. It was gone! He must have lost it when he slithered into the tent. He thought of pulling his sword free but saw a fine blade with a jewel-encrusted handle mounted among other arms along the tent wall. He snagged it and stabbed and sliced his way out of the canvas just as the red-shouldered guards burst in.

Outside again, he glanced back and forth, then turned to race toward the section of readied catapults. He slipped his new knife into his old sheath and sprinted ahead. A Terralain guard turned as he approached and made ready to give the alarm, but the soldier was silenced by a devastating kick from Heyna. She spun and checked the guard, then motioned for Jo to follow.

He followed, rushing past several bound and gagged sentries, as he and Heyna weaved their way toward Cole. Cole was just ahead, sword flashing in the moonlight as he hacked away at the taut rope binding a giant catapult arm.

"They're going to use all this against us!" Jo said, withdrawing the staves from his backpack. He locked them in place and slipped his arms through the straps. "They're going to attack First Warren. Soon!" Heyna, already fitted with her pack, helped Jo secure his buckles.

"They're coming," Cole called.

"Get in!" Heyna cried. Cole nodded and abandoned the thin unbinding line as he leapt into the catapult's massive bucket.

A swarming band of soldiers rushed at them. Jo and the Blackstars hadn't been seen yet, but that would soon change. "Now, Cole!" Jo cried.

Cole swiveled, drew a long thin blade from its sheath, and hurled it at the taut rope that was holding the catapult back. The knife sliced through the remaining rope, breaking the tension to release the catapult arm in a rapid lurching launch that sent the three friends skyward at a nauseating pace.

Jo recovered first. He spun and drew out his bow,

bending to secure its string with expert ease. Reaching his flight zenith, he unlocked his quiver and dragged out a mini blastarrow in one smooth motion. As he began to fall, he nocked the arrow, aimed, and released the string in one deft motion. The heavy-headed arrow zipped away as Jo secured his bow and sent out his arms wide to engage the glider.

The flint-and-fire arrow found its target. The packed blastpowder barrels blew apart in a raucous rupture that showered the night sky with great sprays of orange and gold. Catapults in line broke apart in the shattering blast. The concussive wave reached the glider's wings, and he rose on the dissipating force. He turned, settled into the breeze, and sailed ahead—back toward First Warren. He felt grateful to be alive and happy to have ruined some of the weapons that would soon have been aimed at those he loved. He was glad to strike out against foes who would destroy the cause for which he would gladly lay down his life. After all, Tameth Seer—villain though he was—wasn't wrong about the cost of the cause. It would be won with lives.

Heather. Oh, no. How will I tell Picket?

Jo felt a stab of pain, and he twisted, losing his easy glide. An arrow protruded from his side. He could feel it wasn't deep, that his pack strap had slowed its entry, but it still hurt. More arrows followed. The Terralains, rushing along the ground, shot at the moonlit gliders. Thankfully, Cole and Heyna were far enough ahead of him to be clear of their fire.

An arrow shot through his left glider-wing, causing him to dip. Another ripped through his taut right wing, then another. He was hit again, but this time a buckle blocked the deadly point. His glider was failing, even as he managed to stretch ahead to reach beyond the farthest enemy archer's aim. But the damage was done. His glider, already an imperfect device, was unbalanced by long rips, and he fell lower and lower till he landed roughly in the branches of a tall tree. He was in a grove of trees somewhere between the Terralain war camp and First Warren.

Jo checked his arm, which had turned awkwardly in his landing. He determined it was okay and scrambled down the tree. He landed hard and rolled over. Taking a deep breath, he sprang to his feet and checked the moon. He would run toward First Warren and hope for the best. As he started, he heard a voice from behind.

"Hands up."

Jo stopped.

"I said, hands up." This warning was punctuated by an arrow shot from behind him, which stuck fast in the tree just above his head. Jo raised his hands.

"Turn around slowly."

Jo obeyed, resigned to his fate. He consoled himself that he had taken out some of Terralain's capacity for war and that Cole and Heyna had escaped with the needed intelligence. Well, some of it. When Jo had turned all the way around, he gazed at the figure before him. It was a strong rabbit, though not so tall as the Terralains he had just seen. A hood covered his face. Behind him, a swarthy band held weapons ready.

"Who are you?" Jo asked, peering into the shadowy face, a small spark of hope flickering in his heart. The rabbit peeled back his hood and smiled. Jo laughed. "I thought you were dead!"

"I'm very much alive," came the voice of the archer in the dark. "Where's Picket?"

Chapter Three

Recalled to War

Picket limped along a wide path leading back to Helmer's family farmhouse. He gripped a long, rotting beam of the split rail fence and pulled himself forward. He had rested, as commanded by Princess Emma, but he felt that now he must move. It wasn't only that he wanted to do his part amid the preparations for the coming battle at First Warren but that he felt his fire for the fight waning.

Picket was tired. He felt old, almost. Haggard and weary. His injured leg was stiff and ached with pain. He had all but outrightly defied Emma's insistent order for him to spend a few days at rest, angrily arguing with her so loudly that her staff and court were alarmed. But having grimly accepted his sentence and come to Helmer's rundown family farm for a short retreat, he now found it hard to think of leaving.

Picket hadn't been safe for so long. He hadn't had a home, a proper home, for what felt like years. As for family, he had only had Heather and Uncle Wilfred since that day the wolves attacked and he lost his home, happiness, and, for a while, hope. Picket didn't know if Uncle Wilfred was even still alive. But this farm, Helmer's family's farm where his sister Airen and his niece Weezie lived, felt both homey and safe. *Safe*. He felt a deep, soul-weary longing to stay.

So he knew he must go. Must move. His errand wasn't over, not as long as Heather and the rest of their family might be alive, nor as long as any rabbit in Natalia trembled beneath the vast, ravenous shadow of Morbin Blackhawk and his Preylords.

Picket stopped and retied the long black scarf around his neck. He leaned against the yielding fence and gazed across at the sagging farmhouse set amid an ocean of pale, swaying grass. The setting sun sprayed rays of gold that played along the prancing grass and glinted on the old house. He watched on and on as the sun dipped lower. His hands played absently with sticks he'd gathered along his walk. Picket took his knife and trimmed and scored the stout twigs, fitting them together in their center. From his pocket he withdrew a ribbon, long and blue. Tying the several sticks together, he stared through tears at what he'd made.

Hurried footfalls sounded behind him, and he swung around, hand darting to his sword hilt. It was Weezie, running up with a smile.

"Don't cleave me in two, Picket Packslayer." She raised her hands as she crossed the last yards between them. "I have word from the city."

"Am I recalled?" Picket asked.

"You are, Captain Longtreader," she said. "The princess wants you back tonight for a council. It seems the enemy might be on the move."

Picket nodded, then turned back to glimpse the last glowing light fall on the swaying field. He limped away from the fence, drew back, then launched his creation. He sent the starstick sailing through the air, its blue ribbon rippling in the wind. It rose and fell, disappearing at last amid a dark distant patch of tall grass.

Picket stared at the spot, blinked, then turned back to Weezie.

"Should we go get it?" Weezie asked.

"No," Picket replied, limping ahead. "I'll find it after I find Heather."

He heard Weezie's steps as she caught up to him and they crossed toward the house. The evening settled in as they walked, and the house began to glow with lamplight. Airen emerged onto the porch and gazed out into the deepening evening. Seeing them, she smiled and returned inside.

Picket's leg was getting better, but it still ached. His limp seemed certain to be a lifelong reminder of these days of war, however long his life would last. He gazed up at the first stars, marking the vague traces of the warrior constellation high above.

"Was that my ribbon?" Weezie asked.

"Maybe."

"Maybe?" Weezie frowned in mock severity. "Picket Thingstealer, bane of the does."

Picket sighed. "You're never going to let me forget that song, are you?"

"No. I can't see that ever happening."

They entered the house.

Airen was waiting in her familiar chair. "You seem about to leave me," she said.

"Yes, ma'am," Picket replied, looking down. "The war. The cause."

"I was sitting in this very chair," Airen said, squinting

against tears, "when Helmer first left to join the war. When cause and crown took my brother away."

"How old was he, Mother?" Weezie asked.

"About Picket's age." Airen wiped her eyes. "He told me he planned to come back—to finish his fighting and return to the farm. It's what Father wanted, though he understood the king's need. How I wept! I always wanted him to come home again. I'd stare out the window at the road, believing I might see him top the far rise and walk back into our lives. That he'd carry on what his fathers started. But he never really came home, not to stay. There was always another war, and then . . . well, then the king fell. That was the end of any hope of having him home."

"Helmer was far away then, right?" Picket asked. "With Lord Rake and the army."

"Is that what he told you?" Airen frowned.

"I don't know if he said that or I just assumed," Picket said. "He's not always talkative about the past."

Airen nodded. "For good reason. So much pain." She wiped at her eyes and shook her head, then smiled at Picket and took Weezie's hand in hers. "I'll let you get your things."

Not long after, Picket hugged Airen and took his leave.

"Thank you," he said, taking off and handing her his black scarf. "Will you keep this for me?"

"Of course, Picket," Airen replied, smiling as she took the scarf. "It will be here when you come home." He nodded, wiped at his eyes, then set out along the path as Weezie hugged her mother.

"I'll be back as soon as I'm able," Weezie said. Picket heard their whispered affection and then the sound of the door closing. He thought of his own mother and how long it had been since he'd seen her. Weezie caught up to him and took his arm.

"I can walk without help, Weezie," he said, glancing at her grip on his arm.

"I know," she said.

Chapter Four

The Dawn Alarm

Alongside Weezie, Picket entered the city center of First Warren. By the light of a thousand torches, rabbits crafted elaborate defense works all over the square. Atop the walls, blue-robed votaries and stout soldiers from various citadels installed bowstrikers and other assets. Across the city center, soldiers and staff from all regions of Natalia worked side by side on a hundred urgent errands. Picket smiled to see the unity in the work. Diligent masons stacked long smooth sections of stone beside the palace roof, binding them together, while others stacked still higher sections above, ending in what looked like curling bridgework below. Elsewhere earthworks were being created with long ditches situated around high sturdy mounds. Forges fired, and sweating smiths pounded out arms beneath the starlight.

"I'm angry that she's left me out of this work," Picket said.

"She's no fool, Pick," Weezie answered. "She knew you'd never rest here. And resting's what she needed from you. You're not missing out on the work; you're doing it. She needs you as fresh as possible for what's ahead."

Picket grunted.

"You make a good point," she replied. "It's not hard to see who trained you. Your master—my beloved Uncle Helmer—has the same sweet facility with language."

He grunted again.

Soon they were inside the palace, hurrying past the sentries, who saluted, wide-eyed, as they saw Picket limping past. Weezie smiled at their awe.

"Need a hand?" Weezie asked as they reached the foot of the stairs.

"Actually, they're easier than flat ground," Picket said. Taking the banister in hand and pulling himself up, he took several steps at a time.

They reached the top and moved into the long corridor leading to a large hall, busy with officers and soldiers coming and going.

"Captain," an officer called. It was Lieutenant Warken, saluting as he ran up. "Captain Longtreader, if you please, Princess Emma awaits you in the council room."

"Thank you, Lieutenant," Picket said, then started for the room.

Lieutenant Warken coughed. "Sir, I'm sorry," he said, glancing at Weezie. "The council is for only the highest ranking lords and officers by the princess's invitation."

Picket frowned and was about to speak, but Weezie shook her head at him, then smiled at Lieutenant Warken.

"Of course, Lieutenant. I came only to make sure he didn't get lost. And you should have seen how much help he needed on the stairs. Picket," she said, turning back to him, "I'll be waiting for you beneath the seventh standing stone."

"But Weezie, I'm sure—"

"Go on, Pick. I'll wait for you there." She smiled, turned around, and walked back the way they had come. Picket watched her for a while, then spun and limped ahead.

Picket saluted the guard outside the door, then entered. Inside, lords and captains sat around a large oval table. Emma sat at one end, flanked by Lord Blackstar and Mrs. Weaver. Next to them sat Helmer and Lord Morgan Booker. Lords Ronan and Felson whispered together. They had all been talking, but a silence spread as they noticed Picket come in. An odd reverence, Picket thought, showed on most faces. Some saluted, and others bowed. Helmer frowned.

"So good of you to join us, Lord Layabout," he said. "Find a seat, Picket, if you can manage the strain."

Picket grinned. He much preferred Helmer's needling to the strange awe he seemed to inspire among even the highest ranked rabbits. "Lord High Captain Helmer, Your Royal Lordship, Defender of the Crown and Cause, I thank you," he said, bowing neatly to his master. "It's good to see your manners survived the last battle unaltered."

Helmer shook his head, but a corner of his mouth turned up as he glanced over toward Emma. "Your

Highness, I think we're all here, now that our resident legend of folk songs has arrived from his country estate."

"Welcome, Captain Longtreader," Emma said, smiling tenderly at him. Picket bowed, then found an empty seat beside Heyward. "My lords and captains," Emma continued, "I am reliably informed that Morbin is massing his army north of Grey Grove, and what we have awaited is nearly upon us. We expect his attack within the week." She nodded to Captain Frye.

"Your Royal Highness." Captain Frye bowed before turning to address the room. "We don't expect to be ready with our defenses before ten days." He glanced at Heyward, who nodded. "This intelligence, which was hard won, is ill news for us."

"We must press on," Emma answered. "What else can we do?"

"Press on," Lord Morgan said, and others nodded and echoed his assent.

"Your Highness," Mrs. Weaver said, "we must meet with the Terralains at once. It is vital." Emma nodded, concern playing over her face. She glanced at Helmer, who looked away.

"And we must get the most vulnerable away safely to Harbone," Lord Ronan added. "Unless they are already safely away."

"The last travelers are preparing to leave now," Helmer said. "I'm afraid we must send a sizable escort along, due to the nearness of the enemy."

"I do not like it," Mrs. Weaver said, shaking her head.

"What else can we do, wise Mother?" Helmer asked, without hint of rebuke in his tone.

Mrs. Weaver shook her head. Picket thought he read the meaning of her concerns. *Nowhere is safe. All choices are heavy with peril.*

"They go to Harbone," Emma said firmly. "It is the best decision I can make. I will go with them, and the same escort that sees them there will bring me to meet Prince Kylen of Terralain."

"I will assemble a party, Your Highness," Helmer said, bowing his head quickly to her.

"Lieutenant Heyward," Emma said, "is the coordinated defensive unit working well together?"

"Yes, Your Highness," Heyward said. He coughed nervously and glanced over at Picket. Picket nodded to him confidently, and Heyward continued. "Lord Captain Helmer has scoured every battle burrow with help from Harbone's Captain Brafficks and Lord Ronan's elite guard. We have brought all the weapons we can into the city. Emerson is overseeing the installation and fitting out the bowstrikers and other defensive measures. He has helped equip the Highwall Wardens and has hardly taken a break since your victory."

"Our victory, Lieutenant."

"Yes, Your Highness."

"Go on, Heyward."

"I am heading up the special constructions, under

Captain Helmer, and my team of brother votaries from Halfwind has been excellent. As Captain Frye said, at our current rate of preparation, we need at least ten days."

"Thank you, Heyward. Counterintelligence?" she asked, looking back at Captain Frye.

"Yes, Your Highness," Frye said, looking cautiously around the room. "I will have a full report for you by morning."

Emma nodded, then gazed around the room. Picket thought she looked tired and thinner. "What are we missing?" she asked. "We are doing our best, I know. And I appreciate how hard you're all working. I do. But do any of you have ideas we need to hear? Is there any way to shorten our preparations?"

"Your Highness," Lord Blackstar began, "our messages sent to all secret citadels might yield reinforcements, but it seems unlikely to greatly reduce our need."

"Thank you, Lord Blackstar. If any arrive, you will see to their integration into our forces and preparation."

"Yes, Your Highness."

"The trouble is, we don't have enough personnel or time," Lord Ronan said, frowning, "and we can't manufacture either."

"Which leads us back to the Terralains," Mrs. Weaver said. "So much hinges on what they do."

"I wouldn't expect too much from them," Lord Blackstar said. "Tameth Seer has poisoned them into thinking we betrayed and murdered Prince Bleston."

"And that's not all he's doing," Emma said. "But still, we must try. I sent an embassy for peace days ago, but they haven't returned. Meanwhile, I have taken other, more covert, measures." Another glance at Helmer.

Picket frowned. *I've missed something. Where are Jo and Cole? Where's Heyna?*

"Maybe Picket should sit that meeting out," Helmer said. "The Terralains don't love his folk songs."

Picket's frown turned into a smirk.

There was a knock at the door. Lieutenant Warken entered and, folding his hands behind his back, waited to be acknowledged.

"What is it, Lieutenant?" Emma asked.

"I'm sorry, Your Highness, but a band from Halfwind just arrived," Warken said, "and their leader is demanding to speak to you."

"Their leader?" Emma asked. "Who might that be?"

The door was pushed open, and a gallant grey rabbit strode in. "Wilfred Longtreader, Your Highness," he said, bowing low, "reporting for duty."

Picket leapt to his feet. "Uncle Wilfred!" Sidestepping his chair, he limped quickly across to fold his uncle in an embrace. He felt the strong arms close around him. "I thought we'd lost you. I can't believe you came. How is this possible?"

"There's much to tell, Picket, but you can thank old Jone for my recovery when she arrives," Uncle Wilfred said, giving a final squeeze to his nephew's neck. He broke free and turned to face Emma. "But first I must share urgent intelligence. Forgive me, but that's why I insisted on the interruption, Your Highness," he said, bowing once again.

"Please, go on." Emma stood up.

Uncle Wilfred bowed, then cleared his throat. He looked to the door just as Jo, Cole, and Heyna came in. Lord Blackstar stood. "Your Highness, I found Jo in the forest, then caught up with the Blackstars at the west gate. They learned that Bleston's second son, Naylen, recently arrived with reinforcements. Prince Naylen has emptied their lands of soldiers, and their coming makes the Terralain strength nearly twice what it was. Tameth Seer is rallying the army to attack."

"Attack?" Emma asked, frustration vivid in her drawn face. "Attack where? Who?"

"Here, Your Highness," Uncle Wilfred said. "They mean to attack you here and unite rabbitkind behind Kylen. Then Tameth Seer will finalize a new alliance with Morbin."

"When?" Helmer asked.

"At dawn. They attack at dawn."

Chapter Five

Flight Fall

Picket gazed out over the city from the roof of the palace.

"Are we sure this is the only way?" Lord Ronan asked, fingers raking through the fur between his ears.

"There are other ways," Emma said, fastening a strap tighter, "but they are too slow."

"It's a terrible gamble, but she must go," Mrs. Weaver said, pulling a cloak more tightly around her shivering shoulders. "It's a risk she must take."

Picket and Emma, alongside Cole and Helmer, were being outfitted with Heyward's gliders. Mrs. Weaver, Weezie, Lord Ronan, Lieutenant Warken, Captain Braffeks, and Heyward were helping with the preparations.

"We have more gliders near completion. Production is proceeding rapidly." Heyward's blue robe rippled in the breeze as he checked the princess over with keen attention to every buckle, strap, and fastening. "I do have one more here, Your Royal Highness, and I'd dearly like to go myself."

"No, Heyward," Emma said, glancing at Picket. "I

need you here. Your preparations must go on. And anyway, we're not going to defeat the Terralains in arms. Five of us or four—it makes little difference. I only just got Heyna to leave me."

"Yes, ma'am. It's all secure now, Your Highness," Heyward said, bowing neatly. "Just, please, stick close to Picket."

"How did you get Heyna to let you go without her?" Picket asked.

"She's fiercely loyal, but obedient as well," Emma replied. "I sent her and her father to investigate some rumors. A strange group was sighted by a patrol."

"What was strange about it?"

"It might have my mother in the group."

Picket's eyes widened. "Lady Glen, coming here?"

"I hope so," Emma said. "If it is her, I don't want her walking into a trap—or a tomb. I sent them after her."

Picket nodded, then turned back to the group. "Are we ready?"

They each nodded, but Helmer looked miserable.

"Are we sure Picket should be going?" Lord Ronan asked. "They *do* want to kill him."

"Apparently they want to kill us all, my lord," Picket answered, stepping closer to Emma. "They may be grateful I'm saving them the march."

"No one can fly like Picket," Helmer said. "I wish we didn't, but we need him. I know I'd have preferred to never try this contraption again. But the princess must go. And so must I."

"And I," Picket echoed.

"And I," another voice sounded from behind the shed atop the palace. Jo Shanks stepped out. "I mean, I'm coming too."

"I thought you were being evaluated at the hospital?" Emma asked.

"Surprisingly, it didn't take very long," Jo said, smiling. "Believe me, Emma—I mean, Your Highness—you're going to need me on this little trip."

Emma frowned but nodded for him to join them.

As the urgent—desperate—plans were being made to get Emma to the Terralain camp, Uncle Wilfred had volunteered to lead the escort of the last group leaving First Warren for the hoped-for safety of Harbone. Emma had checked Uncle Wilfred over, marveling at his recovery, and then agreed to his request.

Picket had spent only a few moments with his beloved uncle before they both left again to fulfill their assignments, Uncle Wilfred to Harbone, and Picket to prepare for this flight with the princess.

Weezie added a few supplies to Picket's tight-slung pack and hugged him. "Be careful, Pick."

"I'll see you soon," Picket replied.

"I'll wait for you here," she said, kissing his cheek. Emma looked out into the night sky.

Weezie crossed to hug her uncle, and Helmer asked her to look after Airen.

Emma stepped closer to Picket as Weezie said goodbye to Helmer.

"How are you doing?" Picket asked.

"I don't want to do this," Emma whispered, smiling back. "But neither did I ever want to be queen. I never dreamed of flying, or of ruling. But here I am."

"Dreams do . . . *not* come true," Picket whispered back.

"Inspiring," Emma said flatly. "That's going in my book of *Shuffler's Collected Wisdom*. I'm going to write it after the war—really show Heather who's the true scribe."

"You'll be queen, so you can do whatever you want."

"Obviously, yes. If being a princess is anything like it, then yes; I'll be able to do whatever I want . . . all the time."

"Ready to fly?" Jo stepped near after his new glider pack was checked.

"Ready," Emma said. "Just really, really ready."

"It's been her dream," Picket whispered to Jo, loud enough for Emma to hear.

"Since I was just a little doe, pretending to be a princess," Emma said flatly.

"Hmm," Jo said, raising an eyebrow. "Dreams really do—"

"Let's get going," Emma interrupted.

"Leapers guide you, Your Highness," Weezie said, bowing low.

"Thank you, Louise," Emma replied.

The rest of the court who were gathered atop the palace bowed, and Heyward touched his eyes, ears, and mouth in turn, as did a few others. Emma raised her hand in a blessing, then, balling it into a fist, turned to the edge of the palace.

"Just like we discussed, Emma," Picket said. "It's run and jump, then arms out stiff, wrists twisted in, or forward, to engage the glider. Disengage by twisting your wrists out, or back. I'll be right behind you in case anything goes wrong."

"I could give some advice," Jo said. "Had a pretty eventful flight a bit earlier." He looked around, but no one was paying attention. "Okay, I get it. Let's just focus on Picket here. By all means."

"Have you heard the songs?" Picket asked, feigning a lofty tone.

"More times," Jo replied with a sigh, "than I could have ever believed possible, Captain Packslayer."

Picket smiled. "Are you ready?" he asked Emma. She nodded. "Okay, on the count of—" he began, but Emma took off, darting toward the palace rooftop threshold. "Okay, let's go!" Picket shouted as Emma leapt from the edge.

Picket was right behind her, diving into the darkness in Emma's wake. Behind him he could hear Helmer, Cole, and Jo take flight, but his attention was all ahead as he watched Emma stretch her arms out wide and engage the glider. As he had expected, during the first moments after the device went taut she wobbled and dipped, struggling to master the strange, exhilarating trial of flight.

They were flying. He trailed behind Emma as she circled above the torchlit city, sweeping left and right as she tested the glider's operation. Picket was pleased with her prowess, and he looked back at Jo, who seemed to be okay despite his earlier exertions. A quick glance at Helmer convinced Picket that he should keep an eye on his master more than on the new flyer. But Picket saw that Cole had drifted behind Helmer and was leaving Jo's side to focus on the older buck. *Well done, Cole.*

He was smiling when he turned back to check on Emma, but his smile disappeared quickly when all he saw was empty air before him.

The princess was gone.

Chapter Six

FOLLOWING

Picket, in a panic, scanned left and right, then down. Nothing.

Desperately, he gazed into the gloom. Finally, in the deepening darkness below, Picket caught a glint of torchlight reflecting off what he thought might be a buckle. He twisted his wrists to disengage the glider and pointed his body like a spear.

Down, down, he fell, dropping toward the faded flicker, wind pressing the fur of his face, his mind pushing out the grim insistent doubts and the despair beneath them. He focused and fell, making himself a plunging bolt aimed at the thin strands of his hope.

Scanning as he sped down, his eyes adjusting to the deep darkness, he spotted her at last. She was dropping still, descending limply toward the ground. He cut the arc of his descent, banking hard straight for the ground. Then, angling ahead to intercept the falling form, he engaged the taut wings for a fractional moment. Releasing the mechanism quickly once again, he swept just above the ground to meet Emma, seizing her as his momentum bent upward to offset, even a little, the weight of her plummet.

Picket caught her, but she was falling so fast that he barely held on as they both fell again, slowed somewhat by his upward thrust. Their terrible wreck seemed certain, and Picket braced for the crash, doing all he could to fold Emma into a protective embrace.

Just before impact, he felt strong hands grasp and pull him back roughly. Opening his eyes again, he saw Jo's face, straining to arrest their speed. Cole was beside him, and both bucks had somehow checked his pace, so that Picket was able to land in a rough tumble, turning again and again but without serious hurt to himself or Emma.

Jo hit the ground behind them and rolled in an ungainly tangle, while Cole glided to a smooth landing, never breaking stride as he ran up to Picket and Emma.

"Are you okay?" Cole called, bending to cradle the princess's head in his hands.

Picket groaned and shook his head, trying to see clearly. "Is she?"

"I think so," Cole said, lightly slapping her face. "Your Highness! Emma!"

Emma's eyes opened slowly, and she squinted, then squirmed back and cried out. "Oh, no!"

"It's okay," Cole said gently, gripping her arms and looking calmly into her face. "You're all right, Your Highness. You passed out while gliding. You fell, but you're on the ground again, safe. It's easy to do. It's happened to others."

Jo walked up, rubbing his head, as Picket got slowly to his feet, testing his knee.

"I'm just glad you're okay." Picket leaned back and breathed deeply. His heart was still racing.

"It's embarrassing." Emma frowned, smoothing her fur. "Maybe... don't tell anyone."

"We would never," Jo said. "I mean, half the city saw it happen, but I'm sure they won't say a thing. It's night and they should be asleep, not watching their ruler faint and fall like a stone."

"And there's a code among us Fowlers," Picket said, looking into her eyes and checking for signs of injury. "We don't tell anyone else when something like this happens. Besides, it happened to Helmer."

"It feels like you just told me," Emma said, "one of the things you say you never tell."

"The rules are fluid," Cole said, smiling. "The Fowlers are a relatively new institution. Our fainting founder gave birth to us very recently, as you know."

"Helmer?" Jo asked. "I thought *I* was the Fowlers' founder."

"Where *is* Helmer?" Picket asked, turning around and peering into the night.

An anxious cry, followed by a noise of crashing punctuated with curses, came from the darkness nearby.

"Found him," Jo said.

"Go find the founder, Fowler," Picket said, helping Emma to her feet. "Cole, give him a hand."

Jo smiled and saluted before hurrying toward the angry sounds in the dark. Cole, shaking his head, followed.

"Are you okay, Emma?" Picket asked. "You can't get too upset by it. Rabbits sometimes faint. It can't be helped."

"I'm fine," Emma answered. "It's not the scariest thing I've done lately."

"I suppose you haven't had the easiest time."

"I'm in charge, Picket," she said. "It's awful. The weight of it. It's impossible."

"But you're great at it."

"I'm not the worst," she said.

"Well, it's no great shame you're not a flyer," Picket said. "We just need a new plan."

"What are you talking about?" she asked. "I'm getting back up there. I'm trying again. I'm flying again. Let's go."

"Emma, I can't just let you—" Picket began, but she held up a hand.

"I'm not asking, Shuffler," Emma said. "Remember, I'm in charge. I'm going to meet Kylen. We have to try to stop this attack. Let's get to the launch site and get on our way. We have work to do."

Picket bowed and followed her.

Chapter Seven

Night Flight

Picket grimaced as they hurried up the old stone stairs in the dark. A soldier bearing a torch met them halfway up, calling out a warning.

"Who goes?"

"A herald!" Cole stepped in front of Emma.

"Report," the soldier demanded.

"You did well to require the password, soldier," Helmer said, "but give us the torch and hurry back up and tell them the princess is coming. And look lively, or I may decide to knock your young fluffy backside down these stairs."

"Yes, sir, Lord, sir... Captain Lord, sir," the soldier stammered, eyes wide, as he handed the torch to Cole and turned to bolt back up the steps.

Picket struggled up the stone stairs, his knee aching with the effort. There was no railing he could use to pull himself up, and he strained to see the steps in the darkness. The torchlight helped, but as they ascended, he saw that many of the steps had been damaged in the battle. Jo stepped closer to him while Cole, Helmer, and Emma went ahead.

"Looking out for a poor crippled soul?" Picket asked.

Jo nodded, taking Picket's arm. "I seem to remember a certain soul helping me when I was in a tough spot not too long ago. Not too far from here, in fact."

"Sounds heroic. Lending an arm to help him walk up steps seems a fitting response to his bravery," Picket murmured.

"Well, now we're even," Jo said.

Picket nodded with a grin, and they hurried up the stairs.

In a few minutes they were poised upon five catapults. Lieutenant Meeker was in charge of this battery. Years ago, Meeker had been a young soldier under Helmer's command. So young, they had called him "Meeker the Squeaker." They had met again recently after Helmer and Picket barely escaped from a pack of wild wolves, just getting inside Harbone Citadel, where Meeker was serving as gate commander.

"Remember, Lieutenant," Picket said, "send me right after the princess."

"We will, Captain Longtreader."

"Are you ready, Your Highness?" Meeker asked.

"Yes, Lieutenant," she replied, her hand testing the tension in her harness. "You may launch when ready."

Meeker bowed, then turned to the catapult holding Helmer. He saluted the old soldier but turned away when he saw how nervous Helmer was.

"Squeaker," Helmer said, his voice unsteady.

Meeker turned back, and Picket thought the young officer was bracing for a rebuke. "Yes, sir?"

A pause, and Picket watched his master fix Meeker in his sights.

"I'm proud of you."

Meeker smiled, saluted, then nodded to the bucks stationed at each catapult's release catch. "On my signal," he said, raising his hand. "Go one!" he cried, and Emma's catapult arm raced forward, sending the princess sailing skyward. "Go two!" Picket felt the pressure of the sudden force against his body generated by the leaping arm, then the thrilling ease and speed as he sprang into the sky. Behind, he barely heard Meeker call out, "Go three; go four; go five!" and the entire team was away, speeding through the night sky. Ahead, he saw Emma reach her elevation apex, then calmly engage the glider and fly steadily on. He did the same and, his flight slowed by only slightly less drag, soared up beside her.

Emma was mastering the glider, and he was relieved and delighted to see it. Glancing back, he saw that Cole and Jo flew capably on either side of Helmer, who wobbled as he went but stayed on their course. The bright moon revealed a pale view of the land below. They were following the course of an old road, keeping it always to their right. The Terralain camp was just inland of the road, northwest of First Warren and southeast of Harbone. Jo and Cole had said their flight would not be long, and, depending on the wind, the gliders should get them all the way there.

Picket saw lights in the middle distance and glanced over at Jo. Jo nodded, then dipped and rose, and dipped and rose again. That was the signal for their descent. Emma nodded, then began to increase the drag on her glider and angle down. Picket watched anxiously, but after a few small mistakes she mastered the descent as she had the launch. Jo and Cole took the lead. They dropped low and landed in a clearing not far from the firelights.

Emma kept her feet as she landed, and Picket swept up in an easy flip to land smoothly beside her. "Shuffler the Showoff," she said as he limped up, detaching the back rod, unbinding the two parts, and folding the glider into its pack.

"I'm just taking care of my leg," he protested, helping Emma with her glider pack.

She rolled her eyes. "It's possible *not* flipping before landing might be easier on your injured knee. But what do I know of such things?"

"I'll consult with my doctor," he said, turning to wince as Helmer landed, stumbled, then rose again in a corkscrewing hop that turned him over as he crashed to the ground.

Emma and Picket exchanged a concerned look. "At least he's tough," Emma said.

Jo and Cole hurried to help Helmer up, and he stood unsteadily, arms out wide as if he expected the earth to heave suddenly and knock him off his feet.

They secured their packs, Cole helping Helmer as the

old buck stood still, shaking his head.

"Let's go," Emma said when she was certain he was all right. "We have to hurry."

Just then, a band of tall rabbits emerged from the cover of nearby trees, their black armor dotted with silver stars. "Who goes there?"

"Friends," Emma said.

"Friends?" a large brown buck asked, stepping to the front of the band and holding high a torch so that the light fell on Emma's and Picket's faces. "This looks like Picket Longtreader, the murderer of King Bleston. And, what now? It's the Red Witch usurper herself!" He stepped back a moment, fear in his eyes. Then, glancing left and right, he stepped forward again. "No wonder you fell from out of the sky, like birds of prey. So the legends are all true, I see. Tameth Seer will be pleased to see you both."

"Pleased to kill them both," a white buck said bitterly, drawing his sword. "And I'll be pleased to see that."

Chapter Eight

The Prince's Sword

The Terralain soldiers stood back, eyeing Emma nervously. The brown leader sent a messenger running back to the main camp. Then he stepped closer. "You will come with us."

"We need to speak to Prince Kylen," Emma said.

"The prince is unwell," the white buck said, eyes cold, "but we are led well enough by Tameth Seer and King Bleston's second son."

"Where is Captain Vulm?" Helmer asked, his voice even.

"You pretend not to know?" the leader snapped back. "An assassin from the Red Witch killed honorable Vulm in his sleep. He was a valiant captain! This was the last offense. As the seer said, war is the only answer to such villainy."

Picket thought of Winslow, of how Emma had pardoned him and many more in First Warren. She was merciful and just. That she was being called these vile names and being accused of assassinating a Terralain officer was enraging. But he tried to stay calm. These soldiers needed no provocation.

"Vulm was a good officer," Helmer said. "I would like to meet his murderer and have words with him again."

"So you know the murderer?" the white buck cried, spitting. "You admit it!"

"I have met him," Helmer said, lip curled in a snarl. "But now we must speak with Kylen. We'll discuss these things with him. We didn't fly here to argue with you, Lillywhite."

The leader frowned, then motioned with his head for them to move north, the way the messenger had gone. The white buck stared up at the leader through eyes thinned to slits, then moved alongside the company, flanking Emma's close-packed companions.

They walked on, Picket sticking close to Emma. "You didn't say anything," he said softly.

"They called me a witch! I couldn't think of anything to say that wouldn't get us killed," she answered.

"There wasn't much to choose from," he agreed. "This is a tight furrow to plow."

The Terralain captain walked just beside Helmer, his sword out and his face agitated. The white buck seemed eager for trouble to break out, and he eyed them angrily while fidgeting with his sword. The rest of their band seemed uneasy and angry at once, their faces blurring to black at the edge of the torchlight. Picket couldn't tell how many there were. The nervous leader stepped aside into the shadows, then emerged a few moments later flanked by four massive bucks. They patrolled both sides of Emma and Picket.

Picket heard a burst of laughter and looked back to see Jo and Cole smiling. He stared at them, disbelieving, while Jo stepped forward to walk beside Picket.

"It's a long story," Jo whispered in response to Picket's questioning look.

"I can't wait to hear it," Picket replied, "if we live through this very serious and dangerous situation."

Jo nodded, then turned to the truly hulking buck a few feet away, a grey rabbit with a white ring around one eye. Jo looked back and winked at Picket, then turned back to the huge buck. To Picket's surprise, Jo started singing softly.

"Come, ye fine does, and look upon me,
I'm big as a mountain, but dumb as a tree...
I dance like a dimwit, just about to sneeze,
So come, ye fine does, and look upon me."

Picket grabbed at Jo's arm as the grey buck's eyes grew wide with surprise.

"Tunk, what's happening?" the leader snapped.

The grey buck, obviously Tunk, looked around at his commander, then back over at Jo with alarm. "Captain Granger, they spied on me!"

"Spied on you?" Captain Granger asked. "How am I supposed to believe that? What were you doing that needed spying on?"

Jo smirked. "He was eating one of our soldiers."

"I was..." Tunk began, "er, um...I was..."

Jo just smiled, bobbing a bit to the tune he was humming.

"Just guard them, you great brainless heap," Captain Granger hissed.

Tunk saluted and walked on with an occasional sideways glance at Jo, always puzzled.

Jo edged over to Tunk, who nervously gripped his spear. "The dancing was amazing, Tunky, old fella. I hope you make it home for the festival. Especially if that means you won't be killing me and my friends."

Tunk's mouth fell open and his eyes grew wide.

Picket frowned, then looked over at Emma. She shook her head.

After passing several more fires in a long clearing flanked by woods, they finally approached the main camp and the huge central fire.

The camp was large, spreading far and wide, containing an enormous army capable of the unimaginable. But no, Picket could imagine it. He could see a great sea of soldiers crashing on First Warren, spreading devastation and death until both sides were finally weakened to feeble scraps of their former strength. Easy pickings for the Lords of Prey. Certain victory for Morbin. An end to their hoped-for mending.

The messenger who had been sent ahead came back now and spoke to the leader, Captain Granger.

"The seer is at his rites," the messenger said. "He will be called when he emerges."

"Send for the prince," Granger said.

The messenger nodded and, after a wary glance at Emma, ran off again.

By now a crowd of soldiers had gathered, black-armored and glowering. Picket eyed them warily from the central fire. Some carried torches, and all were angry and armed. They gazed in brazen hatred at him but only glanced at Emma and looked quickly away again.

Fear. Anger. A brooding unrest.

They were silent. All were silent, and this was far more unsettling than noise. Picket could almost wish for insults to fly at him. It would seem better than this quiet, a silence ripe with hate.

"Make way for the prince," came a call from the darkness beyond the edge of the firelight. The gathered soldiers parted and made a lane, those in front bowing on one knee as a hurrying form in the distance approached.

"I hope it's Kylen," Picket whispered, squinting into the dark.

As the form drew nearer, Picket frowned. It was a

shorter, stockier buck. As his face became visible, Picket saw a likeness to Kyle, but where Kyle's face was pleasant and his demeanor winsome, this buck's features were hard-set and only thinly veiled a boiling fury. This was Kyle's brother Naylen, Bleston's second son.

Picket instinctively stepped away from Emma, even as the others stepped closer to her, so that he was distant from the others of his company. He acted on instinct, but it seemed the approaching buck had anger aimed at him, and he didn't want it spilling onto Emma.

"Picket Kingkiller!" Naylen shouted as he reached the edge of the encircling soldiers and came into full view. "You will pay for the betrayal and murder of my father." He was strong, well-built, and ably armored. He ripped free his blade and, bursting forward with surprising speed, rushed at Picket.

"No!" Emma cried, trying to step toward Picket, but Jo and Cole held her back.

The angry prince reached Picket quickly, feinting right before bringing his blade around to strike at Picket's left knee. Picket blocked the stroke and leapt from his good leg, kicking up to meet the wrist of his attacker. His kick knocked the sword free of Naylen's hand as Picket swept back around to drive a darting kick into his middle. Naylen stumbled, tripped, and spilled onto his back. The crowd gasped as Picket caught his attacker's sword out of the air and loomed over the splayed form, bringing both sword points to the prince's neck.

As with many of the moments in flight or battle he had experienced, these seconds, though so few, seemed to stretch past the ordinary limits of time. Picket felt as though he was master of the moment, and though he had only an instant to act, he took the measure of the encounter and knew what he must do.

Picket drew back the prince's sword, as though he would strike. The gathered bucks shouted, and the prince recoiled. But Picket glanced at the sword, then drove its point into the ground. He took Naylen by the hand and dragged him to his feet. Then Picket knelt, offering his own sword, handle first, to the stunned buck. The puzzled prince took Picket's sword but seemed uncertain what to do with it.

"I have not done that thing of which I am accused," Picket said with conviction, looking into Naylen's eyes with complete candor.

Naylen said nothing, only gazed wide-eyed at Picket's face.

Then a shout came from behind. "Lies!"

Picket twisted back to see the white rabbit who had led them to this place darting into the open circle, sword poised to strike Picket's back.

Before Picket could react, Helmer, having anticipated just this, quickly crossed the distance and shot out an arm to meet the attacker's neck. The white buck, stunned by this intervention, was flipped back by the blow and landed crashing on the ground, opening his eyes to see Helmer's blade at his neck.

The crowd pressed in, anger and confusion swelling. Cole and Jo flanked Emma, eyes alert.

Then an ancient, shrill voice screamed out, "Kill them!"

Chapter Nine

The End in Sight

"Kill them, now!"

They turned to see the old soothsayer, Tameth Seer, standing in a new-made gap in the crowd, eyes wild and bony finger pointing at Picket. But when the tall soldiers spun back to execute his order, they saw that another figure had entered the circle. Kylen, thin and sickly, stumbled into their midst, between Tameth Seer and Picket, and shouted in a hoarse retort.

"Stay!" he cried with his hands held high, turning this way and that to address them all. "Stay, by my command!" Around his neck, dangling bright red from a golden chain, was the Whitson Stone.

The poised rabbits paused, glancing back and forth between Tameth Seer and Kylen. Naylen hurried to his brother's side.

"The prince is unwell," Tameth Seer said, eyes crazed as he strode into the circle.

"I am well enough to judge as Terralain's ruler and the heir of all Natalia," Kylen said, clasping his hands together in front of the ruby around his neck, "as you yourself have prophesied."

Tameth Seer scowled; then his face softened and his head fell. "I have seen it, Your Highness," he said, and Picket thought he sounded sincere, almost regretful. "I have seen you in visions, bringing the end. There is a flood. You are brimming over with destiny."

Kylen looked over the visitors and grimaced as Naylen helped support him. He motioned to the few soldiers who had accompanied him, those marked with a red shoulder shield. "Bring them to my pavilion."

Then Picket, swordless and amazed, was led, along with his companions, through the charged camp of Terralain warriors.

Before long they were inside Kylen's tent, large and comfortable but far from lavish. It was long and had a cloth partition midway across. A modest wooden throne sat atop a small rise. Picket winced at the several displays of silver stars on a black field. He had once held such high hopes at the sight of that symbol.

"Leave us," Kylen said, and his guards parted the tent flap and left. "You too," he went on, pointing to Helmer, Jo, and Cole.

Helmer frowned, seemed about to protest, then looked at Picket. Few could read anything in that seemingly plain expression, but Picket read much in it. *I have confidence in you. I'm proud of you.*

Picket nodded, and the three rabbits withdrew, leaving

Kylen with Emma and Picket.

Kylen slumped into the wooden throne and rubbed his eyes. Picket thought he looked weary and weak, a gaunt contrast to the lively, mischievous buck he had first met at Cloud Mountain. Head in his hands, Kylen almost groaned his few words. "Say what you came to say."

"Prince Kylen," Emma began, "we are cousins. It is a desperate time for rabbitkind, and we must unite—"

Kyle cut her off.

"From him," Kyle said, pointing at Picket. "I want... to hear it... from *him*."

Emma glanced nervously over at Picket and seemed about to go on but finally yielded.

"Kyle, you know what's at stake," Picket began. "Our true enemy will attack soon. We are going... we're going to lose. We're going to be routed, in fact. Morbin is coming for us, and he is bringing death and desolation with him. First Warren will fall. Next nearest, Harbone, will fall. Halfwind, Kingston, and Cloud Mountain... you know them. You've seen the faces of the children. The young twins whose parents are already lost will be butchered for the blackhawk's pleasure. As will the votary does and widows of Morbin's murders. They're coming. They won't stop. Please don't make another deal with this evil. Come with us. Fight with us! You are cousins with our queen-to-be. Be my brother on the battlefield, and let's shed blood together. That blood will bond us forever and wash away the problems of our past. This is about rabbitkind's survival now. End your father's feud with King Jupiter's line, or else postpone it until we have gone after our true enemies. Please, Kyle... Prince Kylen, I beg you." Picket dropped to his knees. "We need you. The younglings need you. Come to us, brother. Gain that fame that comes from changing your place in the story. Be for us a hero in our need. Be our ally from now on and Morbin's no more, I beg you!"

Kylen never looked up. But here he held up a hand, and Picket stopped.

"She advised me to stop my treatment." Kylen pointed at Emma, head still down. "She whispered convincing words to me in the forest. Told me to turn on my father's most faithful guide. Told me to renounce my birthright and believe that my father's killer was no true enemy."

"It's true!" Emma said. "Kylen, it's true! Did you stop the medicine?"

"Silence, Emma!" Kylen shouted, lurching to his feet and taking two stumbling steps toward her. "Enchant me no more with... with your words. I see you have this betraying buck in your sway. You have lovely Heather in your thrall too... beautiful, sweet Heather... oh, the shame of it," he went on, tears starting in his wild, sunken eyes, "but not me!"

"Kylen, no," Emma began, her open hands extended before her. "It isn't like that. Let me help you again."

"No more, witch!" he roared.

"Kyle," Picket said urgently, "don't be a fool. Can't you see? Tameth Seer is poisoning you—your body and mind!

We are *not* your enemies."

"If you slander the venerable seer once more in my presence, Longtreader," Kylen said, his voice cold and low, "it will be your last act alive. In my excessive mercy, for love of your sister and because moments ago you let my brother live when you could have killed him, I will allow you all to leave. But you killed my father, Longtreader—do not dare deny it! The next time we meet, it will be on the battlefield." Kylen's voice trailed off as he lurched back to his chair and collapsed into it. He clutched the Whitson Stone and stared, eyes wild, into its red brightness. "And blood will flow. Between you and me, Picket. Blood will flow."

Tears streamed down Emma's face. Picket's heart sank. He felt the war was being lost right here in this Terralain tent, and he didn't know how to stop it. No feat of arms, no risky trick in battle, could solve this riddle. He felt as weak and helpless as he had when Smalls had picked him up and carried him out of danger near Decker's Landing. But there was no Smalls now. Picket's own folly had doomed him to death. Now, more death would surely follow. Dread welled within and was met by a burrowing grief.

"Oh, Kyle," Picket whispered. "You'll kill us all."

"Return his sword, brother," Kylen said, "and escort them away." Prince Naylen parted the stretched curtain behind the throne and walked into view, his square face set in a stern frown.

"As you will, Kylen," the brother said, crossing toward them. He seemed about to speak, but the tent flap parted and a hurrying train of eager rabbits ran in.

Picket saw Helmer, Jo, and Cole among them. And Lallo, a young buck Picket had met at Halfwind but who was now stationed at First Warren. Lallo wore a glider cape and was breathing hard, and his face was distraught.

Before Picket could ask, Kylen cried out, "What's the meaning of this?"

"Your Highness," one of his red-shouldered officers said, bowing, "this buck has come from First Warren, and he reports that Morbin's forces are advancing."

"What?" Emma asked as the pavilion erupted in worried conversation.

"Wait!" Kylen screamed. "Be quiet!" The noise settled and he rose, both hands on the armrests of his throne. "Attacking? Now? But Tameth Seer said Morbin wouldn't attack until—" He stopped when his eyes met Picket's.

"You villain!" Picket cried, rushing at Kylen. Helmer held him back, with help from a Terralain officer, Prince Naylen, and Cole. "Allied with Morbin once more? How dare you accuse me? You're a wretched, grasping usurper like your father! A common villain prepared to betray anyone for gain and glory! Preyfriend! Morbin's pet. Curse you, Kyle!"

"Let us go to fight for our own!" Emma shouted, eyes wet and face grim; "Otherwise, kill us now. There's little difference, since you've killed thousands with your treacherous plots and doomed us all!"

Picket strained to reach Kylen, but Helmer held him

back and spoke. "Let's go, Picket. We have a duty to our own. If these kinslayers want to put arrows in our backs, let them."

Picket stopped straining and nodded. With a last glance of profound malice at Kylen, he turned and followed as Emma's company quit the tent, hurrying into the darkness. An explosion rang out from miles away, and they turned north to see an orange glow, wrapped in a grey haze, in the distance. Terralain soldiers, only moments ago intent on these six interlopers, stared and pointed.

"What's over there?" a young soldier asked.

Picket knew. *Harbone Citadel.* The place where they had sent their most vulnerable for safety. Picket felt his strength drain away. His legs, especially his injured knee, felt too weak to keep him on his feet. He sagged.

"Report!" Emma snapped at Lallo as they gazed on in horror.

"Your Highness," Lallo said, "our scouts picked up a signal from Harbone."

"The warning?" Emma asked. "From that direction?"

"It was both the warning and the signal for under distress."

"What does it mean,

Helmer?" she asked, eyes wild. "For us, now. What should we do?"

"Since I know I can't convince you to flee to a secret location, it means you and Lallo go back to First Warren," Helmer said, "and the Fowlers go to Harbone. We'll be back as soon as we're able."

Emma's head sunk low, and she closed her eyes. "I never should have left. I promised not to leave until Morbin was defeated. And I came here for what? To enrage that poisoned prince even more?"

"We have to go," Helmer said. "Up a tree, all of you. Lallo, stay close to her."

"Yes, sir."

"Wait!" someone called from behind. Picket turned to see Naylen running toward them, sword in hand.

Picket bristled. "This time, I'll not be so kind," he said, fists clenched.

"No," Naylen said, extending the weapon, hilt first. "You never took back your sword. Kylen said to return it. Here it is."

Picket accepted his blade and sheathed it quickly. "We have to go."

Jo stepped toward Naylen. "Check under your brother's throne. I left a note for him there recently when I stood over him while he slept."

"You want me to believe you got past our guard?" Naylen asked.

"I could have killed him." Jo drew a jeweled blade to

display. Naylen's eyes widened slightly. "And if you don't do something, Tameth Seer *will* kill him . . . and then you'll all kill thousands of rabbits you should be fighting beside."

Naylen looked down, eyes thinning to slits.

"Let's go," Helmer growled.

"One more thing," Naylen said, raising his hand. "Three days."

"What?" Picket asked, jaws clenched.

"Kylen has said you have three days."

"Until he attacks," Helmer said in a low rumble. Naylen nodded, head down.

"Tell Morbin's minion we are ever so grateful," Picket said bitterly. "Enjoy picking over the bones of children when you come, princeling."

Chapter Ten

Horror at Harbone

As dawn broke behind them, Picket ascended. Having climbed the highest trees they could find, they leapt to glide away, Emma and Lallo back toward First Warren, and the Fowlers to Harbone Citadel.

Picket outpaced Helmer and Jo, while Cole nearly kept up with him. The fire in the distance made for a foreboding sight, like a second sunrise, and Picket squinted against the drifting smoke. Closer, and closer, and he saw a swarm of shadows in the sky. Morbin's attack squadron.

They were doomed.

He flew on, determined to do what he could amid the ruin.

Nearer now, ash and embers streaked through the air. The skyborne squadron of Preylords was moving away. They had already come and were going. Leaving what?

He could hardly imagine.

Cole shouted at him. Picket couldn't hear the words, but he saw the questioning gesture and knew what it meant. *Should we go on or turn back to First Warren?*

Picket checked the direction of the unnumbered host of Morbin's Preylord raptors. They didn't appear to be heading toward First Warren at the moment. They seemed to be returning north of Grey Grove. Picket pointed forward, toward the ruin of Harbone.

Focusing again on their destination, they could now easily see the ruin. The gate, which he and Helmer had escaped through not so long ago, was smashed, and smoke poured from the black, gaping hole where it had been. Wounded rabbits fled from the ruin, rushing in every direction in terror. He focused on a nurse, her apron more red than white, fleeing with a child in one arm and the other arm extended to hold the hand of another. The children were screaming, and the nurse was running through the smoke and debris, tripping amid the scattered ruins. Then the nurse found her feet and rushed clear of the broken gate. She ran for the relative safety of the nearby woods but stopped suddenly, her horrified scream reaching Picket's ears even through the riotous clamor.

Picket followed her gaze and saw them. *Wolves.* The wild wolves he had first seen when he and Helmer had barely escaped into Harbone, those wolves responsible for killing Lord Hewson, Captain Redthaw, and so many other brave bucks. They were leaping into the ruin of Harbone and preying on the survivors.

Picket felt his anxieties retreat, replaced by a now familiar feeling. A certainty of purpose. Nothing else mattered now. Head down, he sped toward the nurse, who trembled in the midst of several slathering attackers. In his periphery he could see that others were in danger, but for the moment there was only her, those children, and the enemy.

Disengaging the glider, he sped ahead. Faster and faster he fell, until he was ten paces from the pouncing pack. He reengaged the glider, felt it slow him somewhat, then used the drag to keep him just off the ground as he drove into the first wolf. The crunching kick sent the foremost wolf flying and had the same result with the next several as Picket plowed through in a cleaving gash that scattered the astonished wolves. Landing as he unsheathed his sword, Picket sent it slicing at the next nearest enemy, striking down two before they could regroup.

But regroup they did, and they attacked again. Picket rushed back, forgetting his limp as best he could, to stand guard over the kneeling nurse. She had the children hidden beneath her, shielding them as they screamed.

The next wolf leapt, and Picket wanted to twist and let him fly past, but he couldn't let the beast reach those he protected. He gripped his sword with both hands and launched off his good leg, meeting the leaper with a brutal thrust that ended the attacker and knocked Picket back to the ground. As he regained his feet, more wolves rushed in, howling as they attacked in fury. Picket pivoted to protect, but there were so many of them.

The wild host had diminished since his and Helmer's first encounter with them. They seemed weaker, these surviving wolves, and some were wounded. Lord Hewson had killed a great quantity before he fell, but there were still many. Too many for Picket.

Cole glided in, landing nimbly beside Picket and ripping free his sword. Then came Jo, who drew his bow upon landing and sent a single three-arrow shot into the batch of attackers. The next wolf found swift steel from Cole and Picket and died with an agonized cry. Jo kept up a steady fire, finding hearts and heads and leaving dozens dead.

More and more survivors from the smoldering ruin of Harbone hurried to the nurse and children, until the Fowlers finally protected hundreds as the dead wolves piled in heaps around them. Many survivors joined the battle and struck out at the wolves or helped the Fowlers in the fight. Still, it wasn't quite enough. The wild wolves, though fewer and fewer, still pressed in. Picket saw, in snatches between dispatching attackers, a small slice of the horror suffered here. Badly wounded bucks and does in shock at the grisly things they had seen—and were seeing.

And children. Wounded and screaming. Dead and silent. He saw it all amid the smoldering ruin of Harbone Citadel.

Helmer landed and leapt in at last, his furious rally putting final flight to the few remaining wolves of the wild pack. His rage produced a rampage that hit the last attackers with grim results.

Picket winced and fell to his knees, breathing hard and wiping his face with his shaking hand. His master ran after the last wolves, the few remaining attackers scattering in the forest. Helmer turned then, his furious expression fading to a shocked revulsion, and he walked slowly back. Nearing the gate, he collapsed to his knees.

Helmer wept.

Picket got to his feet and turned around and around, looking for the nurse he had rushed in to save. He needed to see her and the children she protected.

Wearily, he moved through the stunned survivors. Amid the shocked, vacant expressions, the hysterical tears, and the angry faces, he walked until he came to one of the many black craters, on the edge of which stood two weeping children.

The nurse lay at their feet, dead.

Chapter Eleven

Cruel Ruin

The next few hours were a nightmare, as Picket and others moved through the devastated remains of the citadel, searching desperately for survivors. After hours of looking through collapsed caverns and burned-out halls, they found only one old doe alive. After two of the searchers were killed in cave-ins and several more wounded, Helmer ordered the search ended.

Picket emerged from the smoking pit that used to be an entrance to Harbone Citadel. It once was a stalwart station for faithful rabbits who waited and worked for the Mended Wood. What his eyes saw now was the farthest thing from the mending. Here, in these ashes, it was hard to believe it could ever come. In his arms he carried the blackened banners once displayed on walls within the citadel. Picket coughed, feeling he might never be rid of the grisly stench of that smoldering dungeon of death. He laid the banners down carefully, stretching them out in the sunlight. A green field bearing a white tree with yellow stars for fruit. Smoke wafted over him, and he coughed again. Looking up, he saw a once beautiful tree, green and glorious, burning yellow-bright while survivors stumbled past, too burdened to even see it. Picket looked down at the banners again. Another that once read "Remember. Resist. Retake." Now it only said "Remember." The rest was burned black.

I'll never forget. He limped into the daylight and met the hopeful looks of the survivors awaiting news of loved ones left inside. He shook his head.

Devastation. Shock. Horror. And more tears. His own tears were spent by now, along with his strength and spirit.

Picket sat on a toppled tree and accepted water from a young buck. "Thank you," he said, drinking deeply. "What's your name?"

"I'm Ikker."

"Are you from Harbone, Ikker?"

"No, sir. I'm from First Warren. Lived there my whole life." Tears came as he continued. "I was . . . excited to leave. I'd never been beyond the walls. I came here yesterday, with my . . . family." He couldn't go on.

"Are they all gone, now?"

"Yes, sir. All gone. My little sister, sir . . . I took care of her. I used to hide her from the Preylords and Daggler's band. They didn't know about her. I hid her hundreds of times. I was her protector! But now . . ."

"I'm so sorry, Ikker," Picket said, his heart aching with the pain. "Did you see them fall?"

"No," Ikker said, "but I was near the gate, and the

guards forced me into the forest when the attack came. They wouldn't let me go back in. I think Morbin's rabbits were inside, along with wolves. I know I saw many rabbits in black wearing red collars striking down our rabbits alongside those wicked wolves. And the birds. Some raptors got inside. They were so big!"

Picket's face formed a snarl. "It wasn't your fault."

Fresh tears. "It doesn't . . . feel like that's true."

"I know, Ikker. But it *is* true. Don't lose heart, or all hope—though it's right to grieve. Maybe your family made it." But Picket had just come from inside, and he had little doubt about their end. "My own sister and brother are lost as well. Parents, too."

"I know about your family, sir," Ikker said, smiling through his tears. "You're Picket Packslayer himself. If only you had been here when they came. If only . . ." Ikker's words trailed off, and he took his water to another nearby band of survivors waiting by the old gate that had become a gaping hole leading down to destruction. Picket winced.

Cole and Jo came and sat beside Picket. None of them spoke. Helmer finished a conversation with the most senior of the survivors by the pit, then crossed to join them, sitting on an overturned cart opposite the three friends.

"We wanted to soar in the sky and save lives, we Fowlers," Helmer said, "but we root in the depths among ruins and find only death. I'm sorry, lads, that you had to do that."

Helmer's sleeve was torn, and Picket saw a long white scar wrapped around his master's arm. Picket had never seen the scar before. It spoke of a brutal past battle and was crossed today by fresh wounds.

"We aren't sorry to do our duty, Captain," Cole replied. "But it was truly awful, and I'll never forget it."

"Where will they go?" Picket asked, nodding to the survivors, now gathering for a conference on the edge of the wood. But no answer came.

They heard a sudden thrashing in the forest, and Uncle Wilfred broke through the tree line and ran to them, his eyes wide. "They're coming back!"

Chapter Twelve

A Longtreader Captive

"Up, bucks!" Uncle Wilfred shouted. "Up and protect the last lives of Harbone. Come on!" He, joined by several young soldiers bearing the symbols of the free citadels, ran past them and stood before the cowering survivors on the edge of the smoldering crater that led down into the ruins. He turned and drew his sword.

The Fowlers were running again, rushing to join Wilfred's small band in protection. Arrows arced overhead as rabbit soldiers in black wearing red around their necks burst from the cover of trees. Jo fired and caught the first two quickly, bringing them down with deadly precision. Soon there were too many for Jo, and the band broke into the clearing and clashed swords with the exhausted defenders.

These traitors were a part of this!

Picket was tired, but the first clash of steel—blocking a powerful strike by a skillful swordsbuck—woke him, and he hammered back an answer that rattled the wrists of his attacker. Dropping low to duck a slicing strike, Picket kicked out to sweep clean his opponent's feet, knocking him down. He did not hesitate with his blade. He felt immediate danger and sidestepped an overhead stroke that ended with his enemy's blade point in the ground. Picket leapt up and kicked out, snapping the buck's blade in half, before spinning to bring his own blade in to finish him.

Now Picket was free to assess the contest, and he saw that the uniformed attackers, those same rabbits that had caused such chaos and enacted so much murder within the citadel, were not so many. Wilfred had several bucks with him, though Picket saw that one was dead and another was on the ground, clutching at a wound. His Fowlers were four, so the defenders, backed against the smoldering pit, neared ten, and the attackers twice that.

"To me!" Helmer shouted. Picket turned and saw his master being overwhelmed by five renegade bucks, with several helpless Harbone survivors behind him. Picket leapt in his direction, then stumbled suddenly as his bad knee gave out. He recovered and slammed into an enemy before he could pin Helmer. Two more fell by arrows from Jo, who, having taken out the enemy archers, was quickly leveling the odds of the encounter.

Picket didn't have time to count combatants now. As soon as he had smashed down one enemy, another's blade snipped the edge of his neck as he skipped backward. Cole's certain stroke ended that attacker, and Picket's first toppled foe sprang up with a scything swipe at Cole's head. Picket deflected the blow and brought his blade back at the buck's

neck. His own stroke was deflected by yet another enemy, and the four battlers traded strikes and blocks in a delicate dance that ended when Jo sent an arrow between Picket's ears and inches from Cole's arm to halve the attacker's strength. As his partner fell dead, the Preylord ally swept his blade across both his opponents, but Picket blocked his blow with ferocity, and Cole drove home his sword in the enemy's middle.

Picket spun to scan the scene and saw Uncle Wilfred battling alone against two foes to protect several survivors. Jo had thrown down his bow and, sword flying at his foes, was engaged in close combat. Picket, seeing that Cole and Helmer had their attackers at even odds, ran for his uncle. Again his leg gave way, but he mastered it faster this time and, drawing close, leapt into the fight by Wilfred's side.

One-on-one now, Uncle Wilfred quickly overcame his enemy. Picket, drawing back to block a sword stroke, tripped on a blackened slab of broken brick and, trying to recover, put too much weight on his bad knee. He crumpled and fell back. His enemy pounced, kicking him in the face, then driving down his blade. Picket just managed to evade the sword, which stuck into the ground. He kicked out at the buck's feet but missed as the attacker leapt up, ripping free the sword and slicing down with a certain killing blow.

Uncle Wilfred's blade crossed in front, deflecting the strike. Wilfred sent a swift kick into the attacker's side, and the enemy crashed hard into a pile of debris. There, Ikker loomed, knife poised.

Picket winced at the ending.

Uncle Wilfred helped drag Picket to his feet, and they hurried to aid Helmer and Cole. Ikker joined them. They quickly ended three enemies, but one last buck ran for the woods in desperate flight. Jo, having snagged an arrow from the field, raised his bow.

"Don't kill him!" Uncle Wilfred shouted. Jo, adjusting at the last moment, sent the arrow into the buck's leg just as he reached the tree line. Ikker scampered after him, red knife raised.

"Hold!" Uncle Wilfred called, and his voice was so commanding that Ikker, enraged as he was, cast down his blade and settled for screaming at the buck amid wild blows.

"You killed my family!"

"I did my duty," the buck cried, defiant.

"Okay, Ikker," Picket said, pulling the furious buck off of the enemy while the rest surrounded him. "We'll deal with him."

Helmer motioned for the captive to be propped against a tree. "What are you? Are you part of Daggler's force?"

"I'm from the High Bleaks...from Akolan," he said, eyes darting all around. "I'm a Longtreader, serving Morbin's ambassador."

Picket and Uncle Wilfred exchanged glances. Wilfred spoke. "You're an assassin, not an ambassador. Why did Morbin attack here and not First Warren?"

The captive laughed, cruel and haughty. "Lord Morbin

wanted you to suffer. He means to end your feeble rebellion, but he wants you to feel the cost of your folly in resisting him. It hurts, doesn't it?" He smiled sickly at Ikker. "We came and made our way in, under guise of aid from First Warren. The fools let us in, and we brought in wolves, then Preylords too. Together, we unleashed destruction below in your dingy tunnels. I enjoyed it."

"You don't even know to be ashamed," Cole said.

"We'll win," he replied, "and that's what matters."

"When does Morbin mean to attack First Warren?" Uncle Wilfred asked, setting his blade to the prisoner's neck. "Be quick to answer. You've condemned yourself by your own testimony, kinslayer."

"We aren't kin!" he spat. "I'm a Longtreader!"

"That's my name too," Wilfred said, and the killer seemed to finally see the resemblance between this buck and Garten.

"And mine," Picket said, adding his blade to his uncle's at the traitor's neck.

"Ambassador Garten's personal guard was called in for this mission. But Lord Morbin's plans for First Warren are known only to himself. Well, I should say the timing is unknown. The plan is settled. He will come in wave after wave with the Six, bringing with him the ancient great wolf king himself. First Warren, and every hunkering hole like this across his lands, will be razed and erased from history. Every enemy rabbit will be killed. Their young, those that survive the purging, will be removed to Akolan and . . . repurposed."

"How have you become so comfortable with the mass murder of your own kind?" Cole asked, eyes aflame.

"Oh, those killed are the lucky ones," he replied, laughing. He looked at Ikker. "I was doing your family a favor when I killed them."

Ikker lunged for him, but Picket held him back.

Helmer said, "Be silent, or I will silence you."

"I'll never be silent—" the prisoner began, but Helmer knelt over him and drove a fist into the murderer's face. The prisoner cried out in pain, then raged at Helmer, trying to bite and scratch him. Cole and Jo held him down till others came to help bind him. Still, the uniformed buck spat as he spoke, blood dribbling down onto his red collar. "He comes, and none will survive! Blood and thunder. Terror and death. It came for this citadel, and it comes for everything and everyone you love!"

The fire of the fight was over, and Picket felt his energy ebbing away. Along with his high spirit, his hope seemed to be draining out in pints. He hated all the rogue buck said, but he had a fearful certainty inside that everything he was saying was true.

Picket turned and walked off a few yards, finding a tree to lean against. But no tears came. Finally, he heard Jo speak up from behind.

"You okay, Picket?"

"I think so, Jo. Just tired."

"Picket!" the prisoner cried, straining his neck against

the grip of a burly buck. "Picket Longtreader?"

Picket turned to face the wild-eyed buck. "I'm Picket Longtreader."

The prisoner laughed loud and long, convulsing in hacking coughs as his bloody smile showed a crazed contempt. "I know your uncle. Ambassador Garten is a great leader. He's bold and—"

"He's a coward," Picket barked, stepping forward. "He betrayed his family, his king, and his kind. Their blood," Picket said, tears starting in his eyes as he pointed to the fallen forms being tended by weeping survivors, "is on his hands."

"He'd be pleased to get credit for their blood," the buck said, snickering with the look of a wicked child with a delicious secret. "That's not all the blood he's pleased to have spilled. There's more and more, and some you would be grieved to hear about."

"Shut him up!" Jo cried, stepping toward him with his fists clenched.

"Wait!" Picket said, sending out an arm to block Jo's progress. Looking into the prisoner's wild eyes, he asked, "What do you mean? Whose blood?"

"I saw it myself, his stained sword." The villain laughed, prolonging Picket's agony.

"Out with it," Helmer said, raising his fist again.

Picket knew what was coming—knew it was true—and the blow still struck his heart like it had never been struck before. Pierced and pounded all at once. Worse than any wound of war.

"Heather Longtreader," the prisoner said, red teeth grinning. "Garten killed her with his own blade and buried her in a desolate place. There was no one there to even mourn her end. She died alone, and it didn't even matter. She's gone, and you're all next."

Chapter Thirteen

Satchels and Stones

A hooded rabbit dashed between districts in the dark. Passing the ash-covered gap in haste, the shadowy figure ran toward the first home and dug into his satchel. He grabbed a stone and hurled it into an open window, then hurried on. He ran to the next house, and the next, hurling stones.

At the end of the block another form joined the first, and together they ran to another cluster of homes, both throwing stones from satchels into the ash-covered homes of Akolan. For the first time in living memory, there had been no sweeping during daylight, and clouds of ash were kicked up around the city. The two forms sprinted up the side stairs of a tall house and crossed the rooftop to its edge. Gazing out across the night, they saw ash rising from every district. Their confederates were everywhere.

"Will they all come, Whittle?" Sween asked, pulling down her hood.

"I don't know," he replied. "I hope most do."

"Do we have room for them all?"

"We'll make room."

"I can't imagine many inwallers will come. They're too far gone, I'm afraid."

Another rabbit, robed like them, appeared at the top of the stairs. "Father Tunneler," he said, "the captains report that the districts are alerted. What now?"

Whittle Longtreader looked at his wife, Sween. She nodded, pulling up her hood again. "Is that you, Dote?"

"Aye, Tunneler," Dote replied.

"Pass the word then," Whittle said, striding toward the stairs, "to rally at the wall." Dote darted down the stairs and could be heard conferring with another rabbit.

"Shouldn't you return to District Seven, Whittle?" Sween asked, catching up to him. "It'll be risky, and there's so much to do."

"You're one to talk," he replied with a smile, "after you risked getting the last assessment from the Commandant."

"I was suited for the job," she said, crossing her arms. "And it was worth it."

"It was." Whittle Longtreader shook his head. "It's hard to believe what they mean to do with... well, with all rabbitkind. They truly are monsters."

"Will they really do it?" Dote asked, swiping at the ash kicked up by his return to the rooftop.

"Yes," Sween answered. "I've listened to them in their lairs, stood mere steps from Morbin himself—massive on his throne—as he spoke of rabbitkind as a disease that needed curing. He'll do it. These last actions of ours have been all the provocation he's needed. He's in earnest, all right, and the Commandant can't be underestimating it."

"Then all the more reason to warn the inwallers too," Whittle said.

"But they're Morbin's pets," Dote said, scowling. "So what if they suffer for their years of collaboration? I won't be sorry to see them skinned."

"They're rabbits, still," Whittle said. "And if they turn back to us, we'll welcome them with open arms."

"I know what you've suffered," Sween said, crossing to lay a hand gently on Dote's arm. "I know it well. But we must think of them not only as they have been but as what they might become."

Dote frowned, then nodded. "I know you're right, but it will be hard to forgive them."

"It's always hard to forgive, but it's never not worth it." Sween put her arm around the younger rabbit. "We'll help each other."

"We'll have to," Whittle said.

"I'll follow you, Father Tunneler," Dote said, "and do as you say, even if that means forgiving these villains."

They heard a whistle from the foot of the stairs.

"Let's go," Whittle said.

They hurried down the steps and turned northeast, joining up with hundreds of runners like themselves, all wearing makeshift satchels stuffed with stones. The ash billowed out in their tracks as they made for the huge wall at the city center.

"Father!" some called as they saw Whittle Longtreader, and he smiled at them and waved. "Tunneler!" they said, and "It's the Tunneler and the Truth!"

"Father," a young buck said, rushing up to him as they made for the wall. "I'm proud to be in your company. My uncle says you'll be the greatest Tunneler in history and will lead us all to freedom."

"We'll do it together," Whittle said, and the young buck fell into rhythm with the rest, marching on.

"Father," another young buck said, hurrying up, "I bet I can throw mine farther than you."

"Jacks?" Whittle asked, peering into the darkness at the figure. "Is that you, son?"

Jacks nodded, pulling down his bandana and hood. "It's me, Father."

"Where's Har—" Sween began, scowling, but a young doe spoke up.

"I'm here," Harmony said, pulling back her hood and jogging up. "I never took my eyes off him."

"Good," Whittle said. "And to answer your question about if you can throw a stone farther than me? No, of course not."

"I'm not so certain," Jacks said, punching his father's shoulder playfully.

"You're getting to be a big lad, Jacks," Whittle said, raising two fists in mock seriousness. "But anytime you want, I can show you the difference between a big young buck and little old buck."

"Maybe after we survive this?" Sween asked, nodding at the wall ahead, which was surrounded by uniformed guards with high pikes and stern expressions. "*If* we survive this."

Whittle gazed ahead and raised his arms. All of the approaching rabbits halted and, making a wide circle around the wall, backed off from the guards. A silence fell.

"Causers and insurrectionists!" called an officer, stepping forward. He wore a red collar and wings on his left shoulder. His right sleeve was ringed with gold bands. "Your doom is near! Meanwhile, do not try to enter District Six. The inwallers want no part of your rebellion and disease. If you attack, we will be forced to destroy you."

Whittle stepped forward. "Wrongtreader Captain, we mean you and your soldiers no harm. We come armed only with truth." He reached into his satchel and drew out a stone. "A hard truth."

Each rabbit rounding the guards drew out a stone and held it, poised to throw.

"I am Captain Tram, and I have served Ambassador Garten for many years," the officer said. "Your stones don't frighten us. You'll only give us cause to engage and end you all."

"Morbin wants us all dead, Tram," Whittle said. "We all know that now. Even the inwallers won't escape his anger—not now that the end's come. I know you soldiers fear infection from us." Tram glanced back at his officers and soldiers, some of whom fidgeted nervously. "We do come with an infection. And we want to pass it on to you." Some of the soldiers stepped back, and Tram stepped forward, urging his officers ahead. Some followed, but others hung back.

"Come no closer!" Captain Tram called. "Away with you all, back to the Leper's District where you belong. You'll infect us all!"

"We are as well as you are. Just look at us. We are no threat to you. It is Morbin who will kill us all," Whittle said, "and he'll use first your hand against us, then another's against you, until we're all gone."

"Causer lies!" Tram cried, but he didn't sound convinced.

"I am no liar," Whittle cried. "I am the Tunneler and the Truth!"

"He is the Tunneler and the Truth," the rabbit host repeated followed by a unified solitary stamp.

"We have no wish to fight you," Whittle continued. "Our attack—our infection—is only this." He raised his rock and, showing it to Captain Tram, tossed it across so that it fell at the agitated captain's feet.

Tram bent to examine the stone and saw words scrawled across it. He held it up carefully with a gloved hand in the dim moonlight. And he read it.

Be free. It's time. Last chance. District Seven by dawn.

As Tram read, Whittle signaled, and all of his company cast their stones at the feet of the soldiers opposite them. Slowly they lifted them up and read, and some crossed at once to friends among the free rabbits. Some argued and seemed ready to fight.

"Archers!" Captain Tram cried, and a team of archers hurried to his side. He pointed at Whittle, who did not move. More archers from down the line of soldiers stepped forward. Some were uncertain, but all nocked arrows to strings and aimed. "Fire on my command."

Captain Tram raised his arm, poised to order death for the ragtag band of satchel-and-stones rabbits. At the last moment, a buck appeared on top of the wall, holding high a torch. His scarred face and eyepatch were notorious among all in Akolan, even were it not for the high rank

displayed on his neat uniform.

"Hold," the Commandant said evenly. "Captain Tram, your bucks will stand down. These rabbits may enter and fulfill their task."

"But, Commandant!" Tram cried, disbelieving. "They'll infect us all... our families! Sir!"

"Hear me, my soldiers," the Commandant shouted in his authoritative rasp. "My last brief to you is this. There is not now, nor has there ever been, a single actual leper in Akolan. It was always a ruse to hide the truth of District Seven, where rescue awaits us all—inwallers too—if we will only be brave and humble-hearted enough to receive it."

"Sir," Tram screamed, "please don't—"

"My last command, officers and soldiers all," the Commandant cried above the swelling din, "is this... it is really an appeal, an invitation." He dropped to one knee, kneeling before them. "Be free. It's time. Bring your families to District Seven, on the other side of the so-called Leper's District. Follow our Father, the Tunneler and the Truth!"

Cheers.

"Now friends," Whittle cried, nodding gratefully to the Commandant, "let us enter in peace." He walked toward the gate, and the rest of his company filed behind him. Captain Tram blocked his way, drawing his sword and planting himself in front of the gate.

"You'll have to go through me to enter this city," Tram said, gritting his teeth.

Whittle glanced around. Few soldiers stood with Tram,

and many were now hurrying back inside the wall, rushing to their families.

"You cannot bar me, Captain," Whittle said. "I am the Tunneler and the Truth."

"He is the Tunneler and the Truth!" they all shouted.

"What's your truth?" Tram spat, "but a sack of stones and a band of ragged lepers?"

"I'm sorry," Whittle said, walking up to the tip of Tram's sword.

"Sorry for what?" the agitated captain cried, ready to strike out at any moment.

Whittle slid the rock-filled satchel off his shoulder and spun, swinging it in a swift strike that stunned and toppled the captain. "For that."

Sween took Whittle's hand, and she, Harmony, Jacks, and all the others marched through the gate.

In the distance, stark against the moon, winged shadows swelled.

Chapter Fourteen

Satchels and Stones and Water

Heather jerked awake, intense pain upsetting the blissful oblivion of sleep. Eyes closed tight with agony, she tried to calm her rapid heartbeat. She listened.

Drip. Drip. *Drip.*

Where am I?

She was aware then of the hand she held, had clasped so tightly even in unstoppable sleep, and her strange ordeal came flooding back.

I was taken by my uncle in Akolan and brought to Forbidden Island. Uncle Garten stabbed me—she winced at the memory—*and kicked me into a pit. This pit. In this pit, doomed to die in a hopeless, dank, dark tomb, I saw light. Light above, a mere mote of brightness. And* him.

And his heart beat.

She opened her eyes, afraid it had been one of her surreal dreams. So much of it seemed a seamless continuation of her visions in the night.

But he was there. *Smalls*. The one she loved. His hand in her hand. His heart…

Painfully, Heather levered up on her elbow and placed her head on his chest once more.

Still beating. But so, so faint.

"How have we come together like this?" she whispered, and her voice was hoarse, her throat dry. "And how have you survived these many days?"

Heather was desperate for water—water!—and knew whatever she needed, Smalls likely needed more.

Drip. Drip. *Drip.*

There is water here. But how to get to it?

She listened intently.

Drip. Drip. *Drip.*

Inhaling deeply and steeling herself against the pain, she faced the sound of dripping.

Letting go of Smalls' hand, she began crawling, in agony, along the moss-covered rock of this vast cavern. She couldn't see well, and half the time she closed her eyes against the pain, but she crossed slowly till the sound was louder and the ground felt damper.

At last Heather reached the trickle and reached out to feel for the drip. But her hand found a small pool. Though she could not see well by the scant light, the pool looked clear enough. She didn't care about dirt at this point but bent and drank in gulps of the cool liquid. It had a mossy taste, almost vegetable in flavor, and she drank on till she could hold no more.

Now, how to get some to Smalls? Maybe he had somehow been drinking from this pool after being dumped in here, half-alive. Maybe that's how he had survived. She started to reach inside her satchel to find something to carry water in when she noticed a clay bowl on the rim of the pool.

She frowned, gazing around in sudden suspicion. Then, as quickly as she could, Heather filled the bowl and carried it painfully back to Smalls. As she crawled, she thought that this bowl had likely been there for uncountable years, and it had surely been ages since anyone used it. She recalled Seven Mounds back in Nick Hollow and how Picket and Smalls had described the disused insides of those series of caves, complete with mundane household items like plates and cups.

Reaching Smalls, she tilted his head up. An agonizing wrench in her wound caused her to nearly faint, but she managed to pour a little water into his mouth. He didn't choke, and she eased his head back down and dropped the bowl onto the soft moss.

She was out of breath, and an insistent weariness deepened till she could barely open her eyes.

Heather knew she needed to examine the wound, or wounds, Smalls no doubt had, but she dreaded confirmation of his peril. And she knew her own wound was mortal. She could feel her life ebbing away.

It won't do to surrender, even here at the end. I must finish life as I have lived it, or have tried to live it.

I am a healer.

Heather had been trained by Emma to tend to herself first in any battle in which she was wounded. This command was so often repeated that it had become an automatic instinct. *You must see to your own condition first, so that you may serve others best.* So, with some hesitation, she tore away the matted fabric around her pierced middle and gazed with grief at her wound.

There could be no doubt. It *was* fatal.

Heather was dying.

Tears came, but she reached for her satchel to apply some ointment and binding. That might slow the process and help her examine Smalls. She felt weak. *So* weak. But the water had helped, and she was determined to carry on till all hope—every last drop of it—was lost.

She drew out Emma's ointment and spread it liberally over her wound, recalling the last patient she had

treated, Master Mills in Akolan. His was a perilous case too. She recalled how she had seen his twin at the Victory Day revolt the next day—so like him it was alarming. She wrapped her wound as best she could, though the wrap could not staunch the bleeding. Heather inhaled deeply, a cough catching her breath, then turned to Smalls.

The small light above brightened, as if the clouds high outside were giving way to full sunshine, and a little trickle of light fell on Smalls. Maybe he had crawled to this spot for the scant heat of the sliver of sun. She opened his bloody shirt and saw the awful wound, now septic in its advanced stage. She fought down an urge to be sick. She was heart-broken but focused on doing what she could.

Reaching inside her bag, she found Aunt Jone's battered

purse, and smiled. She drew out the necklace Smalls had given her, the torch bright on its pendant. She put it on. Then the emerald gem, the symbol of what had been his destiny. She raised the Green Ember and, kissing him gently, she clasped it around his neck. It hung over his heart.

She tossed the small vial of tonic back inside and reached for Emma's treatment. Black edges pushed into the center of her vision, and she blinked furiously as she fumbled with the satchel. Fighting to focus, she pushed away the insistent alarm of her body's peril and worked on. She tore strips for binding, then found Emma's remarkably potent tonic. But she had used this treatment many times and knew its virtues did not extend to wounds as far gone as these. It was no miracle elixir. Still, she poured some into her own mouth, and also Smalls'.

The image of Master Mills appeared in her mind again, and she recalled the excitement with which she had been greeted at the District Four clinic the day after she had helped Doctor Hendow treat him and others. Then . . . the twin brother. She was growing dizzy. Heather believed there was a thread of something important just out of reach, but she could not lay hold of it. She swooned, catching herself just before she fell.

Aunt Jone came to her mind. The old doe had been arrested for stealing Prester Kell's "True Blue," then later insisted she had finally found her long-sought-for cure. Heather thought of her own healthy arm, how it had healed remarkably well while in Akolan. *Was it possible?*

Did Master Mills have no brother? Was it him there on the battlefield?

The tonic. *Aunt Jone's tonic!* She reached in again and dug out the small bottle. She poured several drops into Smalls' awful wound, then more into his mouth. Stoppering the top, she felt a strange sensation.

Fading. Paling.

She felt certain that if she closed her eyes she would never open them again. But she could not—*could not*—keep them open.

Heather touched the Green Ember at his chest. "You would have been a magnificent king," she said, and she collapsed.

The last thing Heather remembered was a guttural gasp from the far side of the cavern and the sound of tumbling rocks.

Chapter Fifteen

Tower of Dreams

Heather had always dreamed. But her dreams had increased in intensity and weight of meaning since she and Picket had become partisans in the cause.

Now she seemed to see, through blurry vision, a scaly hand reaching out to touch a fallen rabbit's chest, gathering into its slithering grip the glowing green gem at his neck. A thin whispering cackle and a darting tongue. "Sleep, or death?"

The hand let go the gem and slipped into the shadows. A rumbling grind of stone on stone sounded from the dim recesses behind, and she gazed on the fallen, unmoving rabbit. A sob stuck in her throat, and despair descended on her like a sudden flood.

The blurry vision faded to darkness.

A vivid scene appeared in its place. She was back home in Nick Hollow with her family, and they were playing a familiar game of Father's invention called Tower Wars. Using small wooden blocks Father had fashioned, she and Picket were building a tower on one side of the room near the fire, and Father was building another on the far side, near the kitchen. He was also wrangling Jacks, who believed he was helping, while Mother made dinner in the kitchen beyond.

"Now, Jacks," Father said, "we cannot allow these upstarts to vanquish us yet again. We must build for strength as well as beauty, son."

The game consisted of building opposing towers and then, when each side was finished, hurling a small ball back and forth to test which tower could withstand the battery longer.

"It's your turn to design the tower," Picket said, "so what are we building?"

"As tall as we can make it," she answered.

"But that won't last long in the battle."

"True," she mused, "but when it falls, it will be spectacular!"

He smiled, nodded, and set to work.

Heather watched Picket as he laid the blocks in succession. She smiled. He looked young and had no scars from battle. His eyes were innocent pools, as yet unclouded by the darker parts that would soon move in through hardships.

This very game had happened, and she remembered it well. She seemed to be the only one with awareness of what was to come, of how soon their parting would be.

"Are you going to help?" Picket asked, gazing up at her. She looked into his eyes once more, and they began to change, to lose their innocence and deepen with the pain of what was to come. With *knowing*. "We should enjoy this while we can, Heather."

She nodded gravely and set to work alongside him. They built their tower with a tall, fragile foundation, but the top rose higher than any they had made before. It was lovely, and they both smiled, even while knowing it would not last. Perhaps *because* it would not last.

Heather smiled at Picket, and he smiled back, eyes damp and with the hint of a wince at their edges. They held hands and looked across to where Father finished his tower, half of it hideous where Jacks had contributed. Mother sang softly in the kitchen just behind them.

"The skies once so blue and beautiful,
Are littered with crass, cruel foes.
Their bleak, black wings beat a dreadful beat,
Over sorrowful songs of woes.

"Songs of suffering and cruel murders,
All lament and never a voice,
Raised in grateful gladness to the heights,
Never reason to rejoice.

"But,
It will not be so in the Mended Wood,
We'll be free and glad again.
It will not be so in the Mended Wood,
When the heir of Jupiter reigns."

Picket squeezed Heather's hand, and they exchanged a significant glance. Mother hummed on, the tune becoming a backdrop as she disappeared from Heather's view.

"Jacks, no!" Father scolded, dragging away his youngest son, who was carrying blocks taken from the base of their tower. "You're unsettling the foundations!"

She came suddenly awake, gasping hoarsely for breath. Dragging in thin measures of air, she sat up, struggling to breathe. Her throat convulsed and a violent spell of coughing ensued that set her writhing in breathless agony for several minutes, sapping the last of her strength.

Finally, eyes streaming and unsteady breath coming in halted, wheezing intervals, she settled on her side and stopped coughing. After a few minutes, she opened her eyes, hoping to gaze on the one she loved, perhaps for the last time.

Smalls was gone.

Chapter Sixteen

Deepening Darkness

Heather tried to scream. A strangled gargle was all that emerged, and she groaned, eyes bulging and wound bleeding freely, as she twisted and tried to rise.

She strained, and an avalanche of pain came as she somehow struggled to her knees. Agony screamed inside her, making everything around her fade into distant rumor. But even there, on the edge of her perception, she heard the tumble and clatter of rock on rock, and a distant part of her mind wondered at it.

Bringing one unsteady knee high, she placed her foot painfully and breathed deeply, trying to find an elusive balance. In a desperate effort, she heaved up, aiming to stand on her own two feet again.

Heather pitched sideways and fell like a plank, rebounded off the mossy stone, and settled into a limp oblivion.

* * *

Darkness, and more darkness. A hazy daze. An eerie lightness of heart. Dreamlike ease. Deep, deep darkness. She tried to open her eyes. A voice, slick as the wet stones on the cavern floor, spoke into the gloom.

"Have you passed over, little doe?"

I think I have. She tried to respond aloud, but nothing would come out. Nothing seemed to work right.

"For generations he has waited for the promised conference," she heard.

What have you done with his body?

"It was promised, you know. A rumor of ancestors, but he thought it only a story. Now, he is not so certain."

Don't separate us.

"Shall he tell you how long he has waited? There is little else to do. All his doing is done. What has he done these long years as keeper? He has kept alive the memory of his kind, as the treaty decrees. He has slept and wakened, eaten and drank, wandering these inescapable passages, tending the countless dormant issues of possibility. He has puzzled over the vault, spent countless hours in grim deliberation."

Heather was confused, but she heard these words on a plane where emotions seemed to be a distant memory. Nothing seemed to touch her heart, and her mind was but distantly interested. Still, she responded in her mind. *I only want to see him again.*

"At last he has cracked it. At last he has the answer. He needed to go around, not through. Around, which meant digging."

Smalls. My dear Smalls. Now Heather's mind, which had been like a long, dim hall, narrowed to the size of a slender tunnel, and meaning fled into the shadows beyond her fading light.

"He is near . . . so very near . . ." the brittle voice intoned, but Heather lost the thread, and the tunnel of her understanding collapsed.

Darkness. Deepening darkness. Nothing.

* * *

Then, an age later, something.

"Heather," a familiar voice whispered. "Drink this . . ."

She drank, somehow getting the thin liquid to slide down her throat without coughing. Then she smiled, or dreamed of smiling, and the darkness came again.

Once more, she drank on command, feeling easy in the presence of that beloved voice.

"Heather, for me," he said. "Drink again."

And later, hours or days later, once again, he spoke to her.

"Drink again, Heather," he said, and she did drink down the cool vegetable-flavored draft. She meant to fade again, as she had again and again, but he squeezed her hand. "Which one, Heather? Which one did you give me?" he asked. "The one in the small battered purse, or the larger one you have more of? Squeeze my hand if it's the small vial in the old purse. Heather, please!"

It was a happy dream, she believed, sleeping and sleeping and waking to drink, feeling every time better and better and—best of all—hearing his voice. She seemed almost able to open her eyes and see him once again, but she slept and slept again, waking only to drink at his command. *He would have been a beautiful king, with kind authority and gentle power. That would be a dream pleasanter even than the one I'm in.*

Darkness. Unknowing. Happy absence of thought and will.

"Again, my dear," he whispered, what seemed a thousand years later. "Drink."

She did drink, eagerly now and with some energy.

Heather began to suspect she was not dead, was not always dreaming. Threads of meaning wove together in her head, making patterns of purpose that began to make sense.

"Are we alive?" she asked and was alarmed at the sound of her own voice.

"Heather!" Smalls cried, coming close and touching her face. "Yes, we're alive!"

She felt joy welling up within her, a deep happiness rich with gratitude. And health—unexpected strength—coursing through her body. She opened her eyes.

Smalls. Smalls was there, gazing down on her with a look of such love and relief that she couldn't believe it was real. She blinked, breathed in deep, and then laughed. Laughed loud and full, without coughing or losing her breath.

Smalls laughed too. They embraced, held each other, and wept for joy in the dim light of the island's deep cavern.

Heather couldn't believe it was real, but it felt more real than anything she had ever experienced. She was alive. She was growing well again, somehow. And he, the hope of the cause and her own heart's love. Here.

Smalls was *alive*.

Chapter Seventeen

Trapped in the Tomb

"How?" Heather asked, breaking their embrace to gaze at him. His eyes were alive with light. *How? How? How!*

"You," Smalls answered. "You came here. You saved me."

"And then . . ."

"And then I saved you."

"We were both abandoned and left for dead here," she said, "but we're alive . . . together. How are we alive, Smalls?"

"This, I think." Smalls reached for her satchel and pulled out Aunt Jone's battered old purse and drew out the small vial. "You squeezed my hand. I poured this in your mouth and in your wound."

"My wound!" she cried, reaching for the spot. It was cleaned, no doubt by Smalls, and it was whole. Somehow, whole. *Healed!* "Aunt Jone!"

"Who?"

"This is Aunt Jone's tonic," Heather said, beaming. "She said she had finally done it, and she had indeed! Oh,

Smalls," she wrapped him in another embrace, "we are truly healed and together!"

"You didn't know?" he asked. "I mean, about the tonic?"

"No, no. I had no idea." She stopped, then began to think back over her short time in the pit. "Wait, no. I did, in my last moments of consciousness, begin to see the possibility...I used it on a patient in Akolan—"

"You went to Akolan?"

"I did," she said, taking his hands in hers. "Oh, there's so much to tell. But I gave a dying buck some of this tonic and took a drop myself. My arm healed quickly and, the next day, I saw him on the battlefield as healthy as any buck half his age."

"Battlefield? In Akolan?" Smalls' eyes went wide. "I need you to catch me up on what's been happening. Is the flame of the cause still burning?"

"I believe it is," Heather answered, "even if it's down to one last, trembling ember. It is burning still."

"Tell me everything, Heather," he asked, passing her a bowl of the greenish water, "if you feel strong enough."

She took a long drink, savoring the satisfying taste. Breathing in deeply several times, she looked up. "I could talk for days. I will tell you how it is, as far as I know, and what hopes we still have for the mending."

She told him all of her adventures since she had seen him last, how Emma had led the resistance and how Picket had fought and flown on high. Of the princes Bleston and Kylen and the betrayals that shook them all at Rockback Valley. How the Terralains, led by Kylen and Tameth Seer, held the Whitson Stone and believed Kylen to be the rightful ruler and heir of all Natalia.

"But the Ruling Stone is a symbol of authority," Smalls said, "not its basis."

"Still," she continued, "the Terralains are a problem that complicates the war with Morbin."

Heather went on, telling of her time in Akolan, of meeting her parents and brother Jacks, of the ruse of the lepers, and the causers' revolt on Victory Day to save the younglings and sneak them away to the secret Seventh District. She told how Father, at the last moment, had become the Tunneler and the Truth. Smalls listened intently, asking questions for clarity from time to time but keenly focusing on her account.

"So, that is my side of the story," she concluded. "What I don't know is how Emma and Picket are situated now. I don't know if they abandoned Cloud Mountain as planned or if they tried to infiltrate First Warren as some advocated. I don't know. I know every avenue for our side is riddled with danger, and it's likely the fight has been costly."

"I've missed so much of the war," Smalls said, hanging his head. "I am so sorry for my folly. I should have listened to my wisest counselors. I should have done many things differently."

"It's true," Heather said, squeezing his hand, "but I know why you did what you did. And you meant well, I know. We all know it. And although Emma has never wanted to be what she now is, she doesn't blame you. Picket blames himself, of course, but he has been a champion for the cause, and the fight goes on."

"Maybe they are better off without me," Smalls mused. "Maybe Emma, who has less ambition, is better suited for the responsibility of ruling."

"Emma would be a great queen," Heather said, "and she has been a bright light in the fight against the darkness. But the cause needs you. Your sister needs you. Rabbitkind and this whole wounded world need you."

"We have to get out of here," Smalls said. Standing, he turned around slowly to gaze at the rocky confines of the cavernous pit. Clusters of smooth rounded stones dotted the floor, half-hidden in thick-grown moss. The scant light revealed high walls, propped up at their base in a few places by stacked stone and wooden support beams. Smalls frowned. "We have to escape."

A shrill, cackling laughter pierced the cavern and echoed off the walls. "Escape?" The shrill voice laughed again. "You seek to leave?"

From the dim recesses of the cave's edge, a dark form glided lithely into view. Moist and muscular, pale-eyed and smooth, with a faint hiss whispering over the silence of the rabbits' arrested breaths. A dragon. It walked slowly into the open to stand before the clusters of slick round stones. "The keeper has abided here for many of your lifetimes," he said. "You will see what the keeper has seen these endless years. You shall spend what remains of your short lives here. There is no escape... no escape possible from the dragon tomb."

Chapter Eighteen

Faded Moonlight

Picket's glider was losing height. He did all he could to prolong his sailing along in the sky, to get as close as he could to First Warren. He was quite near now but was dipping lower and lower. Even in height with the treetops, he flew ahead, scanning all around. To his left, the top of Forbidden Island stood out from the glittering surface of Lake Merle. Beyond it, the River Flint led back toward Grey Grove, north of which Morbin's army massed and plotted doom for rabbitkind.

The dam on the northern border of First Warren, built long ago, created Lake Merle. Forbidden Island rose high above six smaller islands that evenly flanked the bigger central peak—a desolate, foreboding sight. Picket felt a strange desire to go to the island and explore its barren surface. *Why is it Forbidden?* But there was no time for exploration. The war was careening toward its awful climax, and the end seemed certain to be not a glorious battle but a catastrophic massacre.

He glided past the last of the trees and settled into the

space between the forest and the city walls. He landed in the Black Gap, the burned-up barrier between the forest and the city. Small shoots of green grass peeked out beneath the charred mass, but Picket could not be comforted by their significance. Not now.

Picket limped forward, gazing ahead at the broken west wall and the busy city within. This massive breach, so welcome to him when reinforcements had poured in through it during the last battle, now served its original purpose as the main gate of the city. It was the west gate, but some called it simply "the gate."

First Warren was at work, preparing for a fight it could not win. In their flight from the ruin of Harbone, he had flown farther than Helmer, Jo, and Cole—his fellow Fowlers—so he would reach the city first. The rest, including Uncle Wilfred, young Ikker, and his prisoner, would follow on foot.

The sun rose above the ancient towers, and Picket shaded his eyes. He stumbled into the city, exhausted and downcast, walking down the old road toward the city center.

"A cart, there!"

Picket twisted to see who had shouted, then smiled as a tall, gaunt, one-eyed buck with red fur hobbled toward him. "Cap!"

"Aye," Captain Moonlight called back, smiling wide, "it's me."

Picket smiled. "Last I saw you, you were in bed and looked awful. To tell you the truth, you don't look so great now." Captain Moonlight, leader of the resistance movement within First Warren's walls for many years, had been wounded badly as he fought heroically for the city's liberation. He hobbled out to greet Picket, clearly nowhere near his former strength.

"Neither of us, I think, are what might be called 'prime.' But I'm all right," Cap said. "Not quite fit enough to be on the front lines, but I'll do my part. Like my old father years ago at the original Citadel of Dreams—which was just down the way, there—I'm supplying drinks and food. Not so much music, but we're doing our best. I'm a quartermaster now. And you look like you could use some provisions."

"I am pretty low on energy," Picket admitted.

"We have a grand team, and we can find you something quick. Speaking of," he went on, "have you ever met a taverner called Gort?"

Picket smiled. "I have."

"That one's as mad as moonbucks! But I'll be dashed if he can't make a meal fit for a hundred princes. He's been at it for days. He's got all them cooks in line and won't suffer any fools. He's even clapped a stopper over a few high-ranked officers."

"He's quite a force," Picket said.

"He had a run-in with a lovable clown called Eefaw Potter yesterday," Cap said. "I couldn't see why Gort got so bent out of shape over a few broken mugs, but he nearly battered that poor potter."

"There's some history there," Picket said, rubbing his forehead.

"So I gathered. I'll stop yapping, Picket. I can see you're plumb tuckered. Where are ya heading?" Without waiting for Picket's reply, he called to a hulking buck toting a cart piled high with barrels of greens. "Dump that load there, Ray Carter, and take this officer to . . . the palace?" He glanced at Picket, who nodded wearily. "To the palace, Ray." Ray nodded and began unloading his cart, glancing wide-eyed at Picket.

"Thanks, Cap," Picket said.

"Anything for you, General Sunshine."

Picket smiled, leaned against the cart, and shook hands with Ray.

"If it's all right, my lord," Ray said, head down, "we'll go round near the dam wall. The main way, as you can see there, is being worked on, and it's all clogged into the square at the moment."

"Whatever you think best, Ray," Picket replied, choosing to ignore the inaccurate honorific of "lord."

Captain Moonlight raised his voice again. "Weezie, there," he called to a distant band of rabbits serving out meals to weary workers, "bring this buck some provisions!"

Weezie wore an apron and was hard at work amid a busy party of serving rabbits.

"We're overwhelmed here, Cap," she called back. "Why don't you stop shouting orders for ten seconds and do it yourself?" Then she caught sight of Picket easing onto the cart. "Picket!" she cried, dropping her tray and dashing away. Remembering herself, she hurried back and gathered a board stacked with rations, along with a tall jug, and rushed over to the cart.

After setting down her supplies and wrapping him in a hug, she gazed into his face. "What happened?" she asked, seeing the weariness and pain so plain there. "The rumors are all over that an attack is imminent—from Morbin, or Kylen. Or both."

He nodded.

"And what they say about Harbone?"

"The worst is true, I'm afraid. It's bad, Weezie."

"Drink something," she said, raising the jug as the carter, receiving a signal from Captain Moonlight, pulled Picket and Weezie down the old road. Picket saluted Cap, then drank deeply, wiping his mouth after.

"Thank you."

"You must feel destroyed," Weezie said when he had begun to eat a little.

Picket nodded as the cart wound around the busy center of town and Ray carried them past projects on every side. On rooftops all over, new hatches and stairways were being installed. Along the sides of buildings, ladders were being fastened tight. They passed near the dam wall, where Heyward was examining an alcove at the base of the dam while workers installed what appeared to be large stone steps beneath the surface of the river.

"Harbone was hard for you to see," Weezie said. "You're

sad to think of what's going to happen here."

Picket nodded, then turned back to her. "I'm sorry, Weezie. Thank you for taking care of me. I sometimes think you're the last light I've got in an ever-growing darkness. Jo told me that Heather's dead. That Tameth Seer heard it from Garten himself."

Weezie looked down. "I'm so sorry, Pick. Maybe it isn't true, though."

"It feels true." Picket leaned against her, laying his head on her shoulder. "It feels like I will fail everyone in the end, and no one I love will live to see the mending."

Weezie wrapped her arms around him and held him. "If we don't see the mending, it won't be because of you. If any of us ever do see it, then we'll have you—in a big way—to thank."

"I wanted to see her again. I wanted her to be safe."

"But she was brave, like you. She chose to trade her life for the cause. Heather placed more weight on the hope of the mending than she put value on her own life. That's how I want to live. And die, if I must."

Picket nodded. "Of course you're right. And that helps me know what to say to Emma when I report to her."

"I'll see you to the palace, but I've got to get back to my duties." Weezie looked down and wiped her hands on her grimy apron. "I'm a servant here—here at the end. And I don't mind. I have my bow handy for when they come. Until then, I'm a servant. My armor is this apron. It's not very glorious, but it keeps me working the farm—though the farm's never been so shabby—and feeding folks who need it."

"I envy your job. There's nothing I'd rather do than feed folks alongside you."

"But we need you to fight right now," Weezie said, staring into his eyes. "We need you to finish this. So that after . . ."

"It's hard to imagine after," Picket said, trying to shake away the horrors of Harbone. "But I will keep fighting, Weezie. For them all. For Heather's memory, and Smalls' too. For this old city. For you."

"First, you have to rest. After you report to Emma, you must rest," she said.

After he reported to Emma, Picket did rest. At Emma's order, he was placed in a room that also held a perilously wounded officer he knew. Lieutenant Drand lay motionless and silent but for his ragged breathing. Picket could see that he had lost a leg in the last battle. He seemed likely to lose his life. *Will this war leave us with nothing? Will it take every limb, every life, and grind us down to powder? Will Morbin really win?*

Picket closed his eyes, unable to fight off the exhaustion any longer.

Chapter Nineteen

The Last Lord Captain

Picket's sleep was deep and seemed to be impenetrable. But a break came, small at first, and he heard talking.

"He's asleep. I shouldn't wake him."

"He'd want to know."

"He's shattered, Jo." This was Cole's voice. "This might be his last chance for sleep."

"How long have I been out?" Picket asked, blinking and levering up on an elbow.

"You had several hours, Pick," Jo said quietly.

Picket nodded. "What's happening?" he asked softly.

"Wilfred's back, and Mrs. Weaver's been talking to the buck we took prisoner at Harbone," Cole answered. "She's managed to get a lot out of him. He thinks he's outsmarted her, but we've been watching them for a little while with Emma—that is, with the princess—from behind a hidden partition, and Mrs. Weaver has been bleeding away the intelligence from him, all while he thinks he's being clever."

"He's already revealed that Morbin's plan is to release the Six—those most elite raptor lords—in waves of attack,"

Jo went on. "The attack on Harbone was Garten's part, with his best rabbit soldiers, wolves, and minor raptor support, and acted as a preliminary to their main assault. The Six, with their elite Preylord and wolf complements, will attack First Warren in stages, with Morbin coming last of all, to finish the razing of the city."

"Tameth Seer had agreed to attack the city first," Cole said. "Then, whatever is left of us after that, the raptors will finish off in their waves."

"Why don't they come at once and just wipe us out?" Picket asked.

"Prince Winslow—since he was so close to Garten Longtreader and Lord Falcowit when he ran this city as governor—has been explaining this to Emma and helping make sense of the intelligence this prisoner is giving up," Cole explained. "It seems their dark lore demands that the Six be worshiped, and they have a deep belief in the structure of the Six being lords—more than lords—almost like gods to their followers. Their priestess confers this honor during their dark rites. The Six command their own sectors of the High Bleaks, with Morbin as overall king. But if one of the Six falls, all of his sector will be thrown into chaos."

"Are we sure that's true?" Picket asked.

"Winslow was convincing," Cole answered. "Emma and Mrs. Weaver believe he's correct."

"When Falcowit was killed, there was a mess up there in the High Bleaks," Jo said. "That's part of what they're doing north of Grey Grove. Installing the new Sixth. It takes several days."

"So, when they're done and they attack, they don't want to lose them all in one unlucky stroke," Cole said. "They plan to attack in waves."

"It's tactical and, I think... kind of mystically crucial for them," Jo said.

"That helps us, as awful as it sounds. Did he say when they would attack?" Picket asked, swinging his legs off the bed with a groan. He was fully awake now.

"No. He doesn't seem to know," Cole replied. "He only said that after they perform these rites, installing the new raptor king, they will begin to attack."

"Should we glide there and try to learn what they plan?" Picket asked.

"To Morbin's camp? I don't think so," Cole answered. "We'd never get anywhere close without being seen. And we have watchers already as close as can be. We'll know when they're on their way."

"Let's go down," Picket said. He and Jo headed for the door, followed by Cole.

A few minutes later, the three friends had descended to the cells below the palace, where that infamous Captain Daggler had made innocent rabbits disappear—and murdered many—for years. But now the palace was under Emma's command, and the prisons were nearly empty. After creeping quietly past five stout guards and behind the hidden partition, they saw Emma sitting alongside Helmer and two of Emma's brothers in the darkness. Winslow and Whit both listened intently, while Winslow took notes. Picket heard Mrs. Weaver's calm voice.

"You persist in thinking our position indefensible?"

The young buck cackled. "Old hag!" Picket's blood rose. "Our forces will sweep you from this city like a withered old doe maid clears the bones from a Preylord's nest."

"An old doe like your grandmother, perhaps?"

"My grandmother is an inwaller in Akolan and lives in peace and prosperity," he said with a snarl, rattling his chains. "She has ended her rebellion against destiny. She will live out her days while everyone you love is torn to pieces in this war."

"But we are ready for their attack by air," Mrs. Weaver responded, making her voice waver ever so slightly. The young buck seized on it.

"Ha! The lords will come by air in unstoppable numbers, and the wolves will pour in by land and sea! They will come overland from fortresses you've never seen and by sea in ships of death. The ancient great wolf king will come, the cousin of Garlacks, King Farlock. His army alone would end you all! The regular wolf packs will pour out of boats sent from a fort in the Waste by the hundreds and break on these weak defenders with unstoppable appetites."

"King Farlock?" Mrs. Weaver let out a whimper. "Ravaging wolves, like the afterterrors?"

"This attack will make the afterterrors feel like a happy memory. You will all be killed. And I will laugh so loudly!

My howling laughter will be the last thing you hear."

Mrs. Weaver's voice was calm again, and full of pity. "I'm sorry you have been so deceived. I'm sorry you have swallowed these lies. But I am not entirely without hope for you. Maybe, young one, even you might be cured in the mending. I shall always hope it can be so."

He railed on, shaking his chains and shouting curses, as Mrs. Weaver calmly left. They followed her out into the hall, all of them except for Winslow and Whit, leaving the ranting buck to scream his grotesque threats.

After walking down a short hallway, they ascended the steps back up to the higher levels of the palace. Picket walked beside Emma in silence for a while. She stopped when they reached the door to her council room. She looked worried.

Of course she's worried.

"We've got to come up with something to stop them," Emma said. "To slow them down. To tilt the balance significantly. The alcove idea could help, I know. And we might be able to fight off Kylen's forces—might!—but we can't stand one wave of the Preylords' attack, I'm afraid, let alone six. Not to mention wolf hordes led by legendary kings attacking overland and by boat."

Picket felt useless. He had no idea what might make as uneven a battle as could be imagined even remotely more level. "We will do our best, Your Highness. We will..." He was going to say that they would all die bravely, but he didn't think it right to say aloud.

"Did he give up anything more while we were away?" Jo asked.

"Nothing much useful," Mrs. Weaver said. "Maybe Winslow will have more in his full report, some nuance he picked up. I will say that the mention of Farlock does unsettle me deeply. He has been a distant rumor from the north, out beyond the High Bleaks. His cousin, Garlacks, was an early foe of King Jupiter, and his death caused Farlock to send Garlackson and a vast number of his soldiers to fight alongside Morbin against us. If Farlock himself is really coming, then it is ill news indeed."

"All true, wise Mother," Helmer said. "But there isn't much more we can do about that now. We *can* do something with this renegade rabbit."

"Such a proud and energetic evil I have rarely seen among rabbitkind," Mrs. Weaver said. "Perhaps never."

"He's deranged," Cole said.

"The sad thing is that he *isn't* deranged, young Cole," Mrs. Weaver said, not unkindly. "He has his wits. He is not insane. He is wrong, and wicked. He is choosing the part of the enemy. He has every day submitted to the vile lie of Morbin's way, and he cannot even see the road back home. It is sadder than madness, I'm afraid. Far sadder."

"What will we do with him?" Jo asked.

"I would save him if I could," Mrs. Weaver said. "He deserves a trial and swift justice, but he has been useful to us—unwittingly useful—and we have no time for a trial."

"He stays in chains," Emma said. "We have to prepare for this attack—well, these attacks."

"Such attacks have not happened here, at least not of this magnitude," Mrs. Weaver said. "The old captains fought fantastic battles before your time, Your Highness, but this will be on another scale entirely."

"What I wouldn't give to fight alongside the old captains again," Helmer said. "To have them here, even if it is the end."

"Harlan Seer would have some insight, I'm sure," Mrs. Weaver said. "He had such vision. I remember how he changed the way Edward and I pursued our entire vocation because of an offhand comment. He seemed to leak out insights."

"Was he killed in the afterterrors?" Emma asked.

"No, he and two of his fellows went on a quest," Mrs. Weaver answered, "and were never seen again."

"They were gone when the fall happened," Helmer said. "And they never came back."

"They were your friends and fellow lord captains, Helmer," Mrs. Weaver said, "and I am sorry to bring it up."

Helmer looked down. "I was the least worthy of survival," he said. "Would that any of them were with us now. But Stam and Fesslehorn followed Harlan Seer's quest, and the rest all fell after the king's murder."

"Perkin One-Eye, the greatest of your father's friends," Mrs. Weaver said, smiling at Emma, "and Pickwand and Gome. The seven lord captains of Natalia. I would like to put our old seven against the Preylords' six raptor kings. That would help even the odds."

"A little," Helmer said, rubbing his arm absently. "But the least is all that remains of the seven. And I am old."

Emma looked down. Picket felt pity for her, knowing she was struggling to find something to say that might lift spirits and spur action, but she seemed bereft.

"What was Lord Captain Harlan's quest?" Picket asked. "And why did Captains Fesslehorn and Stam go with him?"

"It was a fool's errand," Helmer said. "Those three were the most likely to go on such adventures. Especially Fess and Harlan."

"Lords Fesslehorn and Harlan led the Apothecaries Guild, did they not?" Mrs. Weaver asked.

Helmer nodded, smiling wryly. "They were always so close to some discovery that would 'change everything.'"

"Lord Fesslehorn was a historian," Mrs. Weaver said. "I remember attending his lecture on the Leapers not long after Edward and I met. He had researched the Leaping and the Lost Book for a long time. He had fascinating theories about Flint and Fay."

"The quest was to find some cure, I think," Helmer said, shaking his head. "Harlan told me, before he left, that when they returned everything would be different."

"How different it is," Mrs. Weaver added sadly. "What were they looking for?"

"Fesslehorn said it was a plant," Helmer answered, "something called True Blue."

Emma's head came up. "What did you say?"

Chapter Twenty

Past Masters

Picket listened as Emma probed further.

"It was True Blue?" she asked Helmer. "You're sure of that?"

"That's what he called it," Helmer said, frowning.

"There's something..." she began, her face scrunched up in thought. "Please, tell me more."

Helmer bowed and went on. "They were always researching things with plants and concoctions and took the greatest pleasure in what seemed to me to be minor discoveries. So I wasn't moved when the last breakthrough—I had heard of so many supposed *last* breakthroughs—came and they were thrilled. Though it did seem to be more intense than other times. The king himself knew about their discovery and was, I knew, excited by the quest. He gave them his blessing, and he wanted to go with them himself. But Garten dissuaded him. It was around this time that I was sent away on a ghost mission. Lord Rake was with the main army, far away, when Garten sprang his trap. We fell right into it. I should have..."

Helmer paused and looked away a moment as he rubbed at the bend in his right arm. Wincing, he continued. "I didn't find out till later that Harlan, Stam, and Fess had even made their journey. The other lord captains were killed, along with most of the lords, and I never knew much about Harlan's quest. But it was True Blue they went to find, for certain. What, Your Highness, is True Blue?"

"I don't know," Emma answered. "But I'm certain I heard Heather refer to it back at Halfwind." She opened the door to her council chamber. "Heyward, please come here."

In a moment, Heyward appeared in the hallway, bowing low. "Your Highness?"

"Heyward, is Prester Kell in the city?"

"Yes, ma'am. He's working with Lord Ronan on the gate."

"Please send a brother votary to ask him to come to me as soon as possible. Not you, Heyward; I need you here."

"At once, Your Highness," he said, bowing. He hurried away, his blue robe swishing with his haste as he called out to another blue-robed brother.

"Mrs. Weaver," Emma said, "please take Jo and find the oldest apothecary in the city. See if you can get him or her here. Captain Moonlight, or one of the palace staff from Winslow's time, might be able to help."

"Yes, Your Highness," Mrs. Weaver said, bowing. She ambled away with Jo at her arm.

"Let's have our council," Emma said, sighing. "Maybe someone's unearthed a marvel that will thwart our enemies.

Captain Helmer, update them all on the intelligence we've had from the prisoner. I'll be in soon. Picket, stay a moment."

Helmer bowed, then entered the conference room. Cole followed. Picket wasn't sure what Emma was thinking, and he suspected she was just trying to be proactive amid the crushing reality of what they faced, but he stood by her. She caught his concerned expression.

"You think I'm neglecting the main objective to run down an insignificant mystery?"

"I think you're trying," he replied. "And I'm going to be by your side, trying along with you, until the end."

"There's something about that True Blue," she said. "I almost feel like Heather, on the verge of seeing something important. I can't explain it, but I think it's right to track down this story of Harlan Seer's quest."

He nodded. "And you are doing all you can for the defense of the city already. You knew something was wrong with Kyle before any of us. I trust your instincts. I'll walk beside you wherever you go, Emma."

"Well," she said, smirking in the way she had when they first met, "you'll shuffle beside me."

He smiled. "If we're going to run this mystery down, we need the lords and captains to focus on the fight."

"It sounds like they already are," she said, cocking an ear to the rising volume of conversation within the room. "We need to get in there."

"After you, Your Highness."

They entered amid an intense argument in which several councilors were talking at the same time, and Captain Frye's voice rose above the others.

"Too much risk, you say? It's all a dice throw now, bucks!"

They saw Emma, and the room went suddenly silent. All present rose and bowed to the princess. She nodded and found her seat. Picket sat down beside Helmer, and she began.

"Lords and captains, and Lord Captain," she said, nodding to Helmer. "Please tell me you have some brilliant ideas for how we can counteract the enemy's overwhelming advantage."

A short silence followed before a gravelly voice broke it.

"I do have an idea, Your Highness," Captain Frye said, glancing sideways with a scowl. "Release the prisoner."

Chapter Twenty-One

Yesterflower

Picket limped back down the long stairway toward the cells. His knee ached, but he hurried on. Emma strode silently beside him, distracted by her many cares.

"Cap reminded me of something earlier. Remember when Eefaw Potter shattered all those lovely mugs?" Picket said, smiling over at her.

"What?" she asked, jarred out of her reverie. "Oh, old Master Potter? Ha! Which time?"

"One mug smashing was more memorable for me than the others."

"Of course," she said, laughing harder now at the memory. "I wonder where he is now."

"He's here," Picket replied. "Masters Potter and Gort are helping Captain Moonlight serve out meals."

"I would like to see them," she said.

They had reached the cells. She could hear Captain Frye's harsh voice haranguing the prisoner. "You'll die for these lies, traitor!"

"What's the meaning of this?" Emma shouted, rushing

in. Picket ran in beside her. The prisoner growled at him.

"This villain's being quarrelsome, Your Highness," Captain Frye snarled.

The prisoner smiled defiantly. "I know you'll die soon, you useless old one-armed geezer!"

Picket's blood rose at this insult. He remembered when Captain Frye's arm had been mangled by wolves. It was after Kyle had betrayed his own. Much like this traitor. Picket lunged for the prisoner, tripped on his bad leg, and slid on the floor. The traitor barked a satisfied laugh, rattling his chains with delight.

Picket looked up as Captain Frye drew his sword and pointed it at the prisoner's neck.

"Hold, Captain!" Emma cried. "It's bad enough that you've let our ground defense become irreparably neglected, but now you'll ruin our chance to get anything else from this prisoner."

"As I said, Your Royal Novice," Frye snapped back, "it takes time to prepare for a land invasion by wolves. It'll take us at least two weeks to have them ready!"

Picket sprang up. "That's no way to speak to the princess! If you'd spend less time meddling with prisoners and more on those defenses, they might be ready within the week."

"You have as much experience as she does," Frye shot back. "As in, none. I was going to war before you were born, Junior."

"Why must we argue?" Emma shrieked. "It's nothing

but arguing, all the time!"

"Because of incompetent old fools—" Picket said, just as Captain Frye shouted him down.

"If you think I'll be lectured by a scrub like you, you're wrong!"

Words shot back and forth, angry and harsh, while the prisoner looked on with pleasure.

"Captain Frye!" Emma cried, for the moment silencing the angry argument. "I'm finished with this. Take this traitor outside of the city and . . . do whatever you think best."

The prisoner scowled. This sudden turn enraged him, and he shot an angry look at Emma. "No matter what you do to me," he spat, "in a matter of days there will be nothing left of this place, or any of you. Nothing but broken bricks and bones picked clean."

"Captain," Emma said coolly, "take him away."

"With pleasure," Captain Frye said, face twisted in spite.

"Come with me!" Emma shouted at Picket and stomped out of the cell.

Picket glowered a moment, then followed, muttering to himself.

Once in the hall, Picket sighed and exchanged a fretful look with Emma. She shrugged and headed for the stairs. When they reached the upper levels again, Helmer was speaking closely with Heyward, Jo, and Prester Kell.

"Your Highness," Helmer said, bowing alongside the others as Emma approached.

"Thank you for coming, Prester Kell."

"Of course, Your Highness," he answered, touching his ears, eyes, and mouth, then laying a hand gently on her head in a blessing. "How may I help?"

She turned to Jo. "Any luck?"

"Yes, Your Highness. Mrs. Weaver is waiting with an old apothecary—so old she can't be moved from her bed. It's not far."

"Good. Prester Kell, will you join us?" she asked.

"Of course, ma'am."

"Lead the way, Jo."

Jo led the way, and the small band followed. Heyward, after bowing to the princess and then to Prester Kell, hurried back to his work.

Picket labored to keep up. The pain in his leg was beginning to feel so familiar that he hardly thought of it, but it still required extra effort. They crossed the busy square where the seven standing stones loomed large, holding so much meaning for them all. It was rabbitkind's first parents, Flint and Fay, who long ago were said to have passed over the gap between Immovable Mountain and the Blue Moss Hills by leaping across seven tall stones, leading the other Leapers, who would begin a new world together. Morbin had caused these stones to be topped by statues of the Six and Garten Longtreader, his traitorous ambassador and Picket's uncle. But, having recaptured the city, Emma's liberators had destroyed all traces of this desecration and restored the memorial to its original intent. The stones were meant to honor Flint and Fay and the Leapers and

to serve as a solid reminder to First Warren's residents and visitors of their history and identity. Picket gazed up at the seventh standing stone with a woeful foreboding.

Jo led them past the imposing tall stones and toward the ancient arch marking the boundary of Old Town. Picket's mind was alive with schemes. He remembered his wild flight and fight high above the city, remembered ramming home the flagpole into an attacking raptor. He replayed the battle and considered what forces were certain to invade here soon. They had fought only a few raptors and a garrison of wolves, and it had taken uniting forces, clever strategy, and spectacular heroics to see them through. True, they had killed one of the Six, one of the raptor kings, but now they all would come. Now the sky would truly be blackened with shadows of raptor hordes. King Farlock would descend on them with his wolf army. Other wolves would come. It would be genuinely impossible odds, and he finally fully realized that Emma was right to seek out any angle, however tenuous, that might tilt the scales even slightly their way.

"Just here," Jo said, passing under the stone arch and hurrying down a cobblestone street. He led them past several boarded-up homes and shops and into a neat but ancient establishment that smelled as if a hospital and a cookhouse had been joined. They entered one at a time through the narrow door, Jo, followed by Emma, Prester Kell, Picket, and finally Cole and Helmer. The shopfront was clean, with jars of many sizes staged throughout, most with labels like "stumproot" and "rosewash."

They quickly passed through the front, and, after descending a narrow spiraling stair, they came to a modest living space with a fire glowing on the hearth. In the corner, Mrs. Weaver sat at the bedside of an ancient doe. The older rabbit's eyes were closed, and her face was worn.

"Your Highness," Mrs. Weaver said, unsteadily rising to bow, "this is Missy Dreft. Missy dear, this is the princess, Emma Joveson."

"Bless you, Highness," Missy wheezed, her eyes flickering open a moment to reveal milky-white unseeing pupils. "May you rise and reign."

"Thank you, Aunty," Emma said, kneeling by the old doe's bedside and, with Mrs. Weaver's guidance, taking her hand. "May I trouble you with some questions?"

"Of course," Missy said, her voice catching as she labored to speak. "I will do all I can. I understand that the end is near."

"Yes, ma'am, it is," Emma said, "else I would never trouble you."

"I am your servant, Highness, and I am delighted that you have liberated our city at last. I wasn't sure I would see the day."

"Aunty," Emma said, "have you ever heard of True Blue?"

Missy's eyes widened, and she coughed. "Why, my dear girl," she said when she had recovered, "True Blue is our long-lost source of understanding and ascension. Your Royal Highness, True Blue is Firstflower. It is our path of life."

Chapter Twenty-Two

Aunt Missy's History

"Why is it so called? Why Firstflower?" Mrs. Weaver asked.

"The heir does not know it?" Missy asked, reaching out feeble fingers as if they were searching eyes.

"I do not," Emma replied, "though I fear I have ignored a great source of wisdom."

"Much has been lost, indeed," Missy said. "King Jupiter was doing more than making a peaceful realm; he was recovering the best of a lost one and making it new. But his work was cut short, and all that was being recovered was mislaid again."

"Tell us, Mother," Prester Kell said.

"We have lost knowledge of our first parents, of Flint and Fay. We have forgotten what they found and what the Trekkers left. We have lost our story and remember only Flint and Fay and the other Leapers coming to the Blue Moss Hills, but not why the hills were thus called."

"Was it not the blue moss itself, Aunty?" Emma asked.

"Not at all, Highness," Missy said, coughing. "That

is only what our foreparents thought when they gazed across the chasm from Immovable Mountain. The lore is glossed over or forgotten, but when Flint and Fay led the Leapers across the seven standing stones, what they found on the hills was not blue moss but Firstflower. True Blue. It grew in great swathes across the hills, and the rabbits ate it and grew wise. This is how we first knew language and art and rose up to govern and grow. This is where our first king, Flint himself, became a ruler. It is where Fay, mother of all sages, grew wiser than any before or since and how she made the first book, the heirloom of the royal household."

"True Blue made them wise," Emma said, "but did it heal?"

"They were long-lived as long as they dwelled among the flowers, but after Firstfoe came, many left and trekked inland to Golden Coast. I have never seen Firstflower, so I don't know what properties it has, but a rumor grew among the wise years ago—before the last fall—that Firstflower could heal. Harlan Seer went off to seek it, after a visit to old Jone at Halfwind."

"You know Jone Wissel?" Prester Kell asked.

"I knew her when I was a child. She frightened me—thought I was mischievous—and she used to swat at me and shoo me out of her shop."

"She was of age when you were a child?" Emma asked.

"She was old then," Missy said, "the oldest individual I had ever met. How did you hear of her?"

"Aunty, I know her." Emma spoke reverently. "She is still alive."

"How can this be?" Missy's voice found new energy, and she stirred in her bed. "But it must be tied up with Firstflower. It must be why you're here. Aunt Jone had some . . . somehow! She used it for years—experimenting, always—giving her the long life of the Leapers."

"Did Harlan Seer come during your time, Prester Kell?" Emma asked.

"Lord Captain Harlan came to Halfwind many times before I became prester. I was a votive, of course, and we had some ancient heirlooms that some said held some of the old Blue. But few believed it. Aunt Jone . . . well, she removed some from the old relics and was jailed—despite my protests—by Prince Bleston. But she must have found the mixture she sought and, running low of her own supply, borrowed what we had."

Emma paced the small room, eyes closed and hands clasped before her. "What if we could heal every injury quickly? What if we had an ever-renewing army that could continue the fight even after massive casualties? What if we kept coming back at Morbin again and again?"

"It might give us a chance," Helmer said. "But we don't have the flower, Your Highness."

"True," Picket said, "but Uncle Wilfred was healed, and his healer is on the way here."

"Aunt Jone is coming?" Prester Kell asked.

"That's what Wilfred said," Helmer replied.

"Where is Wilfred Longtreader now?" Emma asked.

When no one answered, Jo said, "I'll find him, Your Highness."

Emma nodded, then closed her eyes again. "If Aunt Jone brings enough of this tonic, somehow, it could give us something to help even the fight."

"It's worth trying," Cole said.

"Aunty," Emma said, turning back to the bed, "did you ever hear any rumors of the plant near here, or anywhere in Natalia?"

Mrs. Weaver shook her head. "Aunt Missy's work is done, I'm afraid."

Picket saw that the old doe's face was frozen in a restful pose. She had breathed her last. Prester Kell knelt beside her and took her hand.

"Let's leave her with the prester," Mrs. Weaver said, rising and taking Emma's hand. Emma nodded, and Picket followed them up the stairs. Picket limped through the shop and out onto the street, his heart heavy.

Emma saw him and put her hand on his shoulder. "It was sad to see her go."

"Yes," Picket replied, "but to think there may be some cure out there to help those who are hurt! To help those in Harbone."

"It can't raise the dead," Mrs. Weaver said, "no matter how healing it may be. And you can't go back in time to be there before they were massacred. It's not your fault."

Picket wiped at his eyes.

"It's not about us now, Pick," Helmer said, "soldiers like you and me. We're arrows aimed at that blackhawk's heart. It's about them," he shot out his chin toward Morbin's distant camp. "It's about a reckoning."

"What now?" Cole asked.

"We find out when to expect Aunt Jone," Emma said, "and we keep preparing as if we don't have a sacred serum that can keep our soldiers fighting beyond hope."

"We are not quite there yet," Prester Kell said, walking up behind them.

"Not quite where?" Emma asked.

"Beyond hope, Your Highness. Not yet."

Chapter Twenty-Three

Vanishing Blue

The prisoner has escaped," Captain Frye said, walking up to meet Emma's party. Picket paused beside the princess, who nodded.

"Good," Emma said. "Well done, Captain."

Captain Frye bowed. "Thank you for trusting me."

"Thank you for being trustworthy, always."

He bowed again, fist over his chest. "My place beside you, dear princess. My blood for yours. Till the Green Ember rises, or the end of the world."

"As Prester Kell said," Emma said, breathing deep, "we are not beyond hope just yet."

"Your Highness," Captain Frye asked, "could I have Captain Longtreader for the Royal Fowlers Auxiliary? Heyward reports they are nearly ready."

"That's much earlier than expected," Emma said. "Well done!"

"We are doing all we can, Your Highness."

"Picket, you're with them," Emma said. "You too, Cole. Helmer?"

"I'll stay with you, Your Highness."

"Where are they, Captain?" Picket asked.

"Up top." The old buck pointed toward the rooftop of the palace, beside which was being built a huge smooth wall tilted in a long curve.

Picket saluted, then turned to head toward the palace. He had limped only a few steps when he heard Emma gasp. He turned to see Uncle Wilfred coming up the old main road, alongside Aunt Jone herself. His heart beat quickly, and he turned back to Cole.

"I'll take care of them," Cole said, nodding up at the palace rooftop, "and you join us when you can."

Picket nodded, and Cole hurried off. Picket turned back and limped behind Emma. The princess ran over to meet Jone, her arms stretching out to embrace the old doe. Aunt Jone bent easily on one knee alongside Uncle Wilfred, bowing to Emma. Emma fell down beside her and covered her in a hug. "Aunt Jone! You're here!"

"I must be, dear Your Highness! I hoped to be some help, if I can," Jone cried. "Instead of hanging around at Halfwind like a quisby, I came along with the last of the healers. I promise I can help, Emma. Do give me a chance, I beg."

"I'm so happy to see you," Emma said. "Are you tired?"

"I'm never tired, Highness," Jone said, getting too close and spitting her words into Emma's face. "I'm as fresh as a fungus on a moon shadow."

Emma glanced sideways at Picket, Helmer, and Prester Kell. Her face carried so much hope.

"What about you, Captain Wilfred?" Emma asked. "Do you need refreshment?"

"I feel amazingly well, Your Highness," he replied. "I could spit in Morbin's eye, if I knew which direction to aim."

Emma glanced over again, then back to the Halfwind team. She pointed northeast. "I think he's that way, Captain."

"Indeed," Uncle Wilfred said, bowing his head. Picket reached him and they embraced. "My nephew... hero of the cause. They sing about you around here, you know? I'm so proud of you, lad!"

"Thank you, Uncle," Picket said, looking down. "I would be useless were it not for you."

"You'd be dead," Helmer said, striding forward to take Wilfred by the hand. "Welcome back, soldier."

Uncle Wilfred grinned. "Thank you, Helm. And thank you for being for Picket... what I couldn't be."

"He's been a trial, for certain," Helmer said, nodding over at Picket. "But I'm sure you can find some way to repay me."

"Well, I still owe you for the bet we made," Uncle Wilfred said.

"What bet?" Picket asked.

"Back at Cloud Mountain," Uncle Wilfred began, grinning, but Helmer cut him off.

"It's none of your business, Ladybug," Helmer said. "Just a friendly wager between two old veterans."

"Old friends," Uncle Wilfred said, smiling. Helmer nodded, rubbing his arm.

"That wound still hurt, Helm?" Wilfred asked, growing suddenly serious.

"Some places never heal," Helmer replied.

"What wound, Master?" Picket asked. "Is it the scar on your arm? What happened?"

"I failed to act, son," he said, and it was clear he would say no more.

Emma looked eagerly at Aunt Jone. "Have you brought medical supplies?"

"Oh, such supplies!" Jone cried. "We brought enough to countermand a raggabrash in a pie pit."

"What about True Blue, Aunt Jone?" Emma asked. "What remains of the True Blue?"

Aunt Jone's face lost its cheerfulness. She frowned and shook her head. Picket's heart sank. "No, my dear," she said, looking away from Prester Kell. "I used the last of that, my little miracle mix, on Wilfred Longtreader here. I'm sad to say there's not another ounce of True Blue in the world."

Chapter Twenty-Four

The Last Dragon Keeper

Heather froze. Amid her overflowing joy in finding Smalls and the bright hope in their sudden recovery, a shadow fell. A shadow cast by a dragon.

"Welcome, young rabbits," the dragon said, stepping closer.

Smalls rose and glided coolly between Heather and the dragon. "What do you want?"

"The keeper awaits the king. The king's conference with the keeper is long overdue." The dragon gave a slight smile, revealing small sharp teeth set in a wide powerful mouth. His split tongue flicked between sentences. Heather winced and her heart raced. She couldn't speak. She couldn't even scream.

"Do you mean us harm?" Smalls asked, his voice even.

"If the keeper meant harm, you would have been dead long ago," he replied, stepping closer still so that the scant light revealed more of his dark form. He was powerful, with short thick arms and legs and a long dangerous tail. His head was large and jutted forward, set atop the slope

of his strong forward-leaning torso. "Who was it, do you think, has kept you alive these many days of your weakening sleep?"

"You took care of him?" Heather asked.

"The keeper keeps," the dragon replied in his low guttural tones. His laughter had been high and shrieking, but his speaking voice was a rumbling rasp. "The keeper kept rabbit buck alive. Cleaned his wound, the keeper did, and made him drink mossdraft again and again."

"Mossdraft?" Smalls asked. "The greenish water—it's more than water, isn't it?"

"Nourishes and slakes, satisfies and strengthens. Mossdraft is life in the tomb."

"Thank you, Keeper," Smalls said. "I am quite sensible of the kindness you have done me. How may I repay you?"

"The keeper seeks a conference with the king," the dragon repeated. "He has waited."

Smalls frowned and looked back at Heather.

"What is this conference?" Smalls asked. "We don't understand."

"Understand more than you show," he muttered, then stepped closer. "The keeper's tale is unknown to the rabbits of Outside and Above?"

"It's unknown to us," Smalls said, and Heather nodded.

"Truthful," the dragon said, eyes squinting at them in the darkness. "The keeper sees it."

"Will you tell us of the conference?"

"The keeper will tell, pale doe," he said, stepping closer still. He now stood almost close enough to touch them, and Heather fought back revulsion, mingled with fear, at his nearness.

"Shall we sit?" Smalls asked, using this gesture to place himself firmly between the keeper and Heather. She sat and took his hand. The keeper shook his head.

"The keeper will stand to tell it," he said. "The weary will sit to hear it."

Heather felt such strange mixtures of emotions. She felt so profoundly well and wasn't sure if this was only in comparison to her narrow escape from death so recently or if she really was healthier than ever. Yet her unease grew as the dragon came closer and spoke more. She tried to recall the many dreams where she had seemed to be in this place. *Why are we here*?

"It was time and time and the times before, when the rabbit king Lander, son of Whitson, closed the hatchery of dragons and could not be convinced by his council to destroy the living eggs of his enemy." The keeper stretched out an arm and waved his scaly claw across the cavern, indicating the smooth, slick tops of moss-covered eggs—*not stones, eggs*—covering the majority of the cavern floor in patches. They stretched, in some sections, all the way to the moss-covered rock walls. Some of the walls were supported by well-placed wooden beams. He continued in his rasping, guttural way. "So the rabbit king had a conference with the last dragon and laid upon him the charge of guarding the eggs and suffering none to be hatched except upon his own near passing, so that the next guardian could be trained to take his place and watch over the last of his kind. The last dragon became the first keeper, and this solemn occupation has come down to the keeper, to the one who stands before you—the last dragon keeper."

"The last?" Heather asked, then quickly regretted speaking.

The keeper smiled that slight smile once again. "The latest," he amended.

"So then, was another conference promised, after King Lander's first conference with the last dragon?" Smalls asked.

"Aye," the dragon said, a rumbling grumble in his throat, "the keeper comes to it."

"By all means," Smalls said, nodding politely.

"Lander King promised that a conference would follow with each new king, and so over the years many keepers have met with many kings, and a record of each has come down in our tales. But the rabbits broke their vows and came not again for a long span of years. And the last keeper has never met a king. He has only heard tales of these meetings long ago. He began to doubt if the tales were true. Then came a small white buck into the dragon tomb, and the keeper thought he might be the king at last. But he was near dead, and the keeper was perplexed." The dragon's powerful right claw scraped the scales of his strong jaw, and he smiled. "The keeper cleaned the rabbit's wounds and fed him mossdraft, doing all he knew from his own lore to cure the weak and wounded buck."

"I thank you, once again," Smalls said, "for preserving my life."

"The keeper could not save the buck, no," he said, shaking his head, "only delay his death and prolong his life. It needed the second descent to cure him."

"Why did you wait to come and greet us?"

"The keeper has waited—done little else but wait—since the days of Lander," he answered, closing his eyes as if in deep thought. "And he waits now for the long-delayed conference..." he ended, opening his eyes and peering at Smalls, "...with the king."

Chapter Twenty-Five

Darkness and Sight

"I am not a king," Smalls said, and Heather nodded.

"Not a king," Heather echoed, grateful for Smalls' elusive answer. "And I am no queen. I come of common rabbits, of an ordinary family."

"The truth, somehow," the dragon said, eyes narrowing at Smalls, "but not all the truth."

Heather looked down.

Cunning creature.

Raising her head, she went on. "The heir of Lander leads the free bucks in revolt against the Preylords even now, and I was with her not long ago. Her name is Emma Joveson, and she is a valiant leader. I wish we were there to fight alongside her."

"There is war outside?" the keeper asked.

"Yes," Smalls said, nodding. "A long war. I'm certain that's why no king or queen has come to meet you. The rulers of rabbits have been overthrown, and they fight to regain what was lost."

"Truth," the keeper said, eyes squinting. "It is the truth

you say."

"Of course," Heather said.

"How came you here?" the keeper asked.

"Stabbed and cast down," Heather said, "both of us. He in battle and me by betrayal. My own uncle's thrust pierced me, and he kicked me in, leaving me for dead."

"So, none will come for either rabbit?" the keeper asked.

"No," Smalls answered, shaking his head. "No one will come for us."

"Then lost you are indeed, both, and forever. There is no way out except and unless an Outside and Above rope is lowered through the only gate, the gate of light high above." He shook his head. "The slick walls slide away, and none can reach the inner peak by climbing. No dragon can, and certainly no rabbit could."

Heather felt panic rising but fought to swallow it down. "We are glad to be alive. That's all we need for now."

"How you have risen up, I cannot tell. But enough talk. The keeper will leave you now and come again tomorrow," he said. "Mossdraft and rest, little rabbits."

"Thank you, Keeper," Smalls said.

The dragon nodded, then turned, and disappeared into the shadows.

They were quiet for a long time, holding hands in the silence.

Finally, Heather leaned on Smalls' shoulder and turned her face to bury it in his embrace. She felt tremendous affection for him, but this tenderness was so she could whisper close to his ear.

"He is listening, you know. He heard all my story catching you up. I'm afraid he must know who you are." His squeeze told her he understood and agreed. She whispered on. "We will have to be careful. I don't trust him, even if he did keep you alive. There's something dishonest at the heart of all his honesty." A hesitation, then another squeeze. "Do you disagree?"

He dipped his head so that it rested next to hers. "No," he whispered. "I can't see all you see, but I trust your understanding. So, when I can't see it all, I trust your sight."

She squeezed him in return.

They broke apart, and Smalls went again to the moss-draft pool. She noticed his movements, calm and unhurried, though with soldierly awareness of everything. Dim by the distant pool, she saw him bend and dip the bowl, then stand and walk back her way.

"The keeper is kind to us," he said, extending the bowl for her.

She received it with gratitude, said, "Yes, very kind," and drank.

A dim rattle in the distance sounded, followed by an extended silence. Smalls returned to the pool and filled the bowl again. Then, a rumbling rattle began in the depths of the cavern and ended in a ground-shaking noise of crashing rock. Smalls tilted, dropped the bowl, then ran back to Heather, knees bent, hand steadying on the ground as he reached her. The rumbling stopped, and an eerie silence followed, interrupted only by the occasional small knocks of settling rock.

They embraced again. Heather whispered, "We have to get out of here."

Then they both looked up as the faint light from the gate, impossibly high above, went out entirely.

Chapter Twenty-Six

Eyes to See

Heather sat in darkness, alongside Smalls, and tried to ignore the dread welling within.

"We should sleep while we can," Smalls said.

"Yes, of course."

She lay down on the soft moss and tried to imagine she was safe at home. Past or future home—it didn't matter. She tried to relax her mind and fill it with the happy thoughts of loved ones. But something wasn't right, and she couldn't sleep. Then, when her heart had sunk low, she heard singing. It was Smalls, and his voice filled the cavern, ringing clear in the hollow space. Warm and sweetly he sang, and her anxious heart calmed.

"I am not made of stone or steel,
but I know my way,
I am only flesh and fur,
But so too were Flint and Fay.

"So, I'll say yes to my call,
Though my heart's afraid.
I will go down this, my road,
Until my part is played.

"I go, I go, and I may die,
But I go, I go, for I must try.
I cannot now stay but must find a way,
So, I go, I go, to leap, to sail, and fly."

Heather reached across and took Smalls' hand. Sleep came.

She did not dream.

* * *

Heather woke with a start as the ground shook and the noise of smashing rock thundered through the cavern. Smalls was by her in a moment, standing, arms spread wide behind him. Light from the distant gate aloft made the cavern feel almost bright in comparison with last night's total darkness. She found that her eyes quickly adjusted, and she could see the dim cavern almost well. Some rocks dropped from the arched roof of the cavern, a few plopping in the mossdraft pool, and a wispy puff of dust wafted across shafts of light high above.

"The Immovable Mountain shakes," she said, as the rumbling subsided and silence ensued.

"But I'm afraid if it shakes more," Smalls replied, "we won't see standing stones to Blue Moss Hills but be crushed, buried, and beyond hope."

"Don't forget drowned."

"Right. I had forgotten. We're underwater here inside Forbidden Island, and if this place goes, we can add drowning to the list of grim endings. Thank you, Heather."

"Anything to keep the mood cheerful," she said, smiling over at him.

He smiled back, then bent to hug her and whisper in her ear again. "You're right, though. The only way out is up. No matter how far these caves stretch sideways, if they don't lead upward anywhere, we're stuck here."

She squeezed him, and they broke apart and both walked to the mossdraft pool. While Smalls dipped their bowl, she made as if to stretch and test her renewing strength, but all the while stealing glances around the edge of the cavern. This was the way the dragon keeper had come and disappeared. Whether or not it was possible to escape by finding the way he had gone, she wanted to know how to get out of the cavern.

Bending low and seeming only to test her legs, she gazed along the dim walls, probing for any kind of break. But the cave walls were covered in moss, and the slick rock wall breaking through in patches seemed impenetrable. She continued to scrutinize the stone.

"How do you feel?" Smalls asked, handing her the mossdraft bowl.

She thanked him and drank deeply, returning the bowl as her eyes flitted back and forth from the pool to the wall. "I cannot imagine feeling any better than I do. And you?"

"The same. I'm not sure if it's that I've been hurt and on the verge of death for so long or if it's true that I, in fact, feel better than ever."

"I think it must be true." Heather smiled up at him.

Smalls grinned back. "Let's go for a walk." He offered her his arm. She took it, and they walked away from the pool, making a slow circuit of the vast cavern. They avoided the smooth patches of dragon eggs but otherwise explored every section of the cave. Heather felt along the smooth wall, then studied the support beams set against some cracking sections of wall. *Who put these here? The keeper?*

"The crashing we heard," she said, nodding to the beams. "Are these intended to keep the cavern from collapsing in and crushing all the eggs?"

Smalls frowned, running his hand along a wide crack in the wall. "It looks like it. Those noises of crashing rock must be other parts of the cavern crumbling in."

"Maybe it won't be long till this all comes down."

"That must be why he's so eager for his conference with the king."

She nodded, and they walked on.

When they had reached the far side of the cavern, opposite the mossdraft pool and the place where the dragon keeper had disappeared, Smalls stopped.

"I think we may speak more freely here."

She looked around and nodded. "I agree. But softly, my dear."

He smiled, then whispered, "How is your history, Heather?"

She looked up, thinking. "Father was a historian and scholar, so we learned quite a bit. But I learned more at Cloud Mountain and Halfwind. We had missed much."

"Did you know about the dragons?"

"Not really. The dragons seemed to belong to legend and not history, to me. I wasn't sure they were real. I don't think Father believed them real."

"I think that might have been intentional."

"What do you mean?" she asked quietly. "Did you know about them?"

"I think most scholars doubt their existence. Wilfred told me that he thought they were real, but I had my doubts. I always got the sense that he believed many important connections to the past were cut off when my father was killed before I could ever speak to him. He lamented the disconnection and felt inadequate, I think, to give me what I needed."

"Dear Uncle Wilfred. I'm sure he did."

"But Wilfred remembered old Lord Booker saying there was always something unusual about me, even as a baby. Father knew something too. He was so convinced that he gave me the Green Ember even before I was old enough to know my own name. Wilfred was there."

"What did he see in you?" Heather asked, but she thought she might somehow know. Or, if not really know in her mind, apprehend with her heart.

"Wilfred couldn't say," Smalls said, stroking his chin absently. "Only that Father sometimes saw the way you sometimes see, Heather. Wilfred didn't understand it. Like I don't understand it or experience it myself. But I experience you experiencing it, if that makes sense. And I trust it."

"So, Uncle Wilfred trusted King Jupiter to know, even though he didn't."

"Yes," Smalls said. "It was the same with Lord Booker. It felt right to Wilfred to see me named Father's heir, even though I was too young to know much or really be known."

"But your father knew you."

"Or maybe he knew he wouldn't be around much longer. Garten was there as well. Wilfred said he didn't know at the time, but, looking back, he thought the king had a premonition of his demise."

"What does this have to do with dragons?" she asked, again peering hard at the slick and mossy wall, looking for any hint of a cleft that might mean a passage.

"It's one of the things I missed. One of the things Father would have shared with me. I'm sure he was the last king to come to Lander's dragon tomb. I think that me missing that part of my training, or my initiation to the throne, has meant that something broke down here. Something that would have been better left intact."

His words reverberated with truth inside her. "You're right. And that explains why we can't stay here. Do you remember anything else from Uncle Wilfred's recollections?" She scanned the wall slowly, looking for some small sign of a break in the slick stone.

"He told me what Father said when he gave me the Green Ember, and I have never forgotten it."

Heather stopped scanning the stone and turned to face Smalls. "What did he say?"

Smalls reached inside his shirt and produced the gem. The emerald signifying his position as heir to the throne hung from the end of its gold chain. Smalls ran his fingers over the contours on its back and the smooth cut surface of its front. "May this be a key for you in dark places and dark times."

Heather's heart swelled at these words, and she turned back to resume her scanning of the rock wall while she thought about what they might mean.

Reptilian eyes stared out at her.

Chapter Twenty-Seven

Splitting

Heather's cry echoed around the cave as she leapt back. Smalls surged ahead, reaching for a sword at his side. There was nothing there, just an empty scabbard. Unarmed, he leapt forward, fists balled.

Heather stepped forward again, reaching for him. "It was eyes," she whispered. "Eyes in the wall."

Smalls nodded, and they stepped carefully back together. For a little while Heather searched the rock wall to see if she could find the eyes again, frightening though the sight had been. She could see nothing but hard slick stone and wet sagging moss. She began to fear that Smalls might think she hadn't seen anything, that her agitated mind had imagined what was not really there. *Is it possible I only saw a shape in the stone and, like a child frightened at night, made it into eyes?*

"I guess we are never alone here," Smalls said with no hint of doubt. "The keeper watches."

"The keeper watches, indeed," came the slick, guttural sound of the dragon. The two rabbits spun around to find the dragon keeper halfway across the cavern, head cocked sideways, gazing at them. "Have the rabbits had a fright? The keeper heard screaming."

Heather started to say it was nothing, but she paused, recalling the dragon's cunning way of telling if something was true. "I was frightened. It's all right now."

"All right?" the dragon asked. "The keeper hopes it is so."

Smalls pointed to the support beams. "Is this why we hear so much falling rock?"

The dragon inclined his head.

"We're not safe here, are we?" Smalls asked.

The dragon's teeth showed a moment, then he looked down. His smooth, slick voice echoed in the open cavern. "Safe? If you are not as safe as the dragon eggs, then for what was the treaty?"

Heather frowned, glancing at the eggs. She tried to make sense of his answer. "Is a cave-in likely?"

"The keeper believes not. He has worked hard to protect against it."

"We can see that," Smalls said. "It must be hard to do all that work by yourself."

The dragon nodded low, then looked away. He seemed to be thinking. After a moment he turned to face Smalls. "Would the rabbit buck like to see the last support made in the tunnels within? He might be able to help us make the tomb more secure. Protect his doe."

Smalls glanced at Heather. She wasn't sure how to

respond, so she nodded. He said, "Yes. I should like it very much."

"Come," the keeper said, extending a scaly hand. Smalls walked forward, and Heather followed. The keeper shook his head. "Rabbit doe must stay. Not enough space for three to travel."

Heather frowned, stopping. Smalls looked back, concern on his face. She smiled at him. He crossed to embrace her. Arms around his neck, she found she was touching the golden chain from which hung the Green Ember. She unclasped the chain, and the emerald fell to the mossy ground. She looked over his shoulder to the dragon and, seeing his attention was diverted, stepped on the gem.

"I'll keep it safe," she whispered.

"Keep yourself safe," he replied. "You are the treasure I care most about."

She squeezed him one last time.

Smalls turned and followed the dragon past the moss-draft pool and into shadow.

Then he was gone.

Heather returned to the spot where she had first fallen and had first found Smalls. The thick, soft section of moss felt almost like a strange home in this dark, sullen place. This cavern had conflicting places in her heart. On one hand, she hated the dank darkness, the absence of clear air or sunshine, the presence of an unsettling dragon, and the impossibility of escape. But this was also where she had found Smalls. Where they had found each other. This was the place where she had recovered from near death and now felt better than she had ever felt before. She reached for her satchel and opened it. She retrieved the battered old purse and placed the Green Ember back within, drawing out the vial. Empty. Nothing at all left of the miraculous cure that had brought them back from the brink of death. She replaced the battered purse inside the satchel.

Automatically, she began to organize the contents of the satchel as if on duty. She thought of Emma as she rolled bandage lengths, checked levels of tonics, and tucked every item, some from Halfwind and some from Akolan's District Four clinic, into its optimum spot. Emma had trained her well, sparing her none of the intense prep she needed simply because they were friends. Emma took her seriously and demanded excellence. She had also helped her, patiently and repeatedly, as she learned.

Oh, Emma dear. How are you getting on? I wish I was with you, that your brother and I were with you now.

When her medical satchel was ready and in the kind of shape she thought Emma would approve of, Heather breathed deeply and gazed around the room. Then she looked back at the satchel's contents and sighed. Taking everything out, she began the routine again, sorting and shifting, imagining the kinds of things that might happen here inside Forbidden Island and call for her healing arts. A cave-in? *Forbid it!* But if Smalls were hurt, trapped, or crushed by some falling rock, how would she help? What supplies would she need ready at hand?

Finally, Heather had done all she could to ready her supplies, and she set aside her satchel and stared past the mossdraft pool to where Smalls had gone. Somehow, she was afraid to walk over there and try to find her own way into the passage. She wasn't sure why.

Heather lay on the soft moss and, staring at the place where she expected him to reappear, waited.

She must have dozed, for the light was nearly gone when she stirred, stretched, and gazed around the cavern. Smalls was there, asleep where she had first found him. She watched him sleep, happy in his presence. But a rivulet of worry sprang up to mingle with her river of joy, and she frowned.

The faint light above faded, and all was darkness.

Chapter Twenty-Eight

Dreams, Memories, and Fear

Heather slept. In the night, visions came and went. She could hardly tell what was real and what was not. Her father stood above a crowded cavern by a long lake filled with ships, his ancient pickaxe raised amid cheers, while he laid out the plan of escape conceived so long ago. Jacks wavered between the Wrongtreaders and the resistance, angrily arguing with Harmony about what was right and what might work. She saw, with eyes grown somehow accustomed to the dark, Smalls bent over her satchel, rooting through it. She saw Emma fretting, with Picket, horribly maimed, by her side. She saw Jacks picking the right side—picking the resistance—then running through the house knocking over everyone's block towers while Heather ran alongside him, laughing. She saw much, and she slept long.

Heather awoke to find Smalls gone once again. Panic quickly gave way to reason, and she assumed he had not wanted to wake her and that he had gone back to work on the support beam deep in the islands. Perhaps it was urgent, and of course he had no way to leave a note.

She sprang up and stretched, readying herself for the day ahead. Even as concerns pricked the edges of her mind, she felt so unbelievably well that almost nothing could touch her sense of health. Her body, so regularly deprived and cruelly injured of late, was as hearty as one could imagine. The tonic. *Dear old Aunt Jone.* How long had she labored to find the right mixture, and what secrets had she inherited and protected, combining them with fresh insights from learned authorities building on generations of wisdom? Aunt Jone had always listened eagerly to discussions of new methods in healing that were effective, and she regularly sat in the back of classes—even novices' classes—taking notes and sometimes uttering awkward exclamations. That was how Heather had first met her, sitting in on a lecture Doctor Zeiger gave on one of his visits to Halfwind.

"Always to be remember," Doctor Zeiger had said, concluding his lecture, "that healing arts is not for bodies—just bodies—but is for minds and hearts. Mind the heart and mind, mine students, and mend the body better."

"Ain't the heart and mind part of the body?" someone had muttered behind her, and Heather turned around to see an ancient doe, ragged and wild-eyed, bent over a small book positively crammed with notes and drawings. A cane leaned against her crossed legs as she looked up from her scribbling. "What are you gawkin' at, young'n? Ain't you never seen an old rabbit before now?"

Heather had answered without thinking. "Not as old

as you."

Aunt Jone barked a laugh that sent spittle spraying over Heather and the next five nearest students. The other trainees wiped their shoulders and, noses scrunched, eased away. But Heather laughed, put her hand over her mouth, and apologized. "I'm so sorry, Aunty! That was rude and wrong. Please forgive me."

"Nothing to forgive!" Aunt Jone had cried, shooting in to hug Heather while her book and cane were dashed onto the floor. "It's truer than you know, I'm quite sure. Maybe you're a true seer or, possibly, something even more awful, if it can be imagined."

"I'm just a trainee. Hoping to be a healer."

"Well, let me tell you something," and the spittle fairly flew once again with these words. "The art of healing ain't all tonics and truisms. I think it's a noble quest to wreck death itself."

"It comes to us all, doesn't it, Aunty…?"

"Jone Wissel, little white learner."

"Aunt Jone," Heather had said. "I'm Heather Longtreader."

"Ah," Aunt Jone had said, peering intently into Heather's eyes. "A dangerous name."

Heather nodded, then returned to the subject. "Aunt Jone, doesn't death come for us all?"

"You might never die, Miss Longtreader," Aunt Jone had said, her eyes sparkling as she smiled her toothless smile. "I never have."

Heather laughed at the memory, as she had laughed that day, thinking Aunt Jone had said something clever. But now?

She headed for the mossdraft pool, wary of being surprised but curious to find the door to the passage. The way to Smalls. She didn't like being cut off from him like this.

Heather bent to fill the bowl and drank deeply, delighting in the refreshing, reviving draft. Looking up at the scant light above, she considered testing the walls for climbing. She felt so strong! *What if it comes to that? What*

if it comes to the whole place caving in and us desperately trying to climb out? It didn't look possible, or anything like it. Still, there might come a desperate moment when that was their only hope.

Gazing into the shadowy corner, if corner it could be called, where the keeper had led Smalls, she stepped forward. Pressing her hands against the wall, she tried to find any way through. It seemed all of one piece, slick rock and thick wet moss. At last she found a small crack, big enough to fit a large hand into but nowhere near large enough for anyone to pass through. She thought of putting her hand inside the crack. Memories of Seven Mounds, where she had become stuck and vulnerable to being killed by the pursuing wolves, including the wicked Redeye Garlackson, flooded her mind. She stepped back. Heather wanted to find Smalls, to know how to get out of this massive cavern, but she also wanted, if possible, to avoid any small passages and tight rock entrances. Even in Akolan, that slave city of Morbin's where Father and Mother and Jacks had long been kept, she had had to crawl through a small cave passage into the ancient Tunneler's first secret meeting place. They had done more tunneling in Akolan since those early years of their captivity, and vast caves were open to them now, and countless rabbits planned a daring escape under the leadership of the newest Tunneler, Whittle Longtreader. *Father.*

Breathing deeply, she stepped forward and reached out for the crevice, determined to probe its depths. When her hand first felt the edges of slick rock, a sound of violent crashing, of tumbling rock on rock, came from deep inside the island.

Smalls!

Chapter Twenty-Nine

The Keeper's Ally

It wasn't only sound. The ground rumbled, the cavern shook, and some rock and moss chunks broke off and plummeted down from the high cavern's arched wall to shatter on the stone floor below. Some just missed patches of dragon eggs. Others fell in the mossdraft pool, and Heather, regaining her balance and unwilling to stand by idly, reached to fish them out. The rumbling stopped, and Heather swallowed. She gazed around the chamber, eerily silent now. She walked quickly over to what she thought of as their own section, brushed away debris, and worked to make all as clean as it had been. Resting on her knees, she gazed across at the large support beam. She thought she could make out, even in this dimness and at this distance, a long crack. *If that beam breaks apart, will this all come down? Maybe not immediately, but soon after, I think.*

"Where are you, Smalls?" she asked in the silence.

"He is working," a scaly voice spoke into the quiet, almost as if into her mind. She spun around to see the keeper, dimly visible, gliding her way. "You worry he will not come again?"

Heather swallowed. "I only want to see him."

"Fear is wicked, little doe," he said, moving closer. "The keeper has no fear."

"That must be comforting."

"The keeper has nothing from which to be comforted. He only does his duty and awaits the conference." He came closer. She looked down, but his gaze drew hers up and she could not resist staring into his pale yellow eyes. He smiled, drawing closer still, then exhaled, enveloping Heather in a noxious cloud of breath. She tried not to gag, but she drew back, coughing from the fumes. "The little doe can help the keeper keep his conference with the king."

"I can help you," she said without even having decided to speak. "Smalls is—" she began; then, shaking her head, she coughed and continued. "Where is Smalls?"

"He is at work, as he should be," the dragon said, smiling. "He wishes to keep you safe in your new home. Does it distress you that you will never leave here, that you share the fate of the keeper and the dragon seeds?"

"Perhaps we will leave when the new queen comes for the conference," she said weakly.

"Oh, the queen will never come," the keeper said, "but I wonder if you might go to her? Bearing a message from the keeper? Asking for her to keep the appointment? Unless she is dead already."

"She's alive," Heather said, louder than she intended.

Her words echoed off the cave walls. "How could we get out?"

"The keeper could let you out," he said, scraping his claws together like two handfuls of knives, "and you could bring the queen here. But the way must be made."

"There is no way now?" she asked.

"No way, but there is a room, and a way inside the room."

"A room?"

"A room, yes. The keeper will show you."

"Won't you show me with Smalls?"

"The buck is working. The keeper will show you now."

She almost stood up but hesitated a moment. She remained seated on the soft moss. "I would rather wait for Smalls."

The dragon smiled, inclined his head. "Would he not be pleased if, when he sees you again, you have made a way for your escape?"

"Our escape, you mean?" she asked. "Mine and Smalls."

"Yes, of course. You will be to him like a queen to a king, even now. And the keeper will see you pleased, and he will reward your work."

"Reward... How?"

"There is treasure here," the keeper said, "and a store of learning. Old knowledge. Here for you, if you only help the keeper."

She was silent for a moment, unsure how to reply. "Help you, how?"

"It comes down to the room," the dragon said, breath rattling in his throat as he stepped closer to Heather. "The keeper will show you the door. It is the way." She stood, heaving the strap of her satchel over her head. "Come now," the dragon continued, stepping away.

Almost thoughtlessly, Heather walked behind him as he headed past the mossdraft pool. Her mind felt foggy, but she knew she wanted to help. And if she could say, when she saw Smalls again, that she had found a way out, he *would* be so pleased. The dragon reached into the small crevice she had found earlier and pulled back. A small fissure appeared, a door sliding sideways to make a way into a dank passage. The keeper led, and she followed him into the darkness.

Inside the faintly lit craggy passage the powerful body of the dragon slid ahead of her. She found it easier going, but that feeling of oppressive closeness, of nearness to being trapped, intensified. Soon, to her relief, the passage widened, and they came into a long, low cave. Water dripped onto her and onto the mossy floor. Ahead, a torch blazed above three arched openings. The keeper passed through the leftmost way, and she, hesitating only a moment at the three doors, heard a distant clatter down the central tunnel. Then she hurried after the keeper into the darkness.

"The door is not far," the dragon said, his long tail swishing back and forth in front of Heather. She could hear him, but sight was almost gone now, and she felt along the mossy wall, stooping as she went. After a few minutes of frightening turns, during which she kept close to the swishing sound and occasional guttural utterances from the dragon, a faint light appeared ahead. She wished Picket were with her. He had a knack for finding his way, for navigating strange places and quickly calculating newly revealed routes.

Finally, the tunnel issued into another torchlit hall, dank like the others and stinking of mildew. The ceiling was high, though not as high as the central cavern. Support beams were everywhere, wedged against each wall. She gazed around to see if she could spot Smalls, but he was nowhere to be seen. The room was round and featured twelve arched tunnel doors all around its edge. A few of these tunnels seemed to have collapsed, their mouths closed by a heaped pile of stone debris. And indeed, debris covered much of the floor, and the dragon dodged between sizable sections of rubble as they entered the hall. Across the hall from where she stood, a long triangular-shaped structure jutted out from the wall. It seemed to Heather to stand in place of the thirteenth tunnel door. The dragon keeper motioned with his long clawed hand to follow. "The door," he said, pointing. She nodded and followed him across.

Reaching the moss-covered exterior of the unusual edifice, the dragon pulled back a tangle of moss, revealing a stone door with a small triangle etched in its center. The triangle outline seemed to bear markings within, but Heather couldn't see them well.

"What does it say?" she asked.

The dragon raised his powerful claws and struck out at the overhanging moss, cutting free a swath so that they both could see more clearly. Heather shrank back at this sudden act. Heart pounding, she stepped forward again. She leaned close and peered at the central triangle, unable to make sense of the marks.

"The doe can read it?"

"I cannot," she said, frowning. "It must be an old language. Is it the dragon tongue?"

"It is not your tongue, nor the tongue of dragons."

"Then what can it be?"

"If little doe can discover," the dragon said, getting closer to Heather and exhaling a putrid breath, "then free she shall be. And free shall her buck be."

Heather coughed, her eagerness to help the dragon swelling, but never took her eyes off the door. For a door she believed it was. And this central triangle was, she was convinced, the key. "I want to get him back. To get out of here, at all costs," she said, peering at the series of slashes around the edges of the structure's front. "Could you bring the light closer?"

The dragon nodded, slipping back to snatch a torch from the wall. While he was gone, she stared intensely at the triangle, trying desperately to locate the clue to unlock the mystery.

The keeper returned, extending the torch to Heather. She held it close to the triangle, and more damage was clear all over the door's front. It looked as though an army had tried to get in there. Scratches, dents, and marks of intense attack—apparently a failed one—aimed at getting inside.

"What's inside here?" she asked. "Why is it so important for you to get inside?"

"The keeper has good reasons. And the doe has good reasons to want to rescue her beloved buck and help the rabbits fighting outside." He drew close again, his fetid breath oppressive to Heather. "You will open the door for the keeper and receive the reward you merit after."

"I will help you," she said automatically, gazing with new intensity at the triangle. "I will get you inside."

"Good little doe." The keeper withdrew a few paces, and Heather shook her head, foggy a moment, then refocused again on the triangle. She felt as though her focus was narrowing to see only those things before her, the thirteenth tunnel door and bringing Smalls news of their imminent escape. Gazing at the triangle, she could see nothing that made sense to her. The strange indentations inside the small triangle were unintelligible. *What can it mean?* She stared and stared, eyes fixed on the problem. Finally, moving to the side a few steps so that she gazed at the triangle from an angle, she thought she saw something familiar. At the same time, some small doubt came to her mind as to why she might help the dragon keeper. *Do I trust him?* She did, at least some, but why did she? Why not? Amid these confused deliberations, she stepped closer still, torch almost up against the impenetrable door. She saw then that someone had tried to burn the door before, among the other forms of destruction attempted on the triangle structure.

Closing her eyes, she tried to clear her mind. But before she could even begin to process the problem, the solution was clear.

The center triangle is not the key. It's the lock.

Chapter Thirty

The Dragon Tongue

Heather reached out with her left hand and felt the small, precise pattern inside the little triangle center. Yes, she had felt that pattern before, or, more accurately, the reverse of that pattern. She patted her satchel, eager to turn and tell the keeper she had figured it out. When she turned back, smiling wide, a crunching rumble began, and the ground shook. The now familiar sound of falling rock filled the hall, louder and closer than before, and she saw shadows of plunging rock and heard their bursting echo join the calamitous crashing all around. Overbalancing, Heather pitched back against the door, and, rebounding with the impact, dropped the torch. It flipped back, scorched her dress, then landed on her foot. She cried out at the sudden pain and kicked the torch away as she patted, then smoothed, the singed fur of her foot. She crouched against the heavy door, arms shielding her head.

As the rattling continued, the dragon keeper seemed to balance easily, and the remaining torchlight beyond revealed him swatting away a rock nearly the size of Heather that fell from above. The next two were too large, and he sprang back and forth to dodge them in succession. Remarkably agile, he eluded a huge section of falling stone and leapt inside one of the tunnels just before the last torch went out.

The rumbling stopped. Her heart beat fast and her gasping breath sounded loud in this settling silence. This episode had been more significant by far than the others she had experienced. And it felt close. She believed that most of the others she had heard were likely to have originated here, or near here.

Heather had just about shared the secret of the triangle door with the dragon, to solve a mystery he had no doubt puzzled over for a long time. *It's our way out.* More urgent now than ever. *But is it right? Why does he want to get inside that structure? What's in there?*

She listened carefully, bending to sit with her back against the old door. Heather hoped to hear Smalls' voice, to see him break into the rubble-covered hall with a torch. But if he could not come, then she hoped for at least the keeper to return. After several minutes, she heard the sound of footfalls, accompanied by a swishing sound. Quite loud, and closer than she would have believed. She almost spoke, nearly called out to the keeper, but an urgent inner voice cautioned silence.

"Yor chey gaba?" she heard. It was the guttural uttering of a dragon voice. "Yor chey, gumbro?"

"Yee shon humva," came an answer. "Voo dorn sitt kaan. Urr atro!"

"Domt nunkolo, gaba gumbro!"

Her mind reeled. The voices frightened her. *Is the keeper talking to himself, using different voices? Was he hit on the head after all?*

More footfalls, and whispers in the distance, as a torch sprang to life. A single dragon, head darting hard one way then the next to survey the room, gazed around eagerly. Heather stayed where she was, easing ever so slightly behind the blocking rock of wreckage lying between her and the dragon. Soon, after making several swipes with his torch along the outside of the hall, he hurried toward one of the tunnels. It seemed to be the one, or very near the one, by which she and the keeper had entered this hall. As quietly as she could, she ran after him. His torchlight, so revealing moments ago, began to fade into the tunnel, and she sprinted across the debris-strewn hall, finally darting inside the tunnel to follow the light.

Heather crept along at a discreet distance, not wanting him to hear. She wasn't sure what her plan was, but she felt compelled to follow him for now. This she did, weaving past debris and sliding along small tunnel walls until the light led to an open chamber, small, but similar to the large hall she had just left. This one—and she realized she had been here before—had three tunnel doors on either side of a bare stretch. She ran into the central one on the near side, following the dimming light inside. She recognized the faint noise from their trek inside not long before, but it grew louder now as she rounded a wide bend and came into a cave entrance on her right, where voices carried to her.

Dragon voices.

She crept to the edge of the tunnel mouth and peered around the side. The cavern was huge, likely ten times the size of the one she and Smalls had been cast into. Torches ringed the hard rock walls, illuminating a terrifying scene.

A vast throng of dragons was packed inside the immense chamber, lined up in staggered columns like an army, all facing a central pavilion, round and raised above the rest. There on the stage stood a cadre of black-robed dragons, and the murmuring crowd grew silent as the torch-bearing dragon she had followed rushed to the stage and whispered urgently with the black-robed leaders.

Heather swallowed hard, gazing in alarm as the dragons huddled, then turned to face the gathered army.

"Looka han drevbo goonsala bancha vose dey!" a dragon chieftain cried. Then all the dragons stomped six times, ending in a unified cry. The shout was a gargling terror, low and haunting. She did not know the words, but she felt their meaning in her gut. And it terrified her. The room shook. Every dragon bent and hissed, filling the space with a noxious stench, a hint of which drifted toward Heather.

Swiping a torch from the wall just inside the large chamber, she dashed back into the tunnel, retracing her steps till she emerged into the small hall with three tunnel doors on both sides of the room. She sprinted into the near side tunnel's leftmost opening and wound around until she came again into the long rubble-covered chamber where the low triangular thirteenth tunnel structure stood. She ran for it, dodging past debris and leaping over wreckage until she finally reached the door.

She lodged the torch between two leaning rocks, where it hung, somewhat precariously, illuminating the scarred door. Reaching out once again, she felt the elaborate indentations in the triangle center and knew for certain it was a lock. And what would every king and heir of Natalia, making regular visits to confer with the conquered dragon's keeper, possess? What token could also be a key? She knew. And she knew where it was.

"Little doe ran off."

Heather spun to see the keeper, and he was ominously close, exhaling as he spoke. Heather coughed and squinted.

"The keeper has been searching for you."

"I followed another dragon," she said, somehow unable to lie or stay silent. "I followed him to the dragon hall and saw the army. I saw the dragon horde."

"A part of the horde, you saw," the keeper said, blowing noxious fumes in her face. "These are only hatchlings of the year. There are more. Many more, in the caverns of the so-called dragon tomb. We are *rising*. We are *ready*. But the keeper must get through this gate!" His split tongue extended, nearly touching Heather, as his yellow eyes hardened. "You will open this gate."

"I will open the gate," she said, but stupidly. Automatically. Meanwhile, another part of her mind, a part so dull she almost couldn't access it, warned her not to cooperate. But the compelling power welling within her felt too strong. She was choosing. "I will open the gate, for I have the key."

Heather reached inside her satchel, snagging the battered old purse where she had long stowed her treasures. She drew out Aunt Jone's pouch and reached inside.

She would surrender the way to the dragons. She would use the heir's most precious token to release the dragon horde to rampage across Natalia once again.

Heather would let them win.

Chapter Thirty-One

The Prince's End

Heather, compelled in a way she couldn't understand, was digging in her satchel, reaching for the emerald gem she knew was the key to this ancient vault. She was going to give it to the keeper.

But the Green Ember was gone.

She looked up at the dragon, eyes wide. Heather saw recognition there that she had failed. His face grew angry, and she heard a low, aggressive growl growing in his throat and then tearing out of his wide mouth in a furious cry.

"Rakafon doo day hoon! You fail me, little doe?" he roared. "You dare fail me?" He raised his head and bellowed a deep, watery call that echoed in the dank halls of the islands. "Bayfooo mon sacha roooo!" Heather covered her ears.

An answering call, from hundreds, perhaps thousands, of dragons, came to Heather's ears through the myriad of tunnels all around. Then footfalls, like the pounding of an army.

"The dragons will break out anyway," the keeper said.

"They grow closer every day."

"What will you do when you are out?" she asked, straining against her almost unstoppable need to comply.

"You are strong," the keeper said, coming closer and gripping both her arms. His razor claws bit into her arms so hard they bled. "If there are many like you, then this conquest will at least be sporting. But the dragons rise, little doe, to do what dragons have ever done. We rise by lies and live to slaughter. We subjugate and sacrifice. We tyrannize and torture. We break rabbits' necks for sport and feast on rabbit young in our devotion."

"I thought," Heather said, squirming against the dragon's painful grip, "you were the keeper. I thought you awaited the conference and kept the old treaty?"

"I killed the keeper years ago, ate him early after my waking," the dragon said. "I am the prince who was to come, the self-waking one destined to lead the rising of our kind. I assumed the mantle of keeper to see if I could entice you to open this gate. But since you cannot, your Small Prince shall be saved to serve at our victory meal. You? I will split you with a swipe of my tail and divide you for the first of my fellows who answer my call. And," he continued, as the sound of footfalls grew and Heather glanced over at the tunnels now teeming with rushing dragons, "here . . . they . . . come."

He threw her hard against the door. She struck the immovable stone, then rebounded to collapse on her knees. Looking up, she saw his claw strike out at her face.

She ducked, shielding as best she could, and the claw cut across her arms and mangled her left ear, knocking her over again. This blow hurt, but it had also shaken her free of the strange compulsion she had. She sprang up, her back to the dragon, then turned slowly, determined to make the best end she could manage. She saw the army of dragons pouring into the room, bearing torches and flocking to their destined prince, the leader of their dark uprising. Tongues flicked and glossy black-scaled armor glinted from the horde. The dragon prince's tail rose slowly, poised above his head. His tongue flicked out, and a malicious smile, venom dripping from his jaws, spread over his face.

"Now, the end," he spat, his tail arcing round.

A sound of a turning lock sounded from behind, and the dragon's tail struck against something hard. Heather watched the dragon prince's expression change from malignant mirth to stunned surprise.

Smalls sprang through the open triangular door, light pouring from behind him as he shot out with a black glowing sword, which reflected light like it was made from a star. *The starsword!*

"Kill and conquer," the dragon prince cried, "the gate is open at last!" and he swiped at Smalls with a razor claw while behind him the dragon horde surged forward.

Smalls ducked the claw strike and, spinning in an agile sweep, brought the sable blade around to cleave clean through the neck of the dragon prince. His head fell among the soldiers, who paused in shock. In a moment,

their enraged cries of anguish rose and they surged ahead with a desperate frenzy.

"Get inside!" Smalls called, rushing back toward the light-filled triangular room, urging Heather on. She dove through the door as he dashed inside behind her, closing it just before the first of the horde arrived.

Heather sat in the small room, shaking, her eyes wide and heart racing.

"Are you okay, Heather, my dear?" Smalls crouched before her, taking her face in his hands. "You're hurt."

"I don't think it's bad," she said, rising to embrace him.

She gazed around the room. There was a bright light she couldn't explain and several crates bearing old inscriptions.

"I'm sorry it took so long. I had to figure out how to unlock the door from the inside."

"You didn't come through the front?" Heather asked, turning back.

"No," he said.

"But that means—"

"—that they can get in. Yes," he said, sighing. He pointed to a gash in the back side of the vault, near the second gate. "They can. They don't know it yet, but they soon will. I was sent to work on that side in a deep tunnel, pounding away with a long maul, and, after the last quaking, rocks tore apart and I found the way in. I think the keeper came, but he couldn't get to me right away because of the fallen rubble behind me in my cave."

"He wasn't the keeper."

"I heard him," Smalls said. "I was trying to figure out the door, but I could hear everything. I was so afraid I'd lose you."

She gazed across at the second door. "The way out?"

"Yes," he said. "It must lead through another tunnel to the surface."

She smiled, rushing to hug him. Then she broke away and ran to the door. She bent to examine its small triangle shape. It looked the same as the other door.

"Oh no, Smalls. I've lost the Green Ember," she said. "We're trapped!"

"No, my dear," Smalls replied, sheathing his sword and reaching into his shirt. "I have it." He drew out the emerald, back around his neck on its golden chain. "I took it with me the last time I left you. I wasn't sure why. It may have been the dragon himself, compelling me in his strange way. But I didn't know it was a key. Not yet. Maybe my subconscious was working on the problem. I'm afraid the dragon prince had quite a sway over me. I was almost in his thrall. That breath. It's poison and . . . far more."

"He had me in his grip too. I nearly gave everything away. What an awful beast. I'm so glad you took off his head."

"I was happy to do it," he growled.

"So, we are free to leave?" she asked, almost not believing it possible. She gazed at the door leading outside. Their hopes were on the verge of being realized. They could be together. They could rejoin the resistance and strengthen their side with the return of the prince. She could see her family again. Smalls would be . . . what he was destined to be. "Smalls! We'll be together and free. It's what we've dreamed might be!" She turned back to him.

But he was not smiling. He looked down. "What is it, Smalls? What's wrong?"

"If we leave," he said, "we'll be leaving the way open for them to follow. They'll clear the cave in an hour at most—perhaps much sooner—and then they'll be in here. I've had time to examine the tunnel's wall. It won't take them long to get past this last barrier. The last quake broke open a way. The old barriers my ancestors built held a long time, but no more. We might make it to the top of the island, and maybe we could swim to First Warren's dam or out to the banks leading into the forest. But by the time we reached either, the dragons would be out. They would be unleashed, in their thousands, into Natalia once again."

Heather closed her eyes. No noxious breath confused her now. She had no doubt about what they had to do. Tears came at the death of her dream, at the loss of their own hopes. She inhaled deeply, then nodded to Smalls.

"Unsettle the foundations," she said.

"What?" he asked.

"We have to finish this. We have to end them all."

"Even if it means, as it certainly does, that we will die doing it? My dear Heather, I wanted us to be together. We could get away. Get away from everything."

"You can't do that, and neither can I. Our love is a treasure, but it's not the house we keep the treasure in." Heather smiled through tears. "There is a bigger world we fit inside, and we can't say yes to our love right here without saying no to that world. I can't. I know you can't either, or you wouldn't be the one I love so much."

Chapter Thirty-Two

The Last Battle in Dragon Tomb

Heather smiled. Smalls looked at her with an admiration and affection she had never known before.

"Oh, Heather. You would have been a magnificent queen. Let's live like we are king and queen—just for now, here among our enemies—and finish an old task together."

Heather nodded. "Defeat the dragons, at last."

"Yes!"

Heather smiled, shaking her head. "We were so close to getting out."

Smalls sighed. "And if we succeed, they'll never know out there what happened down here."

"But we're doing it for them," she said. "We know what it means. We know it's protecting them from adding another enemy to those already out there, another unstoppable foe bent on destroying our kind."

"Would these dragons ever fight against Morbin?" he asked, doubtful.

"They would reach an agreement and divide our kind between them," she answered, "as they no doubt always have. I know it. I see it. We have to do this, Smalls. I'll fight beside you till—"

"—the end of the world."

A sound of clawing came from the door, followed by a series of bashing crashes.

"They can't get in that way," Heather said.

"No, but it won't take long," Smalls replied, eyeing the side breach.

"What wonders are here?" she asked, gazing around the vault at the crates. "Where is this light coming from? Is it wrong for me to look? I'm not a royal, you know."

"You would have been," he said sadly, pointing to a strange lantern in the corner. "I was going to marry you, Heather Longtreader, when the wars were all over. We would have ruled together, you and I, and been happy in the mending."

"It was my dream, too," she said, wiping at her eyes. "I'm glad, at least, that we fight and fall together."

"For the Mended Wood," he said.

"For the Mended Wood," she echoed, and they embraced again.

A noise of hard crashing came from the torn gap in the side of the vault, and Smalls rushed over to look. "We have only a moment, my dear."

"Are there any weapons here?" she asked, "other than... than the starsword?"

"My maul," he said, bending to pick up, then pass to her, the long hammer with a spike on its back side. "How does that feel?"

"It feels good," she said, testing its weight in her hands, "and it's just what I need. Can you make a path?"

"Back home?" he asked, and she knew he meant the spot where they had reunited by the mossdraft pool.

"Back home."

"Let's take what we can. We'll need more weapons."

She peered into an open crate at her feet and saw not a weapon but an ancient book, bound round many times with a rough cord. She picked it up and stuffed it inside her satchel. Breaking open another crate, she saw a small black bag. She stuffed it inside her satchel and secured the satchel tight against her. Heather felt an ache at leaving other treasures, but they had to act and act fast. Finally, she saw a silver knife and secured it in her belt. Smalls donned a steel breastplate, gold-plated with the double diamond etched in its center. Heather fastened the straps in back while he threw on gold-plated armguards that extended to his elbows.

He was rooting through another box when a shattering close by sounded and heavy footfalls filled the nearby cave.

"Let's go!" Heather cried, raising her long-handled hammer.

Smalls crossed quickly to the door and placed the Green Ember inside the inner lock, then twisted right. The door sprang open and, with a cry, they rushed into the darkness.

The dragons were blinded a moment, and Heather saw them flinch back at the intense light. She had a moment to evaluate the dragons and estimate their own slim chances of success. The hall teemed with enemies. They roiled in an eager frenzy to fall upon their prey. Smalls surged ahead, swinging his blade. Heather followed in his wake, staying just out of range of the scything swipes.

She readied the maul, eager to aid in the task. Smalls leapt into the fight, blade singing as it met their enemies with terrible effect. Heather's blood was up, and she rushed into the wake created by his driving charge. A slender dragon sneaked beneath Smalls' stroke and rose up, tail poised to destroy him from behind. Her maul met the dragon's head as she released a wild cry. The enemy fell, senseless, as others rushed in to replace him. On and on they came, met, every one, by Smalls' flashing starsword. It appeared almost weightless in his hands but bit into the seemingly unbreakable scales of the dragons in scores. Heather had almost no time to assess things in the center of the storm, but she could not help marveling at what she was witnessing.

Surely this had never occurred in the history of rabbitkind, such a hero in such a fight. Oh, to have been allowed to tell this tale. These malicious beasts had meant to slaughter rabbitkind, but Smalls had reversed this course and was destroying *them* with awful efficiency. Up they came, rows of killer brutes. And down they fell, each and every enemy meeting the same unstoppable blade. He blocked a dragon pike strike with his left wrist, half-shattering an armguard, then brought his blade back like lightning to strike down the attacker. And so the dragons fell, piled in heaps on either side of Smalls' slashing path. Again and again Heather protected his back and swung her maul to ward off more.

Soon they had reached the edge of the hall, and Smalls called back to her, "Are you clear?"

"Not yet!"

He beat back a sudden attack of several dragons, taking many blows on his chest plate, then pushed ahead, clearing space for Heather. She saw her gap, won by hard-fought heroics on Smalls' part, and she strode into it. Swinging her powerful maul around, she spun and delivered a strike of astonishing force to the support beam they fought beside. The wood split as her heavy hammer tore through it, and the wall tottered and began to come down.

Smalls was already ahead, clearing the way for the next. She leapt into the second strike, her hands still shaking from the first, and smacked a shattering blow on the next support beam. More of the wall gave way, and she had to leap ahead to avoid the crashing stone. Countless dragons, their bloodlust blazing, were crushed in her wake beneath the new-made rubble.

As she dashed for the next beam, Smalls had gotten far enough ahead of her that she was pressed on every side by dragons and he was fading from sight.

"Smalls!" she cried as the scaly creatures reached for her with knife-sharp claws, their tails poised to strike. She raised her hammer as the collapsing avalanche of wall over-took their pursuit, smashing them down as rubble rained all around. With agility that surprised even herself, she dodged the greater part of the debris, brushing off smaller rocks as her enemies were crushed around her.

She rose, leaping from sliding stone to piling rubble, and so ascended beyond the grasp of her attackers. Spotting Smalls, she raced toward him, dodging falling rock and evading the dragon pursuit. She feinted left, then bolted right to head for the exit. Smalls had hacked at another support, then bent his breakaway race her way. They converged in front of the tunnel leading back to the great cavern and hurried inside as the entire cavern roof broke apart and collapsed in a terrific noise.

They sped along the passage, Smalls dealing death to those dragons who pressed in against them, their bodies falling along the path so that Heather had to tread them down as she followed fast after the prince.

They broke into the last hall and rushed through, not stopping as dragons sprang to meet them from every crumbling tunnel. Smalls swung the starsword, and enemies fell in pieces. Heather hurried behind him, ready with her maul to hammer more foes back. They sprinted to the edge of this cavern. Once again, as Smalls fought for space, she drove her hammer into the splintering supports, smashing them to pieces and precipitating a rolling wreck that brought rock crashing down all around in a wave of collapse. They were barely able to stay ahead of the ruin.

Heather was amazed at how strong she felt. She had always been fast, and this last dash had required all of her speed to stay alive long enough to complete the mission, but this heavy hammer felt entirely manageable to her as she raced along.

As they neared the three tunnels on the far side of the collapsing cavern, Heather heaving her hammer to blast through a final support beam, three dragons stood guard at the opening of the one way they must take. Smalls blocked another pike strike with his bright golden armguard and drove his blade through the belly of the first dragon. He turned to the next on his left, but Heather didn't see the result. The starsword flashed in her periphery as she swung her hammer hard, just missing the ducking head of a powerful dragon and smashing through the wall of the tunnel. The dragon leapt back at her, jaws slavering with dripping venom. She was knocked down, her hammer lost to the ground. The dragon's head shot at her, jaws wide. The venom dribbled on her face, burning her as he bent to end her with his bite.

Chapter Thirty-Three

Farewell, Heather and Smalls

Heather shoved up with her hands, trying to block the dragon's death bite. But, as strong as she felt, she wasn't strong enough. He broke through her attempted block and bore down. His head was knocked suddenly sideways, and he bit into stone, breaking teeth. Smalls had kicked him off his killing course and now finished him with the black blade.

Smalls gripped Heather's hand, and she leapt up. She snagged her hefty hammer as rock struck the ground all around them, shattering as it fell. They fled into the tunnel as a last backward glance showed that an avalanche of collapsing stone had fully flattened that hall as well and now carried its devastating wreckage into the tunnel just behind them.

There could be no escape now. No way back to the triangular vault of Smalls' fathers. They would never emerge through that ancient path, unlocked by the Green Ember, to find a way back. Those secrets inside the vault would be secrets forever, just as their own deeds and deaths would never be discovered. But in this exhilarating escape, this sacrificial fight against the dragon hordes, she delighted in their victory and had never been prouder of her prince. He had killed so many enemies, had leapt to meet and defeat their evil uprising. And she had been beside him, striking her own blows against their foes, facing the rising tide of the dragon army's inestimable threat.

Together, they were bringing it all down.

Heather heard the echoing rumble throughout the islands. It was loud, that sound of compounding crashes throughout the vast dragon lair. The ground heaved and they stumbled ahead, rebalancing again and again as they raced on. Amid a plume of rock dust at the edge of the collapsing avalanche, Heather and Smalls shot into the last chamber. The first chamber. The great central cavern of Forbidden Island. They ran on as the collapse stalled behind them, crushed rock vomiting into the cavern and fouling the mossdraft pool. But it stopped. Even while distant rumbles continued, the flow seemed to break and cease in this spot.

Smaller rocks came loose from the curved ceiling, and rubble lay scattered around the cavern; but compared to the ruin behind them, this hall seemed almost stable.

The two rabbits panted, bending over to catch their breath. Smalls fell to his knees, absently cleaning his blade on his shirtsleeve as he shook his head. He gazed at the blade with a kind of holy awe, then sheathed it at his side.

"Flint's own sword. My ancestral arms." Looking over at Heather, he rose. "Are you okay, my dear?"

"I..." Heather began, gasping for air, "...am pretty well."

Smalls laughed, coughing as he crossed to her. "Pretty well?"

They laughed together, leaning against each other in the faint light of the last cavern standing in the ancient lair of dragons. "I feel good," she said, smiling wide. "I'm glad we did what we did."

"As am I."

"Might we...survive in here?" she asked, glancing nervously over at the support beam. The wooden brace was riddled with splintering cracks. "For a while?"

They gazed at one another a moment. Then a hissing bellow sounded, picked up and passed on, repeated again and again by a growing chorus of coarse voices. From hidden vaults throughout the hall came the last part of the dragon army, and they broke into the cavern with an insatiable rage. These came from the other side of the islands, opposite from where the two rabbits had just fled leaving a just destruction in their path. Unless this hall too fell, the dragons would still stand a chance—however slim—of getting out and setting on their friends, ending the hope of the mending.

That cannot be.

With a last, longing look at Smalls, Heather picked up her maul and dashed at the last buttress, that beam that seemed their final chance at somehow surviving. *No*. This was indeed the end.

She reached the beam just as Smalls met the last dragon attackers, hewing them down in succession with his shining black blade. The Small Prince and his sable starsword, a final tale for her to savor and see. The Scribe of the Cause's last story.

Heather spun and sent her hammer tearing through the last beam.

The cavern shook and came apart.

Heather locked eyes with Smalls as the rock rained down.

Chapter Thirty-Four

SIGNALS AND MESSAGES

Jo Shanks had spent the past few days working with the allied archers of Emma's army. He occasionally helped with other errands for the princess or backed up Picket's and Cole's work with the Royal Fowlers Auxiliary. Alongside engineers and many stout soldiers, the archers were folded into the Highwall Wardens, though most called them the Highwallers. They were charged with holding the wall and defending the city. It was a duty many volunteered for but few expected to live through. Jo felt honored to be among them.

The archers were the best ever assembled, if Jo could be trusted to judge. His own former unit, the Bracers, were united with Harbone's best, along with handpicked bucks from every free citadel in Natalia. The Harbone archers were incensed by the slaughter at their citadel. Almost all had lost loved ones—many had lost their entire families. They worked with a fierce determination that inspired the rest. Clay Fletcher, a legendary old archer from the last wars, was in command. Nate Flynn and Harbone's Himson

Forn seconded Commander Fletcher, and Jo slotted in with Nate's division when they practiced maneuvers.

Jo reached the last step up First Warren's outside wall, still wincing as he thought of falling from this height so recently. *Good thing Pick was there.* He dodged past a team of Heyward's brother votary engineers, setting a series of bowstrikers every fifteen feet along the wall. Farther down the wall-top path, amid a band of archers, stood his friends Studge, Owen, and Nate, along with a buck from Vandalia named Deever. Jo had fought alongside Deever's brother Aubray, as had Nate, Studge, and Owen. So the group had quite naturally welcomed Deever in. Jo walked their way, his glider pack on his back and a loose cape draped over his shoulders. He checked the lock on the quiver hanging on one side of his belt, then felt the grip of the sword on the other side.

"Jo Shanks." Studge said as the long-legged buck walked up. "Taking a break from a life of high living among the royals to associate with low fellows like us? How kind."

"You guys aren't low," Jo answered, gazing down on the busy city below, "at least not in location."

"He's probably bringing a message from his best friend, the princess," Deever said.

"I do have a message," Jo said. "Princess Emma wants you all to know that she thinks I'm wonderful, and she has a low opinion of how you bucks both look and smell. There was more, but I'll spare you the most insulting parts."

"Thank you, your lordship," Deever said, making an exaggerated bow. Deever looked so like Aubray, with the same fur pattern as his brother, black with gold around his eyes and the inside of his ears.

"What's happening here?" Jo asked.

"We're waiting on Lord Longshot there," Studge said, nodding toward Nate Flynn, "to let us know when our next in a long line of 'Where Should We Stand During the Fighting' drills will be."

Owen rolled his eyes. "I genuinely cannot wait. I'm so glad you're here with us at this crucial juncture, Jo."

"Otherwise you wouldn't know where to stand," Deever whispered.

"I constantly feel like I'm standing in the wrong place," Jo replied.

"Are we ever going to shoot?" Studge asked, gazing in Nate's direction. "I thought this was a company of archers."

"Stop complaining, Studge," Nate Flynn said, looking up from his notes. "It's possible there are smarter minds at work than yours."

"I'd say *likely*," Deever said.

"We have confirmation," Owen added.

"Yes, sir." Studge saluted and sagged against the parapet. "I just want to shoot an arrow from my bow once or twice as a part of this elite archery company."

"Did you ever consider," Jo asked, tapping his head, "that the commanders already know we can shoot? And maybe they want us to coordinate with the other soldiers, so we don't accidentally kill our own troops or help the enemy some other way."

Studge opened his mouth and extended a finger; then his eyes widened, and he inclined his head, saying nothing.

"I think that's a major military victory right there," Nate said, marking out something on his paper and stepping forward. "You did the impossible, Jo. You shut Studge up."

"Folks use the term *hero* pretty lightly, but—" Jo began, but Nate interrupted.

"Okay, elite archers of Natalia, gather round," Nate called, and the large band of rabbits congregated tightly around him. "We are staging here—at arms—for thirty minutes, then shifting as a body, going light, down to one of three redeployment areas, depending on the signal we get from command. Any questions?" Studge raised his hand. Nate shook his head. "Okay, since there are no questions, to your stations!"

"Yes, sir!" they called. Jo followed Nate to the edge of the wall, where they gazed over at the palace.

Nate sighed. "I bet they've got that dullhead Farns as signaler again. I don't see why the commander trusts him."

"The commander can't keep up with all that chaos up there, sir," Jo said. "His chief of staff is the problem. It's not ill will; he's just overwhelmed with the job."

Nate drew a glass from out of his satchel and set it to his eye. "It is him. And—what? Now he's signaling... two yellow flags followed by three red and then a white with a grey X. He emphasizes the last by shaking it back and forth!" Nate hung his head.

"Oh no, that Farns and his flags again," Owen said, laying down his bow. "Why don't you just fire a shot over there, sir? I'm sure you can hit it from here."

"He might hit the flags by accident," Jo said.

"Shanks," Nate said. "Jump over there and ask command what we are meant to do with a signal hoist of 'Advance with all haste and fall back on the double, we are friends, we are friends,' if you please."

"It's nuanced, sir," Studge said, scratching his chin. "It's got levels."

"Yes, sir," Jo said, saluting his fellows as one of Nate's aides checked his pack over. "I'll report to the palace rooftop, ask what on earth the signal is supposed to say." The aide slapped the pack twice, and Jo looped his hands through the cape's wrist slots, testing the connection. Satisfied, he jumped up to the parapet and, shrugging toward Studge, Owen, and Deever, slowly let himself fall from the high wall.

Engaging the glider, Jo swept out over the old road and then, banking back across the square, up to the palace's high roof, where he alighted in the designated landing zone, on the far side from the giant slide still under construction.

"I need to see the commander," Jo said as an officer approached him, distracted by a list in his hands.

"The commander is very—" the officer began. He was

going to say that Commander Fletcher was busy, but then he looked up and saw who was asking. Jo Shanks, heroic archer and close friend of both Picket Longtreader and the princess herself. "I, uh . . . Lieutenant, I will do my best, sir, to get his attention."

"Thank you." Jo gazed around the rooftop as the officer hurried off. The organization required to get all these rabbits going in the same direction was immense. How it functioned as well as it did was beyond him. *I'm like Studge. Just tell me where to point my arrows.*

"Lieutenant Shanks!"

Jo turned to see Dalla, a young doe from Harbone who served as a runner. "Yes, Dalla?"

"Sir," she said, holding out a folded paper, sealed with wax, "I was charged to give this to you." She handed it over.

"Charged by who?"

"She said her name was Lady Glen, sir," Dalla said. "But she was with Lord Blackstar and Heyna, as well as some others."

"Where have you come from, Dalla?"

"From north of Chelmsford, sir," she said, and Jo could see she was exhausted. "They said it was urgent. I ran all the way."

"Dalla, well done. Get yourself some provisions down below."

She saluted, relief plain on her face, and walked off.

Jo broke the seal and tore open the letter. He read it quickly, then ran to Signaler Farns and snatched away his white flag with the grey X.

"Hey!" Farns shouted, staring at his empty hands. "No one may interfere with or otherwise alter the exact messaging of Her Royal Highness's services—upon pain of death!"

"Then you're a dead buck, Farns," Jo called over his shoulder as he leapt from the rooftop and banked left.

After a flight that took him over the western edge of First Warren and into the forest beyond, he found what he was looking for: the crossroads north of Chelmsford. He dropped low and, increasing the drag on his glider, eased down for a smooth landing. The secluded roadway felt strange after being in a busy city so much lately. It was unnerving. He walked along the road north, as his instructions had stated.

"Ho there," someone called from the forest. Jo stopped, and out stepped several strange bucks wearing odd clothes. They seemed to be travelers—longtime travelers. Their leader, an old buck of mixed brown and silver fur, stepped forward. "You Shanks?"

"Yes."

The stranger nodded. "An archer, right?"

"Like you," Jo said, noticing the same signs. "Where's Lord Blackstar?"

"Come along," the stranger said, nodding into the overgrown forest.

"This feels safe," Jo said with a smirk. But the truth was that he did feel safe. The stranger, as odd as he and his companions looked, felt good. He smelled right. Jo wasn't sure how to word it, but there was something almost sublime in his presence. "What's your name?" Jo asked.

"They call me the Pilgrim."

Entering the forest, they followed a trail to a small camp under a canopy of trees. There was Lord Blackstar, and Heyna, and an old doe with black and silver fur. She wore an elegant dress and long gloves. She might have been Heyna's grandmother.

Jo bowed.

"Welcome, Jo," Lord Blackstar said. "I'm grateful you came."

"My lord."

"You have met the Pilgrim. This is Lady Glen."

Jo bowed again. "Your Majesty," he said.

"So, he's clever, I see," Lady Glen said. "I'm glad to meet you. You are the famous archer of those magnificent shots?"

Jo looked down. "I am . . ." he began, but he stopped.

"You don't wish to lie," she said, smiling. "Either you're always an honorable buck—a rare thing, but it does happen—or you're awed into honesty by the Pilgrim's proximity. He has that effect on many. It's been quite useful lately, I can assure you."

Jo smiled cautiously. "I have hit my mark in important moments, Your Majesty."

"Perhaps your best shot is yet to come."

"I only hope to serve the cause. I fight for the mending, ma'am."

"Very good, Archer Jo. I understand you're quite close to my daughter."

"I serve Princess Emma gladly, Majesty."

"Good. Good. There's someone else here who needs our help, Jo," she said, stepping forward. "Will you help us?"

"I am yours to command, Majesty."

A hooded figure emerged from behind a tree.

Chapter Thirty-Five

PICKET'S APPRENTICE

Picket peeled off his glider pack and laid it down on the palace rooftop as the Royal Fowlers Auxiliary wrapped up training. He watched the young bucks file down the hatchway stairs, recently enlarged alongside several other improvements to the crucial palace roof. These young bucks were doing better. They might be ready. But ready for what? His heart sank at the thought. He sighed and headed for the stairs. The princess would want a report.

Picket dreaded going to see Emma. He hated seeing her grow thinner and more worn with each day. The doom hovering over the city and all its preparations was palpable.

"Captain?"

Picket turned to see young Lallo, an infantrybuck from Halfwind who had made the R.F.A. "Yes?"

"Could I trouble you for a lesson?"

Picket frowned. "We just spent an hour in the air, soldier."

"I want more. More from you," Lallo said, head down. "See, I want to do what you've done, sir. To hit the enemy right between the eyes. To pay them back. To be . . . a . . . to be . . ."

"A legend?" Picket asked. "You want to be a legend?"

"Well, that's what you *are*," Lallo replied sharply. Picket hadn't realized he was wounding the younger buck. "And you once told me I was like you, or you were like me. That we were the same. Infantry."

Picket folded his glider pack and rubbed at his eyes. "We're still in the thick of it together, Lallo. You're in the R.F.A., and you'll do your part."

"I want you to show me how you do it," Lallo said, face set.

"Do what, Lallo?"

"Infantry and airborne. In battle. You fight like no one else. You're different. Better. I want that. I want to be that for the cause and crown."

Picket hadn't thought that way about himself. And he hadn't thought much about how he had become what he had become. He tried to for a moment, closing his eyes. Images appeared in his mind, memories of days he had not thought about in a long time.

"I had a great trainer. I'm not one." Picket smiled, then walked toward the stairs leading down into the palace.

"Ten minutes, sir," Lallo said. "Just give me ten minutes."

Picket stopped by the stairs, hanging his head low.

He didn't want to see Emma right now, anyway.

"How many weapons do I have, Lallo?"

Lallo hesitated. "Sir, you have your sword and . . . uh . . . a knife?"

Picket turned, smiled, and rushed Lallo with a leaping kick, which sent the surprised buck to the ground. Picket didn't leave him there. He kicked his glider pack so that it crashed into Lallo's head, then snagged several signal flags from a nearby shelf and attacked the astonished rabbit with them. Lallo blocked the first blow, then kicked out and missed as Picket dodged to the side and drove a flag's thick handle into his middle. Lallo gasped, sinking to his knees. Picket rose and kicked him down.

"How many weapons do I have?" Picket asked.

"A thousand?" Lallo gasped.

"Lesson one," Picket said, extending a hand to the crumpled buck. "Everything's a weapon."

Chapter Thirty-Six

The Odds of War

After an hour with Lallo, Picket dismissed the young buck and stood gazing at the preparations being made all over the city. They were close. If they could only have a few more days of preparation.

"Captain Longtreader," Lieutenant Bannon, one of the Royal Fowlers Auxiliary officers, called, running up.

"Yes, Lieutenant?"

"R.F.A. patrol reported in, sir. There's an army approaching."

"Whereaway?"

"Northwest, Captain."

So, it is Terralain, come to destroy us before we are fully and finally destroyed by Morbin. "Thank you, Bannon. Please find Lieutenant Shanks and ask him to meet me at the old gate road."

"Sir, Lieutenant Shanks is gone. He left hours ago, taking flight in his glider from this very rooftop."

"Were you here when he left?"

"Yes, sir," Bannon replied. "I saw a young runner—

Dalla, sir—bring him a note. Lieutenant Shanks read it and thanked Dalla. Then he stole a signal flag, ran to the edge, and flew off."

Picket frowned. "Thank you, Bannon. Have Lord Captain Helmer and Captain Frye been alerted about the army?"

"Yes, sir. It was the lord captain himself who sent me to you."

"Well done. Where is Cole?"

"He's at mess, sir. He was scheduled to train the next section after you. Shall I ask him to meet you at the old gate?"

"No. Unless Lord Blackstar's returned, he will have to muster with his father's force from Kingston. Just you and Harmon and Lallo be ready with the R.F.A. Put the second squad on standby and stage the third."

"Yes, sir."

Picket drew his glider pack back on, locked it into place with help from Bannon, and limped to the edge of the roof.

"Oh, and Bannon," he called.

"Yes, sir?"

"Which way did Jo fly?"

"West, sir. Due west."

Picket leapt, closing his eyes as he plunged down, loose cape flapping in the wind. Opening his eyes, he shot out his arms, twisted his wrists to engage the glider, and sailed up in a smooth, swooping arc. Picket glided over the seventh standing stone and gained great height, mastering the wind's sometimes erratic tracks, to survey from high above the city.

He saw them. A massive army, set off in columns, marching toward them. His heart sank, and he descended, bending in an elegant bank to glide over those rabbits working around the west gate, including the provisioners led by Captain Moonlight. Picket swept above the old road, dipping down till a sudden upward whip sent him flipping in a graceful sweep that ended with him landing on his feet. His bad knee only gave way a little, so that he ended by bending in a kneel.

"She's watching," Cap said, hobbling up. "I'm sure you impressed her."

Picket smiled. "Cap, we have to get all your crew to fallback positions."

"To the farm, already?"

"I'm afraid so."

"They won't want to go. I don't want to go."

"It's the princess's orders, Cap. And she's right."

"I know it," he said, frowning. "I'll get right on it."

"And please," Picket said hoarsely, "look after Weezie. I just couldn't lose... not another..."

"I'll stick close by her, Picket."

Picket nodded and hurried ahead as Cap began bellowing orders. He had reached the edge of the city when a column approached from the left with Captain Frye at its head. The veteran soldier looked old and worn. He, like Emma and so many others in positions of leadership, seemed to grow thinner every day.

Helmer approached from the right flank, leading another column of soldiers. Most of the soldiers in the city were situated with their own citadel's units, and the command structures were kept intact as much as possible. These two divisions, one led by Helmer and the other by Frye, were elite handpicked battlers meant to serve as the heart of the army. They were Emma's own force, the Royal Warrenguard.

Picket watched as they marched to the edge of the west gate, then flooded out to form two arching wings to hold the opening of the gate. This part of the wall had been closed up long ago, but the allies had blown it apart when they entered and took the city. It was now the focal point of defense. Picket peered aloft and saw that the Highwall Wardens were ready, with Emerson staged just above the gate on the high parapet.

"Captain Frye," Picket said, saluting his old commander on the left. "Lord Captain Helmer," he said, turning to bow to his master.

"Captain Longtreader," Helmer said, stepping to the center, "assume command of my part of the Warrenguard, if you please."

"Aye, sir," Picket replied, saluting and stepping to Helmer's right.

"I am assuming command of Her Royal Highness's forces entire," Helmer said.

"Aye, sir," Captain Frye said, saluting.

Helmer returned the salute. Picket gazed at the black buck, grey specks stretching across his jaw and flecking most of his fur. Picket had never seen him like this, full weight of the cause assumed with calm expertise and grim defiance. Picket knew that this was what Helmer had run from, what he was so bitter about when Picket first encountered him at Cloud Mountain. The old hero had seen too many young soldiers die under his command, and it took training Picket to once again revive his fire for the cause. Picket wiped at his eyes, seeing him there after all they had been through.

But Helmer had been right, after all. We are here at the end, and no one will survive. Picket's heart sank as he scanned the Warrenguard, seeing faces young and old, all of whom would likely be destroyed by day's end. Behind these troops, the provisioners fell back, and Weezie was among them. *Will I ever see her again?* Some would regroup all the way back to Helmer's family farm. At least she would be with her mother, bow in hand and ready to defend her family's old homestead. Deeper in the city, the lords of each citadel were marching at the head of their own armies, all coming together in long columns stretching back past the palace and all along the river.

The lords left their captains in command and made their way to the gate. Lord Ronan, Lord Booker, Lord Felson, and the others all lined up behind Helmer.

"Lord Ronan for Blackstone," Ronan said, "for the heir and for her cause."

"Lord Booker for Vandalia and my father's memory," Lord Morgan Booker said. "We fight for the princess and her cause."

"Lord Felson for Chelmsford," Felson began, and the remaining lords pledged their forces formally to Emma through Helmer. No one, however, stood there for Kingston. Then Picket saw a black buck glide in quickly. He banked up close by, disengaged one taut wing, then spun down in an expert twist to land before Helmer, alongside the lords.

"Cole Blackstar, sir, for Kingston," Cole said. "Since

our ancestor Fleck and until the end of the world, we stand with Whitson's heir and the cause of the mending!"

Picket nodded to Cole.

"My lords, you are welcome," Helmer said, bowing to them. "You know the plan. Let's begin our defense as we hope to end it."

"With no flinching," Lord Ronan said. "We must treat these rebels like raptors and cut them down."

"Agreed," Helmer said, frowning gravely. "It has come to that."

"Signal hoist at H.Q., Lord Captain," a signal aide named Jefwood called.

"What is it?" he asked, not even trying with his imperfect sight to read the flags.

"Enemy sighted," Jefwood said.

"Thank you," Helmer said, turning back to the lords. "Now, my lords. We must be certain to make them believe we are not coming out—"

"Sir, I beg your pardon," Jefwood said, "but the signal is being repeated again and again."

"What?" Helmer asked, turning to peer up at the palace. "Did we not replace that idiot Farns?"

"Yes, sir, that idiot Farns has been replaced," Jefwood said.

"Signal them to send a flyer."

"Aye, sir," Jefwood called, and he ordered his signaler to send that message.

Picket frowned, then gazed out at the distant army

approaching from the west. He could see them from the ground now, marching ahead in good order. The tall, terrible fighters of Terralain. He had seen them in action now more than once. He did not like the prospect of meeting them again this way.

Picket had hoped for so much more, but Kylen had made his decision clear. That fool would have so much to answer for. Picket recalled with a wince how he could have cut Kyle down in Smalls' chamber so long ago. *But I am no murderer, no matter what the Terralains say.*

The messenger sent from the palace top glided in and landed not far from the command team. The lords and captains parted, and Harmon came through.

"Report," Helmer demanded.

"Lord Captain," Harmon began, then saluted, "enemy in sight, sir."

"We know the enemy's in sight, soldier," Helmer snapped.

"Not them, sir," Harmon said, nodding to the Terralain army. "Another enemy. A wolf army, sir. From out of the northeast. We had an R.F.A. patrol scout report back just now, sir. It's an enormous wolf army, sir, well-armed and coming fast."

Helmer looked straight at Picket, wincing after a moment. Slowly, he looked back at the lords and other captains. "It's King Farlock. We can only face and fight them. Let us show our soldiers courage. There is nothing else for it, now. It has been an honor to serve with you."

The lords nodded and broke up, each heading back to their armies. Picket limped back toward his side of the Warrenguard, trying hard to show a brave face for the watching soldiers. Then, from his periphery, he saw another flyer gliding their way. He turned. *Jo?*

It wasn't Jo. It was Emma, wearing a long hooded black robe that rippled in the wind. She landed smoothly, and Picket crossed to reach her first. "Emma, what are you doing here? It's about to get very, very bad down here."

"I know that, Captain," she replied, hurrying toward Helmer.

"Emma, you can't stay here."

She shrugged him off, hurrying forward, her feet poking out of the long robe with each step. When she reached the command team, each lord and captain bent to bow. "My lords and captains, and Lord Captain Helmer, we have received an additional warning."

"We heard, Your Highness," Helmer said, "King Farlock's wolf army is nearly upon us. Which is why, perhaps, you should—"

"Not that warning," Emma said, looking down. "There is another."

Picket stepped closer as Emma continued. "The first wave of Preylord raptors has embarked from north of Grey Grove. They will be here soon. The end is here."

Chapter Thirty-Seven

The Terralains Attack

Picket staggered back, his knee buckling as he tried to recover. The Terralain army was in sight, just ahead, marching on First Warren from the west. The legendary king of the wolves, Farlock, was bringing his terrible army down from the north. From the northeast, the Lords of Prey, led by the first of the six raptor kings, were launching their attack.

"Leave, Emma," Picket said urgently, getting close to her ear. "You have to go. We'll need some kind of remnant rabbits in hiding after this. Some small group with you as their leader to help pick up the pieces and start again after... after what's about to happen."

"I'm not leaving," Emma said, jaw set.

"Your Highness," Helmer said, coming close. "Please consider leaving with a few loyal courtiers to escort you."

"Please," Lord Booker said, laying his hand on her arm. "Emma, go. I beg you."

"Would you go?" Emma snapped. Lord Booker lowered his head. "Would any of you go?" They all looked down.

"Then neither will I go into hiding. We go on. All of us, together."

"Yes, Your Highness. We will abide by your decision," Helmer said, bowing. "Harmon, please escort the princess back to the palace command center."

"No," Emma said. "I'm staying here."

"At least fall back to the palace, Emma," Picket said. "We can't protect you here."

"Who's protecting you, Picket?" she asked.

"It's not the same. I'm not the heir."

"I know it. I do." She got so close to Picket that her whispered words could only be heard by him. "I also know that we're all going to die here today. All of us. Please let me die up here with you, with those I love most, and not back there... at the end. Not when all's over. I can do some good up here. Back there, I can only wait for the end. I want to speak to these brave soldiers—to do all I can for them and to stand beside them as they go into this, our last battle."

"Okay, Emma," Picket said, bending to bow. "I am yours to command."

Emma sniffed, wiped at her eyes, then turned to the commanders. She threw back her hood and cast off her black robe, revealing a white gown with a silver breastplate fastened over it. On her head gleamed a silver crown. "May I borrow your sword, Picket?"

Astonished, he handed her his sword. She took it and walked toward the wall, Helmer and Frye following close after her, with the lords not far behind. She ran up several flights of stairs, ending on a landing that commanded a view of the Warrenguard and a significant portion of the rest of the army. The Highwallers crowded the wall and leaned down to listen. When they saw her mount the landing, a cheer began, then rose.

They don't know what's coming yet, Picket thought.

After receiving their cheers and applause for a moment, she held up her hand, and the crowd of soldiers grew quiet. "Brothers, the time has come to fight. I call you brothers because today I am more than your princess; I am your sister. I appear to be only this feeble doe, but inside I have the heart of a warrior king. And I will, rather than surrender to these bloodthirsty tyrants and kinslaying traitors, take up the sword. The fight is coming, and from many foes on many fronts. But I am with you. Fight on! I will never sue for terms of surrender or seek a token place in the enemy's evil order. I would rather go down and die, fighting for an entirely new order. And so would all of you. I am a healer, as you know. I mean with everything in me to save life. I will serve among you as a simple medic, bearing my sword where I must and saving some of you if I can. That is always my heart. But today I fight beside you. In our hands lies the hope of rabbitkind. Let nothing keep you from doing your duty; and know that I am beside you." She raised Picket's sword with her left hand and placed her right hand over her heart. The army knelt. "My place beside *you*, *my* blood for yours. Till the Green Ember rises..." she looked out and saw what looked like storm clouds in the east, "...or the end of the world."

The gathered soldiers rose, and a growing cheer began, softly at first as if a reverent moment were passing and there was reluctance to spoil its remains. But it grew. "Fight for the mending!" Emma cried, thrusting the sword up. The soldiers cheered then, shouted loud and long, as Emma descended the stairway amid raucous applause.

"How are we supposed to restore order now?" Lord Ronan asked.

"They were willing to fight before," Captain Frye said, "but now they can't be kept from it. It's worth a little disorder."

"It is that, Frye. And things are about to get very disordered," Helmer said. "Picket, the princess is with you."

Picket saluted and hurried to Emma. "Your Highness," he said, "if you please, you're with me." She nodded. An aide brought Emma her medical satchel, and, after handing the sword back to Picket, she slung it over her shoulder. "Got a spare sword?" she asked.

"Get the princess a sword," Picket called back to an aide. "Do you even know how to use one?" he asked.

"The sharp part at the bad guys?"

"That's the general idea. Listen, Emma. Stay behind me. The first wave will be awful. But there's no way to hide. We'll all be in it soon. Defend yourself first, then start on the healing when there are no enemies around. The Terralains won't kill a medic, I don't think, but the wolves—"

"I know what they do," Emma said. "Don't defend me, Picket. During the battle. Do what you're meant to do. And I'll do what I can."

He nodded, but there was no way he could obey that order. A soldier handed Emma a sword and sheath, and she fastened them around her waist.

There was no sign of the wolves yet, and the Preylords were a growing darkness in the eastern sky. But the Terralains were close now. They came over wide fields in endless rows of stout soldiers, tall and bearing their elegant standard of stars.

"Red Witch usurper!" Tameth Seer cried from the front of the advance troops, tall and menacing. "Surrender this city, and I will spare you. Swear fealty to . . . to the true heir of Natalia, and you will live."

Emma left Picket's side and strode up to stand beside Helmer on an earthen-work heap within bowshot of the Terralains. Picket fought the urge to step forward to protect her. Prince Naylen stood a few paces away from Tameth Seer, scowling. The young buck was barely mastering an indignant rage. *I had hoped he might have changed.*

"I will never surrender," Emma cried, her voice steady. "Fellow rabbits, turn around and go home. Do not do this evil thing."

"It is evil to slay our brave Captain Vulm and to seek to assassinate Prince Kylen himself, which this day you have sent your murderers to do."

"I have never sent killers to your camp," Emma shot back. "But you come to mine to kill your kindred."

"Today," Tameth Seer screeched. "Today, it has occurred! I see it! Prince Kylen is killed in his tent—" The soldiers of Terralain began to grumble and hurl curses at Emma. Helmer stepped forward.

"It's true!" Prince Naylen said, striding forward and

holding up a hand for quiet. "Assassins came to my brother's tent today."

"Let me handle this, Your High—" Tameth Seer began, but Naylen continued.

"They came for him where he slept. And it was the same killers who came for Captain Vulm in his sleep. Should we not attack and kill those who murdered Captain Vulm?" he cried, stepping toward Helmer and turning to his army.

The Terralains shouted, "Yes!"

Helmer's hand drifted down to his sword hilt.

"Should we fight against the source of that treachery?"

They cheered him in a thundering chorus. "Yes. Yes!"

Naylen's jaw was tight, and his eyes were white with rage. "Should we not march to war against any who would align with Morbin Blackhawk, bane of rabbitkind? Should we not oppose the poisoner of princes, the betrayer of brethren, the calculating counselor whose cause has been to play Morbin's part in our camp? Who has been the root and cause of all our woes?" he asked, looking ahead. The army murmured in confusion. Then Naylen spun back and drew his sword, pointing it at Tameth Seer. "You villain!"

"What now, princeling?" Tameth shrieked. "You think you can overthrow me? All I did was for the good of Terralain. I remember before your band of usurpers came. I remember when we followed Father Galt's way purely! I was only restoring—"

"You do not deny my charges, false seer?" Naylen barked. "Did you poison my brother?"

"I gave him what he needed to be reasonable," Tameth Seer said. "I am not ashamed of my actions."

"You should be ashamed," Naylen said, stepping closer. "You have attacked, have been attacking, the prince and heir of Terralain. You have been slowly murdering him. And you sent your assassins to finish the job today."

"Now that he's dead," Tameth cried, "there is no new anointing of an heir apart from my office's sanction. And I will not sanction *your* rise, princeling!"

"You don't have to," Naylen said. And from the army's right flank came a small band of Kylen's guards, their red shoulder armor standing out against black breastplates and armor. In their midst walked Kylen himself. He was thin still, with sunken eyes, but he looked far better than when Picket had last seen him. Naylen continued. "My brother, whom you would have murdered, is alive. Thanks to the warning and help from our allies among these rabbits," he said, motioning toward Emma.

Then Picket saw, among Kylen's guards, a tall, thin rabbit. *Jo?*

"Kill them!" Tameth Seer cried, and his own private guard set arrows to bows and rushed Naylen and Kylen and their guard. An arrow sailed at Emma, but Helmer knocked her out of the way just in time. They eased back down the small hill and recovered a safe position. Helmer motioned for the city's defenders to stay back. Picket watched as Naylen clashed with the first of Tameth's forces, an arrow narrowly missing his head. He held them off a moment, then was relieved by Kylen's guard, who stepped in and beat back Tameth's bucks. Some of Emma's soldiers stepped forward, eager to help in the fight.

"Hold," Captain Frye growled. All was a delicate balance, and Picket knew that interfering openly here could set the entire army into the fray. It was vital that Emma's army stayed out of their internal conflict. The Terralain forces, so notoriously disciplined, were already starting to clamor for explanations, and word was passing back through the army about what was happening at the front.

Naylen broke free and made for Tameth Seer. The old buck squared up to his young attacker and, when Naylen rushed in close, twisted to trip the prince with his staff. Naylen crashed down, and Tameth was upon him in a moment, drawing a blade from a sheath in his breast and driving it down at the exposed back of the splayed prince.

"No!" Kylen cried, rushing ahead. An arrow whizzed past Kylen's head and pierced Tameth Seer's knife hand. He cried out in pain and dropped the dagger, just as Kylen reached him from behind and Naylen rose and turned from the ground. Both princes extended their blades and drove them into the screaming soothsayer.

Tameth Seer fell dead. Picket watched as Jo formed up with the royal guard to protect Kylen and Naylen. Tameth Seer's temple guards surrendered, and Picket gasped, breathing at last. His heart swelled.

Then he heard it, away to his right, the sound of thunderous crashing through the trees.

Wolves.

King Farlock was attacking.

Chapter Thirty-Eight

Heroes Rise and Fall

They came. The wolves of the north, kin of King Garlacks and his bloody son. Huge, powerful, and ruthless in ferocity, King Farlock's army crashed into the clearing.

"Left vanguard, attack!" Helmer cried.

That was Captain Frye's side. Picket had to hold and watch the left flank pour out of the west gate and into the opening, rushing ahead to meet the savage attack of the wolf army. He bristled, holding his hand up for his soldiers to stand at the ready. It was an order he hated. Beyond the first wave of the attacking pack trailed a host of wolves so large Picket could not see its ending.

"Why don't they fire the bowstrikers from above?" Emma asked.

"We have to hold those," Picket replied. "We'll need them soon."

"We need them now!"

"We need more than we have, Emma. Just be ready."

"I'm ready," she said, gritting her teeth.

Out ahead of the first wave of the wolf attack came a massive alpha, white-furred with a black streak down his back and a silver helm on his head. His muzzle was painted with bloodred streaks, and his armor gleamed silver in the sunlight. He was easily twice as large as any wolf Picket had ever seen, and more deadly by far than any other. King Farlock.

Picket winced as Farlock met the first three bucks in the field, strong Warrenguard soldiers, whom the alpha tore apart with two brutal strikes. He bore no spear, but his fore claws were fitted with long silver blades. Farlock hacked through his enemies, his strength and speed unmatched on the field.

"Archers!" Helmer cried. "Fire away!"

The archers were trained to fire mainly at the rear of the attack, thinning the ranks of the reinforcements just behind the line of battle, making sure to avoid hitting fellow soldiers by mistake. But elite archers were among those stationed above, including Nate Flynn, who were expert at picking out targets even amid the melee. Several arrows sped toward the wolf king. But Farlock knew of their presence and had sent a shower of arrows from his own archers up at the Highwallers, dulling their capacity as the clash came. The king also fought in such a way—weaving through the field of battle—to put himself in positions where the rabbit archers couldn't get at him easily. When the rabbit archers were able to fire, a few shots rebounded off his armor, and others stuck in his hide, only to be snapped off and cast aside.

"Please, fall back midway through our division, Emma," Picket asked, "and join the medics there."

"We will have a lot to do," she said, gazing angrily at the wolf king's work, "all of us." With a squeeze of Picket's arm, she fell back, encouraging every soldier as she passed.

The battle was going as badly as possible, with the Warrenguard's left flank taking devastating losses. It could not go on. Helmer had to decide whether to join them or order a retreat to fall back and defend the gate. Farlock killed in batches, swiping aside stout soldiers and tearing through whole units in moments.

Picket glanced at Helmer, who raised a hand.

"Ready, bucks!" Picket cried over his shoulder.

Picket knew the dilemma Helmer faced, knowing that each order meant death for his soldiers, as did each delay. They must save vital assets for the Preylord attack and meet this enemy with what they had on the ground. What they had now was the Warrenguard. And it wouldn't be enough, not by a long shot. Especially while Farlock himself made such a trail of death as he drove closer and closer to the city.

Captain Frye, flanked by two burly bucks, rushed to meet him with a defiant cry. Farlock rounded on him, massive and imposing, his eager jaws glistening.

Captain Frye's one good arm bore his drawn sword, and he pointed it at Farlock. "Attack the alpha!" Frye shouted, and Picket knew, with a sinking heart, that it was the right strategy. Farlock must fall.

The brave captain led the charge, followed by soldiers of the Warrenguard, who broke forward, aiming their strokes at the killing king of the pack. Captain Frye rushed ahead, leaping to bring himself high enough to strike at the great wolf's head.

Frye's sword broke on the wolf's silver helm, while Farlock's blades, from both sides, met in the middle to kill the old captain. Picket looked on through tears, anger bristling inside. Down the valiant captain fell, dead on the field of battle before First Warren. His fellows fared no better as the wolf king cut through brave rabbit attackers with malevolent glee.

As Helmer gave the order for his Warrenguard flank to advance, Picket let loose a defiant cry. He rushed ahead, forgetting his pains, and aimed straight for the wolf king. The monster continued to tear through the gallant rabbits with evident ease. Likewise, his advanced soldiers, attacking in organized packs, were wreaking havoc on the small army of defenders. Picket sped ahead, slipping into the glider's hand clasps as he ran up the small earthen-work hill that Helmer was using to command a view. He leapt off his good leg.

"Picket, no, son!" Helmer cried, but Picket was already in the air.

He engaged the glider and caught a draft of air, speeding him ahead of his soldiers and directly at the alpha wolf. The killer king saw him, smiled wide, and waited, blades poised for his next victim. Picket raced on, aiming straight at the bloody jaws that bellowed out a challenging roar. When Picket reached the edge of the blades' range, he banked up suddenly, feeling the swish of the missing strikes as Farlock stretched to slice him in half, and rose up above the furious wolf. Just above his enemy, Picket twisted his wrists to disengage the glider and drew his blade, falling like lightning down on the shocked beast. Picket's blade bit into and through the hard hide of the stunned wolf's neck. Farlock roared in mortal fury as he tottered and fell, Picket landing beside him with a thump.

The rabbits behind Picket sent up a roaring cheer. But the wolf army, alarmed by the death cry of their king, quit their individual battles and rushed as a pack to avenge their king's killing.

Picket stood over the hulking body of the dead king and yanked back his blade. The wolf army came for him with united howls of anguish and anger as they tore the ground in their haste for revenge. Picket caught a glimpse of Helmer through the haze of flying dirt and wolves closing on him like the center of an ever-tightening circle. Helmer was shouting and rushing ahead, terrible anguish on his face. But he was too far away to reach Picket in time.

Picket braced for the wolves—braced for the end. Widening his stance and breathing deep, he exhaled with a cry.

"Come on!"

Chapter Thirty-Nine

Flood of the Silver Stars

Picket pivoted and picked out an enemy to attack. *I won't wait for you.* He coiled to spring but saw something just over the wolves' heads on his right.

Kylen's army broke in on the edge of the enclosing wolf circle, with Kylen himself at its head. Beside him Naylen ran in, their naked blades slaying as they came. The Terralain royal guard, red shoulder armor plain, drove into the circle of attacking wolves. The odds changed in a moment. Picket, far from being overrun, found himself suddenly relieved and protected. Kylen, weak as he was, pressed in and, along with two stout guards, pushed back the attacker Picket had chosen to engage. Picket joined in the fight, and the four of them overcame the wolf, Kylen finishing the enemy with an angry killing stroke. And so it went up and down the front line as the Terralain army as a whole shifted and rushed in to battle the wolf hosts.

Picket could see it now, as he and Kylen caught their breath. The remainder of Captain Frye's force, shockingly reduced by the first action, was relieved as the Terralain drive broke the wolf lines and pressed them back toward the lake in the east. Picket's fresh arm of the Warrenguard followed on, eager to meet the enemy. Kylen scanned the field and, finding Naylen, motioned for his guards to protect the prince. This they did, with just three staying behind. Picket nodded to Kylen, bringing his sword hilt to his forehead in salute. Kylen returned the salute, then wordlessly hurried toward his brother.

Picket sagged, falling to one knee. He scanned the field and found Emma bent over Captain Frye's body. He rose, with a groan, and jogged over to her.

"Please," Emma was saying to two soldiers, "take his body within the city and lay him somewhere safe. He was a great captain, and he should be buried with honor."

They bowed and reverently took up the captain's body. As they passed, Picket stopped the soldiers, placed a hand tenderly on Captain Frye's head a moment, then nodded for them to carry on. He found Emma kneeling before a wounded warrior.

"You did well, soldier," she said, tying a tourniquet around the soldier's mangled arm. "The war's over for you. We're going to get you back to camp and, even if we can't save your arm, save your life."

"Thank you, Highness," the soldier said through gritted teeth.

"Emma," Picket said. "Let's get back to the commanders."

"I'm needed here," she replied, starting on the next

nearest wounded soldier.

"We have units trained for this, as you know well," he said. "Things have changed since the Terralains turned for us. Not enough to shift the advantage even near to what is needed, but it's a start, and our priorities have changed." He pointed up at the approaching raptor horde in the sky. "We have more wolves on the way, by land and sea, and six waves of Preylord attacks. The first will be here soon. We need to regroup."

She nodded to Picket, finishing up a bandage over the head of a wounded Terralain soldier.

"Thankee, Your Highness," the buck said softly, staring at her with a kind of fearful awe. "May I go and join the fight once again?"

"Just look after that head of yours," she said, patting his arm. "Yes, soldier. Get after them." He leapt up and ran after his comrades while Emma rose and hurried back toward the gate at Picket's side.

They were silent for a while as they crossed the abandoned battlefield. Emma's white gown was stained red in several places—Picket hoped—from others' blood. The sounds of battle nearby and the urgent preparations of the shifting forces in the city were loud all around. Above them, the archers and engineers busily prepared as the lords directed their armies. They passed Lord Ronan's force as it poured out of the gate at double time, hurrying to support the Terralains' rear. Lord Ronan bowed to Emma, gazed wide-eyed at Picket, and then hurried on. They neared

Helmer's command pavilion, where he was issuing orders as messengers came and went. When Helmer saw Picket, he broke off mid-sentence and ran to embrace the young hero.

"My son," Helmer said, letting go of Picket and staring at him. "I thought..."

"I can hardly believe what I saw," Emma said, looking Picket over.

"It looked awfully familiar to me," Uncle Wilfred said, running up to embrace his nephew in his turn. "Seems I've seen something like that before."

"There's more to do," Picket said, returning the embrace. "What's the plan?"

"Helmer is shifting Ronan out and the other armies back to fallback position two."

"And you?" Emma asked.

"I'm taking the Warrenguard reserve east," Uncle Wilfred said.

"Your Highness," Helmer said, as they moved back to his commanders. Lord Booker gazed across at Emma with relief, then over at Picket with awe. His eyes glistened.

"Fallback two?" Emma asked.

"Yes, Your Highness," Helmer said, "but we are sending extra ground forces to the old east wall, Wilfred commanding. The rest to the rooftops."

"Good. What do you advise I do?" Emma asked, her gaze drifting back to the battlefield where medics rushed to help the wounded and dying. Picket realized that she carried the weight of every loss here in a way none of them could understand, even Helmer.

"If you could give a speech like you gave here at each turn in the battle, our bucks would run through walls to fight for you," Helmer said, smiling kindly at her. "But since that isn't practical, I suggest you return to the command center in your palace. I will join you very soon."

"Well done, Lord Captain," she said, voice catching. Then she turned, took a few steps, and stood apart a moment, turning her back to the gathered commanders. Uncle Wilfred and Lord Booker both began to move across and comfort her, but Picket raised a hand. *Give her a moment.* They nodded.

"Is Emerson ready?" Helmer asked a waiting aide.

"Lord Captain, aye. The Highwallers are set. He reports that all stands ready."

"Tell him to be just as careful of our assets as we planned. The Terralain change is welcome, but we still must have enough to hold the city. If we are forced out, there will be no returning."

The aide bowed. "He is entirely of your mind on this, sir."

"Go," Helmer said.

"Master, what can I do?" Picket asked.

"Accompany the princess back to the palace," Helmer said. "Ready the R.F.A. as best you can. I'll be there soon."

Picket saluted, and he crossed to Emma. They hurried together back toward the stairs where she had given her address before the battle. As they passed soldiers, she regained her poise, praising and encouraging them as she made her way up the stairs to the top of the city wall. Picket saw the prepped archers and engineers and mounds of arrows among and in between the catapults and bowstrikers. Barrels and keglets of blastpowder lined the sides, and each soldier seemed eager. The first section of Highwall Wardens stationed near the stairs noticed Emma and dropped to one knee. The honor rolled back, reaching the last of the high defenders. Emma, stepping forward, raised a hand to bless them.

"Your Highness," Emerson said, rising and hurrying over. "How may I help you?"

"We're crossing back to the palace," Emma said.

"Should you like to use a catapult?"

"No, thank you," she said. "Only, be bold and do as Captain Helmer has ordered." She gazed into the distance, where the first wave of raptor attackers—an armada of wide-winged messengers of death—was only minutes away. "I have to believe we may find a victory in this, impossible odds or not. We must believe that the end might be our Mended Wood, even if only a few survive to see it."

"I believe," Emerson said. "We all believe. And we'll die fighting for the peace that must come in the mending."

Chapter Forty

The Archer and the Prince

Jo sent an arrow home into the heart of an angry wolf as it snapped back at two injured bucks. The wolf died, falling onto the bucks. Jo ran on, his quiver nearly spent in ending enemies as the Terralain forces ripped into the wolf army with deadly effect. After the first wave had knocked the vast pack sideways in the wake of their king's astonishing death, the wolves had recovered and were pressing the Terralains back all along the line. Lord Ronan's forces crashed through the middle, splitting the wolf army in two, and Jo stood on the edge of that battle, his bowstring hot with its urgent work.

Now Jo was tired. He had been on the move for hours, this last push an urgent rush that sapped his energy. He sagged there, bending to catch his breath amid the melee. Only one arrow left. A medic found him and went to work on his arm, a free-bleeding wound he hadn't even noticed. He accepted a waterskin and drank from it gratefully as the medic stitched the gash quickly, bandaged it, and sped on to others.

"Thank you," Jo wheezed. He felt a tap on his arm. He turned to see Kylen, huddled with Lord Ronan, Naylen, and a few other captains of both armies. "My lord," Jo said, bowing to Ronan, then to Kylen, "and Your Highness."

"Well done, Lieutenant," Ronan said. "The princes have told me what you did. Do us another service and escort Prince Kylen and some of his guard back to the palace. We believe the prince's gifts will be best used in command there."

"In other words, I'm too weak to keep at it out here," Kylen said with a grimace, breathing hard.

"You're not that great when you're fully healthy, anyway," Naylen said, punching his brother's arm. "Lord Ronan and I will keep up this fight, and we mean to win it. A dozen of Kylen's guards will go with you."

"Do you understand, Shanks?" Ronan asked.

"Yes, my lord," Jo answered, bowing.

Just then the wolf army's southern flank advanced in a sudden surge that came close to the hurried conference, and several large wolves broke through to bound at them. Jo turned, raising his bow as the clash came. He shot one wolf, which slowed, spun, then rose again for one last lurch before crumpling down, never to rise again. He was out of arrows, and the other wolves were nearly upon them. Lord Ronan and Prince Naylen attacked one together. Jo and Kylen drew their swords. Two wolves dashed at them, red teeth slavering as they growled in attack. Near and nearer until—a sudden swish and thud—and the two wolves crumpled as arrows pierced them. The shots came from high above and behind them. The guard surged in and fought back the remaining wolves. Jo turned back to gaze at the distant wall and marveled at the shot that brought down wolves this far away. *Nate. And Owen or Studge.* He had little doubt.

"Let's go, Your Highness," Jo said, taking Kylen's arm.

"Just call me Kylen, Jo," the gaunt prince said as they jogged on, followed by his alert guards. "I think we're all friends again, though I can't help feeling incredibly guilty for what I've put Emma and Picket—and all of you—through."

"You were being poisoned," Jo said, bending to pluck used arrows from the field and adding them to his quiver.

"It's no excuse. Emma warned me, and I had every chance to do what was right. I was obstinate and wrong. If not for Naylen—"

"What do you say we express our profound regrets about it later, Kylen?" Jo said, dodging a destroyed cart where many fallen of both sides lay. "Right now, we've got a war to win."

"Let's go back to *Your Highness*," Kylen said, smirking.

"Too late, Kylen old pal."

They were making for the west gate, which looked oddly barren in the wake of the clash that almost happened there so recently. The wolf battle had veered off to the east, and the rear guard of the Terralain army was still far off, turning toward the north split of the wolf forces.

By the time they reached the palace, the raptor force was nearly to the city walls. The Preylords banked and circled, falling into position in a pattern of gliding that puzzled Jo.

Jo led Kylen, humbled and weak, onto the porch where Emma's command was centered. Helmer had made it back there. He stood on Emma's right, with Picket on her left. Picket was sticking close to Emma, his eyes intent on the looming enemy. Aides rushed back and forth with messages. Whit was there, Emma's cruelly scarred brother who had joined the resistance and fought against their oldest brother, Winslow. Winslow, who had been pardoned by Emma, was now at his battle station in the hospital, working as an assistant.

Kylen fell on his knees, not far from the very place Winslow had done the same so recently. "Your Highness," he said, head low, "I am so sorry. Could you ever forgive me?"

"Get up, Kylen," she said, crossing to give him a hand up. "We have work to do. Together."

He looked up at her, staying on his knees. "Please," he said, taking the Whitson Stone from around his neck and handing it to Emma, "take this. It belongs to you."

Emma bent and accepted the necklace with its brilliant ruby. She put it on. "You gave us a chance today, Kylen. I won't forget that. Come now, get up."

"You were always right about me, Emma. You knew long ago, though I had others fooled. I'm so, so sorry."

"All is forgiven," she said, "and this reunion—for we are family—will, I hope, be a glimpse of the mending on the way."

"May it be," Kylen whispered, squeezing his eyes shut tight on tears.

"They are coming, at last," Helmer said, stepping forward.

Jo spun around, eyeing the descending horde, their darkness casting a long shadow over the city. Jo grabbed an aide as he passed. "Get me as many arrows as you can and as many of the flint-and-fire kind as possible."

Whit stared at the enemy armada. "There aren't enough arrows in the world."

Chapter Forty-One

The Destroyers Come

Picket instinctively stepped in front of Emma as the Preylords dropped lower and lower, nearing the edge of the city.

"Shuffler, you're going to have to stop doing that," Emma said, hooking him with her arm. "It's 'my place beside you,' not 'my place blocking your view.'"

Picket shrugged and stepped aside, smiling. "You'll miss me when I'm gone."

Emma smiled sadly.

"Let's hope the scheme works," Whit said, stepping to the edge of the porch.

Picket lifted a glass to his eye and gazed at the raptors. Many were armed with what seemed like long spears, others with some kind of smoking black circle on the end of a long chain. Some kind of incendiary. All bore shields in their other talons. There was a collective groan from those on the porch. They had all seen the shields.

"Perhaps they aren't strong shields," Jo mused.

The raptors approached in a pyramid formation, with

the front line the wide base and each line smaller all the way back to the single massive raptor at the back. One of the Six.

"Can you tell which it is?" Emma asked Whit, passing him her glass.

"It's a white falcon—no doubt the heir of Falcowit. Winslow says he believes they either slaughter all the family of one of the Six who dies or sometimes promote an heir if he is powerful enough to have survived the maddening aftermath of his sire's demise and has a spirit of revenge that is useful to Morbin's plans. They appear to have chosen the latter. This is Falcowit's son; I'm sure of it."

"May he meet the same end," Jo said. Falcowit had been blasted apart by a bowstriker shot in the battle to retake First Warren.

The first line of Preylords neared the rim of the city wall, and the bowstrikers, all lined along the wall, released a barrage of blastarrows. The raptors raised their shields and broke into an evasion pattern, clearly planned, as the blastarrows missed their mark in many cases and exploded against the shields in others. Some raptors were blown from the sky, injured or killed, to plummet down in a spiral. But many more surged past the walls, dropping their smoking black circles on the walls and into the city with an exploding impact that blasted apart sections of the wall and sent rabbits rushing away from blazes all along the ramparts while bowstrikers and catapults broke apart.

It could hardly have gone any worse. And this with a

defensive strategy that required near perfection to have a chance. Emma cried out, eyes filling with tears, as bucks were blown off the top of the wall and cut down in midair by darting talons from swooping birds.

Picket grabbed Helmer's arm. "Should we deploy?"

Helmer shook his head, his face set in a disgusted fury. "We have to give the plan a chance. Otherwise, we are already surrendering."

"Should we consider surrender?" Whit asked, spinning back to lock eyes with Emma. "I don't like it one bit, Sister, but it's only just begun and it's virtually over."

"Never," Emma cried, above the noise of the bursting rock and raining debris. "Look!"

On the wall, the soldiers were recovering their positions on what remained of the bowstrikers. They sent a diminished second volley off against the second line, this time waiting till after the attackers had exposed their bodies in the act of slinging their bombs. The simultaneous fire made a terrific display as the Highwallers suffered another barrage of bombs. But the Preylords suffered too, coming apart in a line of lethal explosions that sent feathers flying and raptors diving to their deaths. A volley of small flint-and-fire arrows sailed into the sky, setting off smaller explosions that wounded many and brought down some of the attackers. The second wave was decimated, and a muffled cheer rose from the wall. Emma turned to Helmer with a clenched fist raised before her, just as a raptor spear sped at the porch.

Jo knocked Emma down as the spear smashed into the far side of the porch, shattering the stonework there in a spray that sent the command center scrambling.

Picket glanced aside to be certain Emma was unhurt. Then he leapt up and ran for the edge of the porch as the raptor who had slung the spear followed its flight and bore down on the porch. The raptor raised its talons, razor sharp blades attached to the already deadly claws, and slashed at Picket. Picket's sword stroke met the powerful raptor talon blades, sending up sparks as the sword was knocked aside. It was all Picket could do to hold on to his blade as he was slammed sideways. The raptor struck out, but archers fired a volley of arrows at its middle while Whit and Kylen led a band of bladed rabbits to hack at the flailing creature. Finally, Helmer's thunderous drive sent the raptor falling back, lifeless, to crash in the city square.

"Get the princess inside!" Picket cried, as more enemies poured into the city center, spreading death and destruction as they came.

Emma rushed into the palace as Picket, Kylen, and Whit covered the retreat from the exposed porch. Picket watched, heart racing, as raptors wheeled around the city center, dodging the defenses and wreaking havoc all around. They veered toward the porch once more, and Picket sprinted behind the princess.

Crashing inside the palace, Picket slid for cover amid a hail of shattered stone as the building was rocked by a series of explosions. He scanned the shaking hall for Emma and found her huddled with Helmer hovering over her. The palace felt sure to fall apart.

Cracks climbed around pillars, and large chunks of ceiling crashed around scurrying rabbits in uniform.

Lieutenant Warken ran up, panting hard as he found Emma.

"Your Highness! The east wall is breached. Another wolf army is coming in."

Chapter Forty-Two

The Blackhawk Option

The hall stopped shaking, and Emma rose, tentatively, while Helmer looked aloft anxiously for more crumbling chunks of ceiling.

Emma's voice rose over the settling chaos. "The first of the six raptor kings is wreaking havoc on the city. The wolves are at the east gate, far earlier than we had planned. What now, my captains?"

"The ground invasion scheme is still sound, and the alcove is secure," Helmer said, shaking off shards of rock, "but we had hoped to repel the first waves of the Preylords. It's not clear what is next."

"We must kill the alphas," Emma said, "as Picket did with King Farlock. If we kill their lord, in this case this Falcowitson, then the rest will fall apart."

"I'll go," Picket growled, heading for the stairs to the rooftop.

"No," Helmer said. "No, Picket. You are needed here. And no one can defeat one of the Six one-on-one." He spoke calmly, but Picket saw the worry in his master's eyes.

"Then how do we deal with the alpha—with Falcowit's son?" Kylen asked.

"He's far above and beyond the rest," Jo called back from his spot back out on the damaged porch. Coming back into the hall, he continued. "There's no archer that could hit him."

"The Blackhawk Option?" Picket asked.

"We were saving it..." Emma began, but trailed off.

"At this point there'll be nothing to save it for," Picket said. "If we survive long enough to get to Morbin, we'll figure it out then."

"Agreed," Helmer said.

Emma glanced around the faces of her commanders, then nodded. "Do it."

Helmer wasted no time. "Warken, send the signal for Emerson's Blackhawk Measure."

"Yes, sir!" Warken called, rushing up the stairs. Picket followed, alongside Jo. Reaching the roof, he saw the long, curved slide and several catapults still operational, while crews worked on damaged assets and cast aside those ruined beyond repair.

Harrowing screeches filled the air as birds of prey swept around the city, wrecking fortifications and heavy weapons stations. On top of the wall nearest the dam the fighting was fiercest, as Nate Flynn's archers and Emerson's bowstrikers strove to contend with the swarming Lords of Prey. The Highwallers fought bravely amid the chaos. The former wolves' garrison atop the dam wall was shattered in several places, and they were under heavy assault now. Falcowitson loomed above, shrieking orders as his thralls fought on.

To the east, Uncle Wilfred and the Warrenguard fought hard in the gap that had opened in the wall. The bridge they had built, making a wide passage from the east wall to the city center, was crammed with rabbits advancing on the attackers, bent on holding them off. The old east gate was breached again, and Uncle Wilfred's elite soldiers battled with a host of wolves so numerous it dwarfed even King Farlock's forces.

To the west, the Terralain army, alongside the Blackstone army, was still fighting beside Lake Merle. Farlock's northern wolves, though kingless, were gaining again with help from the newly arrived Preylord cover. And they were slowly making up ground, fighting their way back to the west gate. The balance was breaking heavily for the Preylords and their wolf allies. The rabbits were mere moments away from being crushed in an unstoppable landslide on all sides.

Turning back to the signal office, Picket saw Warken arguing with the signal officer. The Blackhawk Option was supposed to be reserved for Morbin's arrival, and the signal officer was balking. Picket rushed over and shouted at the officer. "Follow orders! Send it, now!"

The signal was sent, and Picket turned to see if the wall's signal office would reply and pass the signal on. But there was no response. They were too occupied with the fight, and it seemed likely their signal corps might be disabled, or worse.

"Come on, Jo," Picket said, snapping his glider rods in place and fitting his wrists in their holds. As a soldier ran up to check his pack, he leapt from the backside of the roof. Jo raced behind him, and they flew over the forces fighting along the east wall. The bridge was holding, and Uncle Wilfred was rotating soldiers around to the gate, pushing the wolf army back.

Their prisoner from Harbone had given them details about the attack, and they had prepared accordingly, even pretending to lose the prisoner in order that he could carry back flawed intelligence to influence where and how their foes should attack. They had expected this wolf attack in the east, and the previous one in the west. They expected another wolf army to attack by sea at any time, but they couldn't worry about that now. Terralain showing up had shifted the battle plan, and they still had a ground force solution in play. But their plan had counted on being able to take out the first few waves of raptors with their bowstrikers.

That had not happened. At least, not nearly so well as they had hoped.

Picket and Jo soared over the east wall and banked left, dropping low over the secret battle burrow poised just on the eastern shore of Lake Merle.

"Rouse out! White Falcon!" Picket cried as they swept low to the ground. The two flyers swept up and, noticed by

the Preylord attackers, turned again, banking back toward the hidden team. Fearing their message had not been heard, they flew toward the hidden battle burrow once again. But just as they began to swoop down, the dirt shook loose, boards were cast aside, and a bowstriker emerged from a hidden hollow in the earth. Picket and Jo banked hard left, pushing away from the city and out over the long lake.

The battle burrow's hidden assets emerged into view, with several bucks operating the bowstriker. Wolves from the east gate attack broke off and sped toward the isolated fighters, and Preylords bore down on them from the main assault near the dam. But the bucks were working to arm and aim their asset. Ignoring the targets all around, they fired at the unsuspecting commander of the attack.

Falcowitson.

The white falcon turned in time to see the speeding blastarrow just as it reached him.

Boom!

Chapter Forty-Three

Meetings and Reunions

Jo Shanks banked back and headed for the palace, following Picket's path. Many birds of prey faltered as Falcowitson's pale feathers scattered over the dam wall in the wake of the fantastic explosion. The defenders, so hard pressed in this battle, now gave back to their attackers with vigor. More birds fell, and many fled as a roar emerged from the defenders on the wall. Jo rejoiced to see many of his friends shouting defiantly from the ravaged wall top.

The wolf battle on the edge of Lake Merle raged on with Terralain soldiers locked in intense combat with fallen King Farlock's vengeful army. He could not tell which way it would go. He longed to rejoin those brave fighters alongside Prince Naylen.

Jo glanced left. The Warrenguard, with Wilfred Longtreader at their head, were now pushing back the wolf invaders at the east gate. With their raptor support lost, at least for the moment, the wolves gave up ground. Still, the number of wolves pressing the gate was astonishing. They *would* break through. It was just a matter of time.

Sweeping in for a landing amid a busy palace rooftop, he found Emma alongside Helmer. Kylen stood nearby, looking fretful and worn.

"Are you okay, Jo?" Emma asked, offering him a waterskin. He took it gratefully.

"He looks fine," Helmer said, frowning. "What's the situation near the dam? Is the alcove secure?"

"Give him a second to breathe, Lord Captain," Emma said, making him drink.

Picket landed, breathing hard. "The alcove is secure, though we didn't spend a long time staring at it, of course. The Warrenguard is relieved by the Preylord's setback—"

"Some setback," Emma said, shaking her head. "Go on."

"The east gate seems certain to hold for a while longer."

"And the west?" Kylen asked, stepping closer. "Could you see them?"

"It's balanced," Jo said, wiping his mouth. "It could go either way."

"I have to get back down there," Kylen said. "My brother…"

"I understand," Emma said, nodding. "Do you feel strong enough?"

"I do. I took the physic from the Pilgrim's herbmaster. I've rested here. I'm ready."

"The Pilgrim's herbmaster?" Emma asked. "Pilgrim? Who is that?"

"You don't know?" Kylen asked. "I thought you must know."

"Know what?"

Just then, a crowd parted near the stairs, and Lord Blackstar led an old doe, elegant in a long dress, her fur black and silver, toward Emma.

"Mother?" Emma asked, wide eyes suddenly shining.

Lady Glen held out her arms. Emma rushed to embrace her mother, and the Pilgrim's band emerged behind the Queen Mother and her daughter. Lord Blackstar came, and Heyna automatically drew near to Emma, scanning the busy rooftop with concern.

"Pilgrim," Jo said, as the old traveler walked up, "may I introduce Picket Longtreader and our commander, the lord captain?"

"I am honored," the Pilgrim said, bowing to both in turn. He shook Helmer's hand and smiled at him with his head cocked sideways. "Helmer, is it?"

"It is, sir," Helmer said, clearly feeling what Jo had felt—still felt—from the Pilgrim's presence. The Pilgrim exuded serenity, seemed at ease in every movement, though he was obviously old. His eyes seemed older still but somehow wonderfully alive with an ageless grace. "Have we met before, my lord?" Helmer asked.

The Pilgrim grinned. "I'm no lord, Helmer there. And no, we haven't ever met. But you remind me of an old friend."

"Have you traveled far, sir?" Picket asked. "Can we get you anything?"

"We have, sure," the Pilgrim said, smiling back at his

band, "but we need nothing now. We are pleased to be here in this fight with you, and"—this while bowing to Helmer—"Lord Captain, I would like to formally volunteer for whatever errand seems best to you to help in the defense of our ancient capitol."

Kylen stepped into the group, saluting Helmer. "Lord Captain, might these brave bucks accompany me back to the field to fight alongside my brother?"

Helmer looked over at the Pilgrim, who nodded. "We would be delighted to fight alongside the prince. We have worked together before."

"They helped us rescue Kylen," Jo said.

Helmer nodded. "We must hold that line and win that battle. I can think of nothing better than to reinforce our Terralain allies with such fighters as you appear to be."

"May I go with them?" Jo asked, feeling an eagerness to be with the Pilgrim he couldn't explain.

"Yes, Jo," Helmer said. "But meet us at the appointed time before the alcove. Your arrows might buy us some time if it doesn't go as planned. And I don't want Picket out there alone."

"Yes, sir," Jo said, saluting. He gathered a fresh pack of arrows and handed the Pilgrim's band more. They added these to what they had, and it was then that Jo noticed the Pilgrim's quiver. It seemed ancient and was packed tight with black arrows. The Pilgrim alone took no extra arrows for his quiver.

They passed Emma, bowing as she and her mother

spoke quickly back and forth. Mrs. Weaver had joined them, and the reunion of old friends was sweet, though brief. Mrs. Weaver returned to the stairway top as Lady Glen and Emma joined Helmer and Picket. Jo waited for the Pilgrim's band to descend and took Mrs. Weaver's extended hand. Her eyes were wet and her face kind.

"Dear Jo," she said, "what a day this may be."

"It's the end, Mrs. Weaver."

"Maybe it's the beginning."

She motioned for him to follow behind the odd band, and he hurried down the stairs.

Chapter Forty-Four

The Archer and the Pilgrim

Jo led the way out of the palace and across the old city. They jogged, with Kylen and the Pilgrim on Jo's heels as the party advanced. Jo glanced right to the dam wall, saw that the small alcove on which so much of their hope rested was still secure, and hurried on.

They passed a broken building, one of many damaged in the last attack. Rabbits ran through the streets with urgent messages, rejoining lost forces or transporting the wounded back toward the palace or one of the other hospitals. Jo grimaced at the injuries but jogged on toward the west gate.

Seeing that Kylen was growing tired, Jo slowed and called for a halt.

"A quick break, if that's all right?" Jo asked.

"By all means," the Pilgrim replied, stopping to drink from a waterskin.

Jo eyed an obliterated building, with only one long stone wall standing against mostly shattered adjoining walls. The charred inside stank of soot and death.

"What will you do when the war's over?" Kylen asked. The Pilgrim nodded to Jo.

"Probably rebel and try to start my own rival kingdom," Jo said, then shrugged to Kylen. "Sorry, might be a little soon for that one."

Kylen laughed and shook his head. "I like you, Shanks. You remind me of me—well, me a long time ago."

"That's pretty insulting," Jo said, "but I've heard worse."

The Pilgrim laughed, and Kylen smiled at Jo.

"Tameth Seer would have killed you for that," Kylen said.

"Yeah, but he wasn't very good at killing, obviously," Jo replied, nodding back at Kylen.

"Your note, Jo. It saved me, I think."

"Note?" the Pilgrim asked.

"Yes, Jo left me a note when he paid an unannounced visit to my camp."

"What did the note say?" the Pilgrim asked.

"That's not really important," Jo began. "We'd better get moving—"

"It said," Kylen broke in, "'Dear Kyle, You are the great nitwit of the world. Love, Jo Shanks.'"

The Pilgrim whistled. "It has a certain style."

"It got straight to the point, I'm sure," Kylen agreed, chuckling.

"I was on a tight schedule," Jo said. "Kylen's killers were trying to kill me, and so were his protectors."

"Sounds like a busy night," the Pilgrim said.

"Almost getting killed is stressful," Kylen said, wiping his eyes. "I feel like I've been doing it my whole life."

"We have so much in common," Jo said as they resumed their march. The Pilgrim grinned and shook his head.

Screaming. Close by. Urgent.

Jo pivoted back, an arrow already drawn and nocked.

The Pilgrim's band fanned out as another scream came. "Whereaway?" the Pilgrim asked, eyes squinted as he scanned around.

Jo started to speak, but the Pilgrim silenced him with a swift motion of his hand. They both looked right to find that one of the band had scampered wide and was now turned toward them, sending hand signals back. Two fingers pointed up with thumbs crossed, then a stiff open hand aimed at the spot where the sound came.

More screams and a howling sounded. Jo stepped toward the sound, which came from the other side of the burned-out building before them. The Pilgrim's bow was off his shoulder and a black arrow set to its string. He closed his eyes, listened intently, then mumbled, "Half speed," and released his arrow straight at the building's wall.

Jo gazed in amazement as the black arrow flew into the thick stone wall, breaking through in a spray of grey dust. A whining howl followed, then silence.

Jo stared open-mouthed at the archer, who calmly hung his bow over his shoulder again.

"Good . . . shot?" Jo said.

"If that's a question, Jo," the Pilgrim replied, "then the answer is yes. Yes, it was. Not my best, but I think he's dead. Unlike Tameth Seer, I *am* fairly good at it."

"Clearly," Kylen said. "Let's get you out there against those wolves, relieving my brother."

"I am with you," the Pilgrim said.

They jogged on until they came near the gate, where frightened cries sounded from the ramparts of the wall above and several rooftops.

"What's the word?" Jo called up the devastated wall. Smoke curled into the sky, and an odd silence settled.

"Preylord swarm spotted," a soldier, voice panicked and ragged, called down. "Twice the size at least of the last."

"I want to have a look," Jo said, turning back to the group. "Something's not right up there."

"I'm going on," Kylen said. "I have to find my brother and help where I can in this war."

"Go with him, friends," the Pilgrim said, and his band followed Kyle out the west gate and toward the Terralain battle.

Jo hurried to the stairs, the Pilgrim running behind him with no apparent difficulty, despite his age. Glancing back, Jo assumed the Pilgrim was quite a bit older than Helmer. But he ran like a young buck. They reached the last steps and emerged onto the platform. What a change. The wall top was lined with shattered assets, pieces of bowstrikers and catapults clotted the way, and wounded

Highwallers leaned against the parapets while too few medics tried to save some.

"Who's in charge here?" Jo shouted.

"I am," a familiar voice said. Jo hurried ahead, finding Nate Flynn was being treated not five yards away. One side of his face was burned and bleeding, his eye on that side destroyed. His arm and shirt were torn terribly on that side as well. "What's the good word, Jo?"

"They're coming again, Nate," Jo said, bending to give his friend water. The Pilgrim silently helped the medics nearby care for other wounded bucks.

"I know," Nate replied, tears in his eyes. "And we'll knock 'em back again."

"You have to go below, Nate," Jo said. "Where are Owen and Studge?"

"I don't know where Owen or Studge are, Jo. But I know this. I'm not going anywhere till this war's over, or I'm dead. This is what it's all been for. I have trained for this day my entire life. Don't dare tell me to leave my post." He rose, unsteadily, and stretched his cruelly marred arm, wincing as the tears flowed.

"Here's your bow, soldier," the Pilgrim said, handing Nate his weapon. "Aim at their eyes."

"Who are you?" Nate asked.

"Just an old archer," the Pilgrim said, laying a gentle hand on Nate's neck. "Now lean here, son." The old buck guided Nate to a place on the wall where he could lean and watch. "And take your shot when it comes."

Jo's eyes filled with tears, and he hurried ahead, dodging through wrecked wood and shattered rock, scanning for an officer. He glanced at the approaching swarm and made out two massive raptors at the head of the attack. They bore huge spears and wore crowned helms on their heads.

"Is there an officer in charge?" Jo called, panic welling.

"Aye, sir," a husky voice called. "I'm Lieutenant Meeker, sir."

"Meeker," Jo said, "I'm sorry. I had no idea it was so bad up here."

"I'm doing my best, sir. Most of the archers are dead, and all the catapults are destroyed. No bowstrikers. We don't have much left to fight with."

"They're coming, you know?"

"Aye, sir. I do. I guess this is the end. Is the princess secure?"

"She's fine."

"Good. I'm doing my best here, sir. We won't let the lord captain down."

"I know it."

"Jo," the Pilgrim said, eyes on the coming raptor throng, "follow me."

Jo saluted Meeker and darted after the old buck, who ran with incredible agility. Jo was winded by the time they made it all the way around to the edge of the wall where it began to form the dam. Jo peeked at the covered alcove below, then followed the Pilgrim into what was left of the old wolf barracks. It still stank of the pack but now bore signs of the rabbit defenses, though those were broken and scattered throughout. Up they clambered, until they reached the top of the barracks. Climbing onto the roof—the part that was still intact—they scanned the approaching horde.

"If we can take the two leaders out," the Pilgrim said, passing Jo one of his black shafts, "I think we have a chance."

"Agreed." Jo examined the arrow back to front, and at first he didn't see anything different about it. Then, reaching the arrowhead, he saw the black carved rock that sparkled. He was surprised it was no heavier than a normal arrow.

"It's lighter," the Pilgrim said. "The range is longer by at least a hundred yards. It won't dip. Aim true. Center of the body."

Jo nodded. They set their feet, and Jo closed his eyes and felt along the arrow for imperfections. Finding none, he opened his eyes again. "Ready."

He eyed the raptor king on his side, a huge eagle with hooked beak, razor talons, and crowned points on his silver helm. One of the dreaded Six. He breathed out, trying to find his focus as the eagle approached range. *Almost there.*

The eagle drew back and fired his spear with frightful force.

Jo flinched, then saw with a moment's relief that the spear would miss them low. He readied to shoot. The eagle just came into range as the spear he had thrown smashed into the barracks below, shattering the walls that held up the roof.

The rooftop shook, then collapsed in a compounding avalanche of wreckage. Jo and the Pilgrim tumbled down as the Preylords unleashed their fury on the tops of the walls and swept into the city with ear-splitting shrieks.

Chapter Forty-Five

The Archer's Last

Jo was falling, tumbling through the air among the shattering of the barracks below him. This time he had not gotten his shot off. Neither had the Pilgrim. Jo landed with a bounce in a heap of spraying debris amid the rubble of the fallen barracks. The Pilgrim was gone, along with his incredible black arrows. Jo lurched to his knees, wiping from his eyes the blood trickling down his forehead.

Amid the fresh rubble, Jo saw the one black arrow he had meant to bury in the eagle's heart lying alongside his bow. He grabbed both, but the bow came apart in his hands. It had snapped in the fall and now dangled uselessly as Jo shouted in anger.

Screams and wild cries echoed in the air above the city and all along the wall. The raptor horde, now doubled and led by two of the Six, wreaked havoc on First Warren.

Jo stood slowly, groaning at the pain in his back as he shook loose some of the debris caked in his fur. He lumbered a few, awkward steps, realizing he had fallen only one story down. He stumbled around a jagged rend in the floor, which must have been where the Pilgrim had crashed through to the bottom floor.

"Pilgrim?" he called through the breach, setting off a coughing fit that he gasped to recover from. He heard nothing and ran ahead, taking several steps before he began to feel his legs working again. He ran faster, rushing to the edge of the barracks.

There came a thundering crash, and the roof above him tore free at the cleaving strike of a colossal raptor's talons. The Preylord's open-beaked screech nearly knocked Jo over and deafened him at once. He stumbled, then balanced, drawing his sword as the great eagle beat his wings and slashed back with his powerful talons. Jo readied to spring over the slicing strike, knowing he would have to jump high. Driving into the floor, he made to leap, but the floor came apart under him and gave way. He plummeted below, narrowly ducking below the raptor's slash.

Falling once more, Jo hit and rebounded off the solid bottom floor. He rolled over in pain and reached out for his throbbing hip. His back screamed at the reach, and he writhed on the ground in agony. His sword was gone.

The Preylord hovered just above, and Jo lay as still as he could. He clenched the black arrow tightly, listening to the eagle's breath and his awful beating wings. Another screech, and those powerful talons shredded the next level of the barracks, exposing Jo once again as rubble rained all around him. Ignoring the pain, he shot up and darted for the door. The raptor tore ever more of the crumbling structure, and Jo outran, sometimes by inches, the Preylord's killing strokes. Finally, Jo dove free of the crumbling barracks and rolled onto the wall top. He scrambled to his feet and turned back amid the chaotic noise.

Jo saw with terror not only the huge predator eagle but the second of the Six—the massive hawk the Pilgrim had meant to kill.

Two raptors, and one rabbit. Not ordinary raptors, but enormous kings of their kind, worshiped by their followers and evil beyond imagination. Jo was injured, his clothes in tatters and his body battered. He had no sword, nor his famous bow. All he had in his hands was the Pilgrim's black arrow.

Useless. Hopeless.

He closed his eyes as the raptors drew back to cut him down.

A cry rose from behind him, and he turned to see the soldiers of the wall, led by Meeker and an arrow-firing one-eyed Nate Flynn. *And Owen!* They shouted and shot and leapt into the impossible contest with the towering raptors. They were few, perilously few, but their well-aimed arrows sent the monstrous enemies banking back, giving a moment's reprieve.

But it did not last. The wall guards were not enough—nowhere near enough—and the Preylords soon swept back at the vulnerable bucks on the wall. Jo's eyes grew wide, and he turned and ran back to his fellows. He dove for an abandoned bow as the eagle's beak snapped into the defenders and his talons tore through the wall they tottered on.

Jo was struck hard by the incredible force of the awful talon, swiped sideways with a great gash torn along his side. He flew out and away from the wall into open air amid a spray of rock. He cried out in pain and terror.

Jo opened his eyes at the height of his fall and saw the two raptors kings in a line, one in front of the other, atop the shattered wall, striking at his surviving allies with savage zeal. He closed his eyes and felt what was still gripped in his hands.

A bow in his right hand. A black arrow in his left.

Automatically, without thought of what would follow, he brought the two together and smoothly nocked the arrow to the string. Aiming as he fell back, he drew hard, waited a moment, and exhaled with a smile as he released the speeding shaft.

It raced through a shower of debris, narrowly missing a chunk of parapet, to sink inside and rip through the angry eagle's heart.

But the arrow did not stop.

It sped on through the raptor king with a shocking pace and caught the heedless hawk behind him directly between the eyes.

The raptors tottered, then fell dead, plunging limply from the top of the wall.

Jo watched until he saw his shot go home. He sent out his arms and twisted his wrists, activating his mangled glider. It went taut, though only barely as its stitching began to tear apart in the tension. He glided low, weaving uncontrollably till he landed roughly among a band of soldiers, who surged up to protect and give him aid. They bore the arms of Chelmsford.

"Where's Lord Felson?" Jo asked, panting.

"Dead, sir," an officer said, face showing amazement. "What did you just do?" Above them the surviving raptors went mad, and many fled. A medic bent beside Jo and eased him back onto the ground. He felt a stinging on his side.

"I helped the Highwallers up there... We killed two of the raptor kings. Can you send up reinforcements... and medics for them? They're heroes up there... there aren't many left."

"Yes, sir," the officer said, nodding to his colleagues to send a detachment that way.

"You should all go, in fact," Jo said trying to get up. The medic held him back.

"Wait, Lieutenant Shanks," the officer said. "Please lie back a bit. Let her stitch you up, at least. We'll relieve them up there."

"There's an old buck up... in the old wolf barracks," Jo said, wincing. "He's on the... bottom floor. Please find him."

The officer gazed up at the devastated barracks, then back down to Jo. "We'll do our best, sir."

"He's stitched up and bandaged for the worst wounds," the medic said. "Recommend evac to field triage."

“The palace,” Jo groaned, sitting up. “I’ve got to get back . . . to the palace. Picket needs me.”

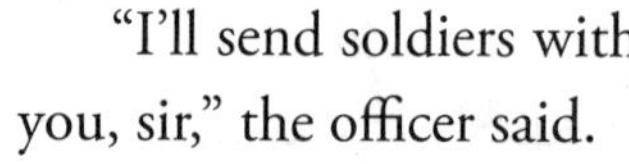

“I’ll send soldiers with you, sir,” the officer said.

“Send everyone you’ve got aloft,” Jo said, accepting help getting to his feet. “There’ll be more enemy . . . here in no time. They need you up there on the wall. And anyway . . . it’s nearly time to clear the field here.” He glanced over at the alcove beneath the dam.

The officer frowned, hesitated, but finally saluted and hurried off toward the steps, followed by the medic. Jo took a last look up at the shattered wall and wrecked barracks. He shook his head and hurried—limping painfully—toward the palace.

Chapter Forty-Six

Accepted

Picket stepped closer, listening intently to Lady Glen. Jo and Kylen, accompanied by the mysterious Pilgrim and his band, had left not long ago. He was back inside the palace in Emma's council chamber. Helmer and Heyward had just laid out their long-planned scheme to thwart the ground invasion.

"So all our hopes hang on the timing of the blast," Helmer said. "It must all come apart in time. Otherwise, all those young soldiers..."

Picket caught his master's eye, saw there through a dewy veil the old soldier's affection.

"Do we have any chance of survival if the alcove scheme fails?" Emma asked.

"None," Helmer said.

Lord Blackstar nodded gravely. "It has to work."

"It's a gamble," Lady Glen said, leaning back in her chair, "but it's all in the balance now. We have to turn the tide, so to speak."

"I don't think Morbin expected us to survive the first

wave of attack," Lord Blackstar said.

Picket nodded. *He's not the only one surprised.*

Mrs. Weaver leaned forward, hands clasped beneath her chin. "Having thwarted the first invasion—though at great cost, to be sure—we must be prepared for anything. Morbin might decide to send the next waves in pairs."

"Agreed," Helmer said. "But even if he does, I still believe we should hold the alcove back, Your Highness. We have already used the Blackhawk Option. I don't want to squander this until the wolves are in position."

Emma nodded. "We proceed as planned. Heyward, make sure the primary line is working."

"Yes, Your Highness." Heyward bowed quickly and hurried off.

"Picket," Emma said, "is the R.F.A. ready?"

"Standing by, Your Highness. I just checked in with Harmon and Lallo a moment ago. They have done well in my absence. Somehow the ramp is still intact, and they are itching to get into the fight."

"You have trained them well. And... their time will come," Emma said, a grimace flickering across her worried face. "Lord Blackstar, try to find out if we have any reparable bowstrikers or anything that might help us repel the next wave."

"Yes, Your Highness," Blackstar said, bowing. He left too.

The room, which had been a hive of activity over the past week, felt ominously empty. Picket glanced at Captain

Frye's seat and felt a sharp sadness. He thought of Heather, of his parents, and his little brother, Jacks. Glancing over at Helmer, he saw the old buck was looking at him with an expression that matched his own.

"I think that's all," Emma said, rising. Those left in the room rose and bowed; then most hurried back to their stations.

"Mother," Emma said, when only she, Helmer, Picket, Mrs. Weaver, and Lady Glen remained in the chamber, "who is this Pilgrim?"

"He's an old friend, Emma, my dear."

"A friend of Father's?"

"No, your father never had the honor, I'm sorry to say," Lady Glen said, smiling kindly at her daughter. "Trust me when I tell you that his loyalty to our family and this cause runs deep and goes back far. And how are you, my love? You are doing a wonderful job here. Your father would be very proud. I am."

Emma smiled. "I hope we come through this, Mother, so we can be together at last."

Picket looked down, thinking of his own mother with grief.

"It is my greatest hope," Lady Glen said. "But the place of a queen, whether ruling or not, is to give everything for the cause. I have no doubt you will say yes to your subjects before you say yes to yourself. I see it in you."

"Thank you, Mother," Emma said. "I wish Father were here, or Lord Rake. But I'm glad I have you."

"Picket Longtreader, son of those faithful old friends Whittle and Sween. It has been some time since I last saw you," Lady Glen said. "You have grown, in so many ways. Your father and mother would be proud of you. I am so sorry. I am afraid my coming to Nick Hollow endangered your family. I meant to warn them. I was heartbroken to see them fall. And your sister..." She hung her head.

Those horrible words echoed in his heart. *Heather is dead.*

"We have all lost so much, Your Majesty," Picket said, "you not least of all. I miss my family, and I still feel their loss keenly. I wasn't ready. I was weak. I feel responsible. But I can't fix that. I can only try to save those I love now." He looked over at Emma. "Heather gave her life for Emma. I will do the same."

"You have been a flame for us in the dark part of our story," Lady Glen said. "Shine on, while you have the fire."

"I will, Your Majesty," Picket said, bowing low.

"Now I must speak to Lord Captain Helmer," she said, as Helmer drew nearer to her.

Mrs. Weaver crossed to embrace Picket, and Emma followed them to the far side of the room, near the door.

"How are you, my dear Picket?" Mrs. Weaver asked. "You've come a long way since Helmer nearly killed you in training and you smiled at me with your bloody teeth."

"Heather didn't love that," Picket said, smiling.

"No, she didn't. Dear Heather, how I miss her." Mrs. Weaver looked past their small huddle to where Helmer and Lady Glen were speaking quietly together across the room.

"Heather would have been a great queen," Emma said. "Was Mother a good queen, Mrs. Weaver?"

"She was. There was glory there, and she wore it well. You can still feel the remnants of our golden age when you're with her. Heather would have, perhaps, surpassed them all. But you, dear, will be our spark in the darkness."

"I only wanted to heal," Emma said, head down.

"Queens can heal," Mrs. Weaver replied, gazing across as Helmer knelt before Lady Glen. She put her hands tenderly on his head in a blessing. Helmer rose, bowed low to the Queen Mother, then turned and hurried out the door with a quick sideways glance at Picket.

There were tears in his eyes.

After a quiet moment, Lady Glen crossed to join them.

"He still feels it, doesn't he?" Mrs. Weaver asked. "Guilt over the king's death."

"Helmer feels he could have done more," Lady Glen replied. "And maybe he could have. He could have lost his arm and died fighting them all. I think he wishes he had."

Picket winced. "Wait, what? Excuse me, Your Majesty, but did you say he might have lost his arm? What do you mean?"

"He never told you about the scar on his arm?" Lady Glen asked.

"No. I hadn't even seen the scar until Harbone fell. What happened?"

Lady Glen exchanged a look with Mrs. Weaver. "I think you ought to tell him," Mrs. Weaver said.

Lady Glen nodded. "You see, Picket, in those last days before my beloved husband, King Jupiter the Great, was killed, Helmer felt uneasy about your uncle Garten. By other betrayals, Garten found out and had Helmer and his squad sent on a meaningless errand. Helmer's team of elite young bucks was known as the King's Arm. Their motto was *My arm for the cause and crown. My all for the cause and crown.* Helmer grew suspicious of his mission and turned around, returning unexpectedly with his young soldiers. Finding the traitor on the verge of his betrayal, Helmer and his unit tried to kill Garten and foil the plot. But they failed. He failed."

"And the young bucks under his command were all executed in front of him," Mrs. Weaver said. "This was worse than killing Helmer a thousand times. He cared for his soldiers unlike any other commander, looked after their families and treated them like sons. But for Helmer himself, Garten had far darker plans."

"Indeed." Lady Glen picked up the telling. "Garten sought to teach Helmer a lesson on the futility of resistance, a sick lesson from a corrupt and wicked mind. He had Helmer chained to a tree in sight of the clearing at Jupiter's Crossing, where he could witness the defeat of the king. Garten did not think the king would be killed, but he savored his rival witnessing what he believed was his crowning achievement."

"Garten had only Helmer's right arm chained tightly to the tree," Mrs. Weaver said, her mouth drawn down in disgust, "and the cruel villain left Helmer his sword."

Lady Glen went on. "'If you want to die fighting for your king,' Garten said, 'then use your famous blade and cut down this tree, or else take off that strong arm you've used to win so many battles.' And Garten left him there with this twisted, unwinnable dilemma."

"In the end, Helmer watched," Mrs. Weaver said, tears in her eyes, "thinking, quite wisely at the time, that his death in attack would do nothing to serve the crown and cause, but if he survived to fight, he might right this wrong. But ever after, he was convinced he had failed and should have given his arm and his all to stand up for the king. He called himself *oathbreaker* and brooded for years."

"Oh, Master!" Picket groaned, so much of his mentor's pain making sense like it never had before. "Oh, my master."

"All the young bucks died, and his king was murdered," Lady Glen said. "He saw it all. He knew he could cut himself free, losing an arm, and charge into the clearing to be killed in a vain and valiant final stand. Afterwards, his heart beat, but he was dead inside. He lived only for revenge against Garten and Morbin. But he kept his arm. He kept his life, and his body unmarred. Except for the scar on his arm. The arm he should have, in his mind, cut free to die in an honorable ending. Yes, he kept his arm, and his life. But he lost all hope."

"Until you came," Mrs. Weaver said. "Until you gave him hope again."

"I suppose you know," Lady Glen said, turning to Picket, "that he loves you."

"I know it, Your Majesty." Picket wiped at his eyes. "And I love him. He accepted me—me, with the same name as his tormentor and traitor—when I couldn't accept myself." An image of Helmer as Picket had seen him that fateful day appeared in his mind, fist over his heart, making his surprising vow. *I accept you.* Picket hadn't known then how brave Helmer had been to do that.

Mrs. Weaver took Picket's hand. "You accepted him too, my dear. You were just what he needed."

The building shook with a sudden thundering above. Picket glanced at Emma, then rushed for the stairs to the roof.

Chapter Forty-Seven

A Desperate Skyfight

Picket labored up the stairs and emerged onto the palace roof amid the chaos of battle. Birds of prey swept in, sending long shafts that shattered stone and tore through troops who tried to repel them. The command pavilion was in pieces, and Picket scanned the scene for Helmer.

Unable to locate his master, he drew his sword and rushed at the nearest raptor, joining with several soldiers bearing long pikes. The bird broke through the pikes with ease, swatting away the soldiers. The blow drove Picket hard across the rooftop and over the edge.

A few moments later he swept over the lip of the roof and landed again, narrowly rising over a hurled spear that blasted apart the palace's original rooftop shed. Rushing on, he leapt from his good leg off the roof again, this time with more speed, and caught an updraft that he rode back to attack the raptor.

The bird turned, beating its wings as it adjusted to strike at Picket. Just as he neared the Preylord attacker, Picket disengaged the glider and flew straight at his enemy, sword flashing in the sun.

The raptor slashed out, but its killing stroke was thwarted when a hail of arrows went home and several pikes found their mark. The bird faltered, eyes wide in shock. Picket, his way now clear, drove home the killing blow with his blade.

The raptor fell dead as Picket landed roughly on the palace roof, amid scattered cheers. Picket limped away and collapsed a few yards from the signal station.

"Are you all right, son?"

Picket turned to see Helmer rushing up, a bleeding wound on his head but a smile on his face.

"I'm fine. Let me at the next one."

"On your feet," Helmer said. "They're coming."

They *were* coming.

The raptor that had reached them first had outstripped its comrades, and now more were nearly on them. Beyond, over near the dam at the top of the wall, a pitched battle was raging as two massive Preylord raptors tore into the remains of the wolf barracks and loomed over the edge of the battered wall.

Picket grabbed a glass and saw that the monster raptors were two of the Six. He cried out as Jo was swept off the wall in a terrible strike from the eagle's talon.

As he fell, Jo nocked and shot an arrow at the foremost, the eagle. The shot went home in the eagle's heart, but the arrow somehow followed on through the enemy, emerging to sink into the next raptor's head. Picket gasped, dropping the glass as both raptor kings fell dead.

Picket started for the edge of the roof, but Helmer grabbed him firmly. "Stay here, son."

"But Jo's in—"

"He's fine. See." Helmer pointed to Jo's uneasy landing below. "We need to see them off." Helmer pointed at the raptors who remained, now undone in a shocking frenzy while the defenders' energetic efforts began to pay off. Picket nodded and took his place alongside the soldiers holding the rooftop. Alongside his master.

Soon, to the rabbits' stunned disbelief, the raptor horde of the second and third waves was beaten back.

Emma emerged on the roof the moment Helmer gave the okay. She thanked the soldiers as she helped tend the wounded.

"Well done, Lord Captain," she said. "How can this be?"

"It was Jo," Helmer replied, "and the Highwallers. I can't believe what I've seen."

They explained what Jo had done, and she shook her head in disbelief.

"Is the alcove still secure?" she asked.

"Yes, Your Highness." Helmer, as if waking from a dream, sheathed his sword. He seemed shocked to be doing so, as if he never expected to put his blade away again.

"You will need it again, soon, Lord Captain," Emma said. "You're certain it was two of the Six?"

Whit trudged over, stumbling as he came. "It was two of the Six, all right. I saw them straight off. Had them in my glass and saw them tear through the barracks. Then that speedy fiend got here quick and sent spears that nearly took my head off."

Emma hurried over to tend to her brother's fresh wounds. "Oh, Whit!"

"I'm okay, Emma. But I saw Jo's shot too. I would never have believed it had I not seen it with my own eyes."

"Mrs. Weaver was right, then," Emma said, expertly assessing Whit's injuries and reaching into her satchel to find the right supplies. "They came in a pair, two of the Six. Now three are dead. We can expect them to double up again."

"They might all come, along with Morbin himself," Helmer said. "Then we may be forced to use the alcove early."

"Do we still have the red flare?" Emma asked, looking past the bandage she was applying to Whit's leg to the signal station.

"Warken!" Helmer called. "Find out if we still have the red flare."

"Yes, sir!"

"Lord Captain," Emma said, frowning at the free-bleeding wound on Helmer's head. "You are hurt."

"It was a rough round," Whit said, groaning as Emma tied off his wrap and turned to Helmer.

"I'm fine," Helmer said, wiping fresh blood from his eyes.

"You can't see," Emma said, "but you're fine? You don't

need to see to lead my army?"

Helmer squirmed a moment, then frowned as Emma cleaned the wound quickly and sewed the gash closed.

Lallo and Harmon appeared, glider packs strapped on. Lallo bowed to Emma, then to Picket. Helmer's brow raised, causing Emma to slap his head lightly.

"Sir," Lallo said, "the bucks heard the blasts and are restless. They sent us to beg you to let us into the battle."

Helmer twitched, but Emma shook her head. "Hold. Still."

"Harmon, get back and help them settle down," Picket said. "The princess will need them soon. The first challenge is to get them ready to fight. The second is to help them understand how they fit into the overall strategy. The first is done. Give them the second, if you can."

Helmer clapped his mouth shut.

Harmon nodded.

"What about me, sir?" Lallo asked.

"You stay with me," Picket answered, "and I'll send you for the rest when the time comes. Harmon, be ready with the alcove squad soon. Keep the rest steady and ready."

Harmon saluted and hurried back, his face set in a respectful frown.

Lallo tried to hide his smile. Picket thought he looked like a youngster who had managed to escape punishment after a reckless caper. *He is so young. I must not fail him.*

Picket looked over at Helmer. His master's tender expression was surprising in that moment.

Lord Blackstar ran up, breathing hard. "Your Highness," he said, bowing to Emma. "There are no known assets left in the city capable of firing. We are down to our own arms."

"May they be strong," Emma said.

"The wolves are breaking through," Warken called, pointing east.

Picket ran to the edge and gazed at the battle for the east wall. The Highwallers were trying to re-form after the last attack, but there was no covering fire from the rabbit archers, and the wolf host surged ahead, pressing the gap with renewed ferocity.

Picket turned to Helmer. "We have to help! Let's relieve them, get the Warrenguard out, and then bring the flood."

Helmer looked from side to side, face pinched. At last he met Picket's eye. "I'll meet you there."

Chapter Forty-Eight

Helmer and Picket

Picket leapt from the rooftop and sailed down toward the east wall. Wolves were tearing through the gap, and the valiant bucks battled back, trying to hold the line.

Uncle Wilfred was at their head, fighting like a hero. Picket's heart swelled to see his kin fight so bravely. He descended rapidly, aiming for Uncle Wilfred's place at the head of the defenders. Glancing back, he saw Helmer, flying uneasily, and a few other soldiers who had been on the rooftop. More were on the way.

Just before Picket turned to focus once again on the enemy, Lallo looped around behind Helmer, a determined expression on his face. Picket's heart sank.

There's nothing for it now. He knew Lallo was a good fighter, having seen the young buck and his fellows fight with great tenacity at the Battle of Rockback Valley.

Picket set his jaw and flew low, sweeping up to deliver a crushing kick on the wolf his uncle was desperately trying to hold off. Landing, Picket drew his sword and scanned the field. A tall wolf sped toward him, swinging a long blade at Picket's head. Picket ducked but was knocked sideways at once by another bounding wolf. The wolf's jaws opened wide and went for Picket with savage eagerness. Picket couldn't bring his sword entirely around, so he used the pommel of his hilt to clip the attacker in the lower jaw, slowing him just long enough for Helmer to end the enemy with a two-handed slice.

Picket leapt up, nodding to Helmer, and together they attacked a wolf that had pinned another defender.

Helmer drew the wolf away with exaggerated swordplay, while Picket swept in and stabbed the beast in his middle. Helmer finished the villain, and they stepped away from his collapse to immediately meet another. Helmer hewed him down with an overhead hack that caught the wolf between his shoulder and neck. He fell, and Helmer followed on with Picket to the next of their foes. This wolf leapt as they came, and Picket sidestepped the swiping claws and struck the beast with a slice to his side. Helmer dove in, but his sword swipe was turned aside by the angry wolf's strong parry. His driving reply would have split Helmer in two but for Picket's blade turning it aside at the last moment. Instead, it caught Helmer's left arm, tearing a bloody trench that sent the old buck to his knees with a low groan. Picket stepped in front of his master, blocking the next strike from the wolf and driving his blade into his enemy. After kicking the dead wolf free of his sword, Picket spun to see Helmer up and protecting his back from another attack. Picket surged ahead to Helmer's left side, and the two of them took down this enemy with a feint and plunge as they had done so many times before.

Free of this enemy, he and Helmer leaned on their swords and gasped for air. Picket scanned the field and saw Uncle Wilfred near the wall striving with a wolf many times his size. Knocked on his back, Wilfred fought with determined poise. The gap in the wall behind him was just barely being held by a thin band of rabbits that Uncle Wilfred had been trying to reinforce.

Picket and Helmer exchanged a glance. They surged ahead, apprentice and master, reaching Wilfred just as the frenzied wolf drove his blade down at the overwhelmed rabbit.

The blade drove deep into the earth as Uncle Wilfred rolled aside, and Helmer leapt, connecting a powerful kick against the large enemy. Picket followed with an overhead strike, but the wolf parried and thrust a spear at Picket's head. He dodged the spear, bringing his sword back to attack the wolf's neck, but this again was blocked with such force that Picket lost his grip. His blade fell and the wolf struck him with a strong claw across the face, scraping him cruelly. Picket whirled and fell, rolling on the ground as a fiery pain erupted in his face and neck. He could feel blood coming, but he turned, trying to rise again as Helmer hewed the wolf's head off with a cry of such anger it caused the nearby fighters to glance back.

The bucks rallied, and they fought on, harder than ever. The wolves battled back, their ferocity in no way diminished. Picket rose and, taking a moment to gain his balance, rushed back as Helmer plunged ahead, making for the wall. Helmer cut down wolves as he went, a fierce energy in him that, paired with his experience and intelligence, made a warrior unlike any other. He broke the wolf lines and relieved those soldiers at the gap in the wall. Battling so that the defenders cheered, Helmer led a surge that forced the wolf army back again. All those enemies left within the wall were cut down by the reinvigorated Warrenguard and their well-timed relief.

Picket charged up to hold the line with Helmer while Uncle Wilfred rallied his forces to them.

Picket fought on, and Lallo wedged in beside him. Picket was relieved to see the young fighter alive, though he saw evidence that it had not been easy.

Helmer had turned back a moment to call out a command to strengthen the right side of the gap when a huge claw tore at the old buck. His eyes bulged and his neck showed red. Picket and Lallo teamed to beat back the attacker, who fell in the gap as his comrades rushed over him to get at the rabbits.

Fresh cries erupted in the city, and Picket risked an upward glance. He saw two raptors, silver-crowned and towering, enter the city. They were followed by a host of raptors carrying incendiaries.

With a terrifying screech by the two raptor kings, the Preylords released their smoking black bombs. They landed all around the city, exploding and setting fire to the entire Old Town and beyond.

Smoke billowed into the sky, and everywhere Picket looked, fire blazed.

Chapter Forty-Nine

Fall and Rise

Picket swiveled to find his master.

"It's time!" Helmer cried amid the terrible din, and Uncle Wilfred nodded. Picket relayed the order as his uncle surged ahead, alongside many brave bucks. Helmer turned and ran back toward the city center.

Picket was knocked back by a fresh surge of attacking wolves. He scrambled to his feet and ran straight ahead, dodging a killing strike from a wolf as he reached the wall and leapt up to rebound off it, while wolves snapped at his legs.

Engaging the glider, he swept low and followed Helmer over the bridge and into the city center opposite the dam wall. They made for a point midway between both city walls, where several young soldiers were already gathering amid the chaos of fire and death. After sweeping wide near the dam base, where the critical alcove remained undisturbed, Picket turned back and dipped toward their planned rendezvous.

Picket landed badly, twisting his already injured

knee so that he stumbled in the dust. Jo and Cole were there, battered and unbowed. They bent to lift Picket. At last, Helmer and Lallo charged up, alongside Heyward, Harmon, and a detachment of young bucks from the R.F.A.

"It's thick now, lads," Helmer shouted, panting. His left arm was bleeding through his torn sleeve. "But stand firm and we may tip this thing."

"Heyward," Cole called, "is the secondary trigger set for the dam?"

"It should be," Heyward answered. "The first line is gone now, but the failsafe should operate as designed. Tug that line hard," he cried, pointing to the rope coiled beside Cole, "and the dam will come down."

Picket steadied on his good leg and rubbed at his bad knee. Glancing aloft, he saw the Preylord swarm descending from on high amid the billowing smoke. Their leaders came on ahead—two of the Six—with nothing to fear, as the last bowstrikers and every catapult had been disabled or destroyed. It was body to body, rabbit against wolf and raptor. The wolves were pressing the last of the Warrenguard. Uncle Wilfred's band had bravely held them back beyond the east gate—at a horrific cost. Picket strained his eyes to find Uncle Wilfred but saw only a tangle of steel and fur amid twisting smoke and rising fire.

They couldn't hold the wolves any longer—nor should they. It was time. A sheet of smoke cleared in a sudden gust as the last defenders fell beneath the ravaging advance of the wolf host. The breach teemed with wolves.

They poured in, all snapping jaws and slicing claws. They were armed with every weapon for war that might tear through the heart of the rabbit city and wreak havoc not seen since the afterterrors. In the desolate days following the fall of King Jupiter, wolf armies ravaged the Great Wood, burning and murdering up and down the forest. In First Warren, they brought fire and death, leaving a long trail of desecrated places, widowed wives, and fatherless children.

So it was with unfeigned terror that they watched the wolves race in on the young band of rabbits standing ready at the city center. Picket watched them come. A collective gasp sounded from the gathered watchers on rooftops around the embattled city. A raucous rumble of hundreds of growls sounded from behind, and Picket spun to see the west gate overrun with wolves. They had fought through the Terralain army at last and were pouring into the city. Now Picket and his friends faced foes attacking from both sides, as well as the raptors above. Anguished cries rose up from the rabbits watching, and Picket heard the warning shouts. These wolves, amid the blazing fires all around, were set to meet in the middle with an easy victory over these few young defenders. That fast massacre would fuel new afterterrors and finish off the resistance once and for all.

Picket stood amid his fierce fellows, eyeing both sides with anticipation. This was the ground war's last stand, and all the rest hinged on the slim hope of what happened here.

The wolves charged closer, and Helmer nodded to Cole. Cole yanked the rope, squinting as he did, and the Fowlers all bent in anticipation.

Nothing happened.

Heyward's plan to blow the dam by packing the alcove with stacks of explosives and tripping the flint firing mechanism remotely had failed. Now the enemy pressed in, as planned, on the young rabbits positioned as bait. But there was no trap.

Overhead, a terrifying screech sounded. Picket glanced around, seeing everything poised in the balance.

He knew what he had to do.

Picket started for the dam wall, but Helmer held him back.

"Son, stay."

Picket had no time to argue. Helmer was tearing toward the dam, sprinting with every ounce of energy he had. He ran along the river's surface, on the barely submerged walkways made by Heyward, finally reaching the small alcove at the base of the dam. The cove was packed with blastpowder in quantities never before collected. Barrels lined the walls of the cove, and Helmer bent to draw free his flint and light his torch.

No. No. No! Picket fell on his knees, agonizing over what he was seeing.

More screeches followed as the raptor kings pursued Helmer toward the alcove, a sudden suspicion driving them to dive at the scrambling rabbit captain.

Helmer lit his torch and lifted it high, then turned to face Picket. The old buck stood, illumined in the alcove's arched opening, barrels of blastpowder piled around him, left hand holding his torch aloft and right hand clenched in a fist over his heart.

Picket could see the pale scar wrapped around the bend in his arm.

My arm for the cause and crown.

My all for the cause and crown.

Never taking his eyes off of Picket, he let go his torch.

Picket lurched forward. "No!"

Then he was knocked back, as the great grey dam exploded in a shattering bloom of orange. Jo rushed to Picket's side, dragging him back to his spot as the dam came apart, spraying colossal chunks of rock into the sky and belching out jets of fire. The host of Preylords around the dam, including the pursuing two raptor kings, burst into flames and were shredded by the hot rock shrapnel blasting out in a wild hail of crippling shards.

The Fowlers tripped their small hidden catapults in turn as the wolf army closed around them, teeth snapping and claws slicing. The young bucks launched in a sudden shot to fly back near the edge of the dam's calamitous detonation. Picket rose in the blinding brightness, then was hit by the concussive wave emanating from the all-pervading blast. He was driven back in the sudden gust of the explosion's aftermath, amid the falling rock and fiery spray. He came to himself in the air and banked back automatically to follow the other Fowlers to loop up and land on the palace roof where cheering soldiers shouted for joy and hugged one another.

Picket shoved celebrating bucks away and hurried to the edge of the rooftop, where he gazed at the ruin of the now-flooding dam breach, tears streaming from his eyes. Heyward's trap had worked better than they had dared imagine. Fires were everywhere in the city center, and the damage was extensive, but the explosion killed countless enemies, and the furious flood that now rushed into the city swept away the great army of wolves on both sides, carrying them past rooftops crammed with rabbits long-prepared for this maneuver.

Fires were doused. Foes were destroyed. Heyward's gambit had paid off, and he had been there himself to see it through. They had tried to plan for the least cost in lives, but Picket knew Helmer would have chosen this ending for himself every time. He had saved Picket and the other young soldiers in his charge. He had saved them all. *Cause and crown.*

Picket fell to his knees, weeping for more reasons than he could even understand himself.

Somehow, against all hope, the cause was still alive.

But Helmer was dead.

Chapter Fifty

The Final Foe

Picket sagged on the edge of the palace roof.

Rabbits on rooftops all over the city launched everything they had at the surviving Preylords who fought on. But, as before, many raptors turned back in retreat to fly back to Morbin's forces. The flood rushed in, covering the city in high water. But the rabbits had been planning this tactic, and they were well-drilled in its execution. Hordes of wolves were washed away and drowned in the flood, many sinking down into the pit that had once held the original First Warren, where Daggler and his band were destroyed and where enemies of the last battle had been cast. The Brute's Gorge. The pit became a swirling vortex of death, spinning down countless wolves to their end.

They had dealt with all but the final attack waves, had killed five of the vile Six, and the two principal wolf armies were being swept away in the flood. They still expected a wolf attack by sea, still expected the worst of the air attack led by Morbin himself, but the enemy's land forces were defeated.

Water poured through the shattered dam, and the islands beyond it were open to view. Forbidden Island's desolate gloom showed clear in the north.

A hand touched Picket's shoulder, and he turned to see Emma. "Let's finish what he started," she said.

He nodded, wiping his eyes, and followed her to the huddle of surviving rabbits atop the palace. Lords Blackstar and Booker were there, along with Lady Glen and Mrs. Weaver. The Blackstar twins, Jo, Harmon, Heyward, Lallo, and the sturdy old Pilgrim—returned from his misadventure with Jo—rounded out the group.

"The true end is upon us now," Emma said, "and you are all that remains of my council."

"We have no plan left for killing Morbin," Lord Booker said. "It was spent on Falcowitson. Father told me what Morbin was like in battle. Helmer—may his memory endure—has given us this chance, but we are not ready, Your Highness."

"I have seen him at war," Lord Blackstar said, "and Morgan is right. It is . . ." He trailed off.

"We have come this far," Emma replied. "There is a way, even if the odds aren't good."

"Beyond a plan to answer Morbin," Lady Glen said, "we must hope for an unexpected bequest. I have seen it happen before."

"We can only do our part," Mrs. Weaver said. "The next right thing."

"What is that?" Emma asked.

"Fighting them," Heyna said, pointing at Lake Merle, where a fleet of ships appeared in the lake bay behind the islands.

"And them," the Pilgrim added, pointing high and far, where a black mass formed like rainclouds on the horizon.

"My eyes are not so keen as yours, Pilgrim," Emma said. "I see the ships—so many—but is that . . . ?" Her voice trailed off as she gazed into the sky.

The Pilgrim peered into the distance, while Picket reached for a glass offered by an aide and set it to his eye. It seemed a swarm of some kind, but of an unbelievable number. His heart sank. Out in front of the innumerable horde flew a great black bird bearing a long scythe.

"That's him," Lord Blackstar said, shaking his head. "Morbin Blackhawk comes at last."

"They're all coming," the Pilgrim said.

Picket clenched his fist as he stared into the distant host. "Let them come."

* * *

Morbin Blackhawk hit the city at the same time as the forbidding ships. Diving in with his scythe, he carved an avenue of destruction through the midst of First Warren. He raised his scythe as he approached the wall but did not use it. Instead his powerful talon tore through the top of the wall, shattering stone and sending scores of defenders plummeting to their doom. He scythed them out of the sky as they fell, as if so eager for their deaths that he could not wait for them to strike the earth. His cruel, cackling cry echoed around the city and stilled the hearts of its defenders.

Morbin made for the city center, shattering the rooftop armies with great swiping strikes. Many fled, but brave bucks fell at every swing of his deadly weapon, and his breastplate deflected any arrow sent his way. Others stuck in his hide to be snapped off in turn. Nothing could penetrate his armor, nor anyone resist his coming. He came like an angry king retaking his throne with a heart bent on vengeance. Buildings crumbled before his wrath. Even Forbidden Island, visible behind his brutal attack, rumbled and collapsed in a series of unsettling tremors that shook the entire city. The islands on either side of Forbidden shivered and shook, then fell themselves into the ruinous deluge.

Forbidden Island and its six sister islands were gone.

First Warren was falling.

Chapter Fifty-One

Attack by Sea

Heather cried out as the hall came apart all around them. Smalls' starsword and her massive maul were no match for the last of their foes, the avalanche of falling rock they had themselves created. They embraced in the center of the cavern, the dazzling spread of light falling on them from above. She gazed up while the world rumbled and dragon death-wails joined the noise of bursting rock all around.

The light high above grew, and Heather winced against the sudden sharp brightness. *It must be that the high gate is crashing in.* Just before she closed her eyes, she saw a shape against the brightness.

"Take the rope!" came the call of a familiar voice from far above.

A long rope uncoiled above them, falling in a rippling descent until its unraveling end landed with a muted thud beside them. Heather's eyes flared and Smalls urged her onto the surprising lifeline. She gripped the rope and was heaved up amid the ongoing chaotic collapse of the dragon tomb. Halfway up she saw more forms above, but one looked familiar.

"Heather!" Father cried, and she was drawn up into the light, out of the gate and onto the surface of the quaking island. Father gripped her hand and pulled her into an embrace.

She could not believe what she was seeing as her eyes slowly adjusted to the blinding light. Father stood among others, many of whom she recognized from Akolan, as, in the background, the stout ships packed with battlebucks from District Seven sailed by. One was moored to the edge of the rocky Forbidden Island. They had come, just as had long been planned, and just in time.

Behind her, Smalls emerged and was pulled out onto the faltering rock.

"We have to hurry!" Father cried, gazing up with a shudder as the crew urged them ahead to the ship while the ground rumbled, gave way, and split apart behind them, opening ever-widening gaps that flooded with rushing water. Heather leapt onto the deck of a long narrow ship as the island behind her collapsed entirely in a thundering rumble of ruin.

"Give way!" Father cried as the ship's crew pushed off with long poles extended, and a huge wave generated in the wake of the island's demise shoved them ahead. Heather, unbalanced by the sudden surge, fell on a coil of rope. Gentle hands reached out for her, steadying her shoulders amid the swelling sea's rise and plunge as the ship sped ahead.

"I've got you, Heather dear." Heather squinted up to see Mother bending over her.

"Mother!" was all she could say; all else was lost in an astonished babble.

"Are you okay?" Mother asked.

"I'm . . ." Heather paused, glancing around as her eyes adjusted further to the light, ". . . I'm very well."

"I'm glad to hear it, my dear girl," Mother said, "because you will have to be brave for what we are facing."

Smalls stood beside Father only a few paces away, and Father was pointing ahead as he spoke in the prince's ear. Heather gasped at what she saw.

First Warren was under siege. Everywhere fires blazed, but a sudden gushing flood—the current of which the ships seemed caught in—was extinguishing many. She squinted to make out an enormous raptor above the city with a long scythe tearing through defenders with alarming ease.

"Morbin!" she cried, stumbling ahead.

"It's him," Father said. "Hold on!"

The ship entered a rough gap and shot down into the city itself. The dam, Heather saw with ever-rising alarm, had been blown apart, and the ships of District Seven's long-prepared fleet were sailing into the city. Heather saw Father and Smalls on the prow, stark against the brutal battling all around. The Tunneler and the Truth and Whitson Mariner's Heir, sailing into the ancient city on its darkest day.

"Fire away!" Mother cried, as raptors flew low overhead.

Small, coiled, wooden devices were tripped, and great nets shot out from bow to stern of the long ship, enveloping enemies in a tightening net fitted with weights. They brought down several raptors, and the ship's company of battlebucks, who had trained their whole lives inside the caves of District Seven in Akolan, leapt from the ship to finish off their foes.

Battlebucks from every ship followed hard after the netapult attacks on the raptors, and soon the rooftops of the flooded city were relieved by teams of eager rabbit soldiers—all born slaves in Akolan—surging into the fight.

Heather saw, with satisfaction, that Father's forces from Akolan were helping to even the odds against Morbin's raptors and the smaller number of wolves who fought against the rabbits atop the roofs of First Warren. These Akolan rabbits had planned their battle with raptors for decades and had spent countless hours and resources preparing for this war.

The netapults were joined by other devices and strategies, ably adapted by shrewd commanders to the battle blazing all around them. A kind of iron blastpowder barrel sprayed shrapnel skyward, tearing through and bringing down countless Preylord foes. Bucks throughout the fleet set fire to touchholes on these devices and a cheer followed their roaring blasts.

The bedraggled rabbits of First Warren's defenders rallied, and the intense fight continued all around. But there was that part of the enemy's arsenal for which no preparation could be made.

Morbin.

The Preylord king carried all in his wake. There was no answer for him, and defenders fled or fell at his coming, cut to pieces. He tore through every defense, and no strategy could withstand his invincible advance. Morbin swept into the city center and hovered above the last of the tall standing stones lining the square.

Smalls, sailing into the city by sea like an ancient king, gazed with hatred at the massive hawk, the eternal enemy of his kind.

"Steer for the standing stones!" Smalls commanded.

"Aye, Your Highness," the pilot cried, and they swerved past a huge half-shattered building upon which rabbits and raptors battled.

Along the tops of the buildings a new thing was happening. Some of the enemy raptors bore rabbits on their backs, and these uniformed soldiers leapt from the birds and landed on the rooftops, joining battle against the city's defenders. Heather fumed as she noted the red bands at their necks, preymarks of the so-called Longtreaders of Akolan.

These were her uncle's—Garten Longtreader's—own soldiers, and she scanned the rooftops for their leader.

A shriek spun Heather around as a pale raptor dodged past a desperate netapult blast and winged back to strike at the sleek ship. The massive talons tore through the mainmast, sending shattered wood spraying out in splinters, killing many of the crew, including the pilot. The ship swerved left, back toward the main surge of the current, knocking Heather sideways. The raptor circled back, beating his wings to fly in and strike at the scattering crew atop the ship.

"Pikes!" Father cried, and the rabbits left on deck reached for the long poles that they had used to shove off Forbidden Island and turned the reverse sides, with points carved into sharp-ended javelins, up at the attacking raptor.

The raptor balked, then came again, swiping sideways with his talons to tear apart several of the long pikes. But the brave crew drove the remaining pikes back at him again and found their mark. The wounded bird broke off, rising only to dip and dive into the surging flood before washing down toward the swirling sinkhole in the near distance. While the pikes were stowed along the ship's sides, Heather sprinted in to help the hurt, swinging off her satchel and going to work at once on a badly wounded buck knocked senseless by the raptor attack.

Father ran for the helm, and, arresting its reckless roll with help from a strong sailor, he steered the ship back around, aiming for the prince's destination: the standing stones. The mainmast was down, but they had enough steerageway to correct the course with the remaining smaller sails. The hands were busy clearing the wreckage away as Father called out orders.

Heather looked up from her latest patient, having done all she could do quickly, and saw with satisfaction that Morbin's forces were diminished, and the Wrongtreaders and remaining wolves were facing hard fighting atop the roofs. Morbin himself fought on with savage expertise, his impenetrable breastplate repelling every advance and his swift killing strokes ending any defender in reach. The killer king brooded above the seventh standing stone, slaughtering all around him.

As their ship drew nearer to the first standing stone, Smalls stood poised on the bow, angry eyes aimed at Morbin. Heather felt a hush fall over First Warren. A vast shadow from above blocked out the sun, and her heart sank.

More of these endless enemies? More of Morbin's forces? She shuddered, then willed herself to gaze up at the titanic shadow.

Chapter Fifty-Two

The Death of Longtreader

Heather's heart swelled. Looking up, she saw a host of rabbits flying, gliding in the sky. At their head, unmistakable to Heather's keen eyes, flew Picket Longtreader.

"Picket!" she cried, leaping high as Father and Mother looked up, astonished. Father left the helm to a reliable hand and ran to stand with his family.

Elation gave way to fear as she saw the target of his flight. The enemy raptors still filled the sky and, beyond them, Morbin himself.

"They'll be killed," Mother said, "all of them."

Father grabbed his pickaxe and called out, "Signal all ships to converge on us!"

"Aye, Tunneler!" came a drenched buck's reply. It was Dote.

Dote sent the signal, and several of the vessels began a slow turn. They steered toward their leader, the Tunneler and the Truth. Heather hoped they wouldn't be too late to help. As their ship drew nearer the first standing stone, a diving raptor flashed in and slashed at them again.

Heather dove down alongside Mother and Father as the raptor tore a long gash amidships. Heather lay on the edge of the gap, nearly rolling in with the sudden pitch of the deck. The raptor reappeared and swept low to finish off the rabbits.

Behind the raptor's raking dive, she saw Smalls swing in from a foremast rope. As the rope's arc swung upward, Smalls let go and drew. The starsword flashed out, catching the poised raptor and cleaving it so that the bird fell to splash in the flood, both port and starboard.

The helm came around, and they sailed through a surge as wind filled the sails. They were crossing the first standing stone from the west, gaining speed.

"Can you slow the ship?" Smalls called.

"No, Highness!" Dote cried from the helm. "Anchor's cut free and our crew's been mostly killed, so we can't take in sail."

"I have to go!" Smalls cried, staring a long moment at Heather before he sprinted to the edge and leapt high, landing roughly on the stone stairs spiraling up to the top of the first standing stone.

Heather watched with growing dread as the one she loved took the stairs three at a time in a desperate climb. The ship sailed by, and she rushed to the helm. As she ran, a volley of spears from swarming raptors tore through the ship. A lurch sent Heather sprawling, and she leapt up to see Dote recovering the helm.

Heather glanced back at Smalls as he ascended. "Turn us around, Dote!"

"It don't answer, Heather!" Dote cried back, spinning the wheel uselessly.

"Rudder's knocked away," Mother called from aft; then she ran up to join them alongside the rift amidships.

"Hull's opened and we have water coming in too fast to pump out," Father said, appearing from belowdecks.

"We're adrift, I'm afraid," Mother said, pointing ahead, "and going wherever the current's going."

"And where's that?" Heather asked, then saw their horrified faces. Spinning around, she saw the great swirling sinkhole ahead taking chunks of debris, and many fallen foes, down into a watery doom.

"We have to abandon ship!" Dote cried, lurching for the side. Father caught his arm.

"No, Dote. If you jump over, you're into that pit," Father said, "and there's no coming back from that."

"What do we do, Father?" Heather asked, trying to keep her voice calm.

Father lunged for a rope and began tying it around his waist. "Tie this fast to the mizzenmast, and I'll try to ship the rudder."

Heather nodded, leaped to the mizzen, and sent the rope around in a quick knot. "It's secure!"

Father hurried to the stern rail and gazed over, testing the tension.

A swift raptor swept in, aimed straight at Father. On its

back rode a grey rabbit.

"Get down!" Heather cried as the raptor's talons reached out for Father. He dodged sideways, striking the rail so hard he pitched overboard.

The raptor rushed on, tearing through the mizzenmast as the grey rabbit leapt from its back and landed on the deck with a roll.

Garten Longtreader sprang up on the aft deck, drawing his sword with an angry cry. Heather saw rage and indignation combined in his face. He seemed the offended party in an ancient feud, finally finding his foe.

He caught Heather's eye and looked surprised. "You? How are you still alive?"

Mother stepped ahead of Heather. "Garten, don't do this."

"Will you see me now, Sween?" he screamed. "Am I still invisible? Will I be invisible if I run this rabbit through?" He stepped ahead and met Dote's brave charge with a sideways step and slicing sword stroke across Dote's middle. The young buck fell motionless on the deck.

Heather and Mother stepped back. "No!" Mother cried. "What are you doing, Garten?"

"What I should have done long ago," Garten said through gritted teeth. He stepped ahead, his sword hand shaking with anger.

"Look what you've done, Garten!" Sween cried, sweeping her hands around the city at war. "This is all your doing."

"Me? *You* started all this, Sween!" Garten said. "Where could I go when you turned me away? Your refusal sent me straight to Morbin. I didn't know it then, but I *wanted* all this. I wanted it all to burn."

Heather glanced around the deck, seeking for some defense against this attack.

"If you want to kill me, then do it," Sween said, stepping forward with her arms out wide. "I chose your brother, yes, but I never hated you then. We were family then. We are family now. Won't you come home again?"

"Your home is destroyed," Garten said, nodding over where Morbin's scythe filled the sky with the dying cries of rabbits. "And this is your end."

Heather felt an urgent presence from behind, and she shoved Mother over as Garten advanced. A shrill shriek came from behind, and Garten's raptor swept in, set to slice Mother with its talons. Heather rolled to the rail, grabbed a pike, and swiveled it quickly around, bracing the dull base against the joining between rail and deck.

The raptor was focused fully on its impending kill and didn't see the pike until it was too late. Its shriek was cut short as it struck Heather's pike, snapping the long stave in two as it plunged into the water. Heather swiveled back to see Garten surge ahead, sword poised to strike down Mother.

"No!" Heather cried.

Father emerged then, pulling himself over the rail with an effort. At the last moment, he leapt between his wife and his brother's killing stroke. Father's pickaxe rattled with the force of Garten's furious strike, but he brought it back around to block a second stroke aimed at his own head. Father ventured a kick at Garten's middle. The kick went home, and Garten stumbled back, doubled over. A swift recovering stab from Garten caused Father to dart sideways and bring his pickaxe back across his brother's front. Garten's sword came up, but the heavy axe snapped the sword and sent Garten back, staggering, to the rail. Another kick sent Garten over the side with a cry.

Heather rushed to the edge and saw Garten clinging to the rail as his dead raptor circled the whirlpool nearby. Round and down it went, the watery pit its grim fate. The ship, whose ruined masts hanging overboard were a drag holding back its descent into the sinkhole, was still nearly to the brink of the irresistible swirling pit.

"Give me your hand!" Father cried, extending his to his brother.

"I'll not take pity from you!" Garten screamed back.

"It's not too late, brother! Please, take my hand! Please, Garten. There is a way back! Take my hand!"

Garten's face seemed to soften for a fleeting moment, then harden again as he snarled. "I would do it all again."

Garten Longtreader let go the side and dropped into the water. He appeared again on the edge of the twisting pit and soon swirled down and out of sight.

The ship was on the very edge of the whirlpool now, and Heather looked around for any way to escape.

Nothing.

Heather felt her mother's arms around her as the ship entered the spiraling flood. Father, eyes wide with shock, turned to his wife and daughter.

"I love you both."

Just as the ship dipped and began its first circling of the swirling pit, breaking apart as it dropped, they heard a faint voice amid the raucous noise.

"Jump for it!"

Heather let go of her mother and ran to the rail. A ship under full sail was racing toward them. Two ropes were launched at them, landing in the water below.

"Come on!" Heather cried.

Mother ran to the edge as Father lifted the slumped form of Dote. They leapt as the ship broke apart. Heather snagged the end of one rope as the whirlpool drew her down. She held fast and reached back for Father, who would not let go of Dote. Mother grabbed the other line.

Father seized Heather's hand, and she held with all her might. They were pulled free of the vortex by the sudden force of the swiftly turning ship. On the rescue ship's deck, Jacks and Harmony, together with some others, hauled on the ropes with a desperate effort.

They were dragged free of the swirling sinkhole's pull and up toward the waiting arms of their saviors.

Once on board, they embraced in exhausted relief, and an on-ship medic went to work on Dote.

"Look!" Jacks said, pointing up to the seventh standing stone.

Heather ran to the edge of the ship, staring in disbelief. "No!"

Chapter Fifty-Three

The Last Charge of Picket Longtreader

Picket turned to the eager band of rabbits rushing behind him, all fastening buckles and checking their partners' glider packs.

"See them come, the last of our enemies!" Picket shouted, pointing at the foes pouring in. "You are Fowlers now, and you must fight as our founder fought—fall, if necessary, as our founder fell. Say it with me: My arm for the cause and crown!"

"My arm for the cause and crown!" they roared.

"My all for the cause and crown!" Picket cried.

"My all for the cause and crown!" they thundered in reply.

"Come on! Follow me into this last fight, my friends, and let's together forge a brotherhood of blood that will outlive this battle and stay with us all our days. I will fight beside you!" Cheers. "I will fly beside you!" Louder cheers. "I will die beside you!" They roared as they came on.

Picket leapt from the palace roof onto the long slide and raced down at a thrilling speed. After him came Jo and Cole, alongside Harmon and Lallo, and behind them a countless mass of trained young Fowlers of the R.F.A.

Picket glanced across as Morbin slashed through the city, his huge cruel band in his wake. Then Picket focused again on the long wide slide that had somehow survived every attack on the city so far. Now he reached the curved end and shot up along the ramp, launching high and fast into the sky. In groups of five behind him, the R.F.A., those young soldiers held back against the last need, shot into the acrid air above First Warren to meet the evil armada of Morbin Blackhawk.

The clashes came at once, and the Fowlers threw themselves into fierce fighting. Picket saw Lallo struck by a raptor's blow, then plucked out of the air in the beast's talon. Picket banked hard in pursuit, correcting course to intercept the fast raptor. Lallo sagged in the enemy's grip, and Picket bent his flight to come at the raptor in the sun's eye, appearing beneath it from a blurry brightness.

Disengaging his glider, Picket drew his sword and sliced the raptor's talon clean off, sending Lallo plunging below. The bird twisted in fury and sped at Picket with a long cleaving strike of its blade. Picket engaged the glider again, caught an updraft that sent him just clear of the slice, and then, banking sharply, killed his glider again so that he fell like a stone toward the city. Lallo, he saw with great relief, was being helped to a rooftop by two of his fellow Fowlers.

Picket felt the raptor's pursuit hot behind him. He

turned back and saw the one-clawed fowl bearing down hard. Picket twisted into a spin, corkscrewing down by engaging one side of his glider, then disengaging it in quick succession. The raptor screamed behind him, beating its wings in a furious trail. Breaking the corkscrew, Picket rotated both wrists and came up in a sudden rush. Twisting to disengage again as he rose suddenly, he whipped his sword out in a slashing strike that cut deeply into one of the raptor's wings.

Just holding on to his sword, Picket spun away as the raptor, flapping madly, crashed into the east wall and then down into the flood.

Rising in a sharp upward climb, Picket banked back to survey the scene.

It was a nightmare.

Nearly all the young flyers were trying to get to Morbin. None succeeded. But they all saw what he saw: If Morbin wasn't defeated, this battle—this war for all Natalia—would never end.

Picket sped toward Morbin but was forced to watch the massive and agile raptor rip through rabbit defenders with murderous potency. The gliding rabbits flew at the huge hawk, swarming him in their desperation to defend their liberty and loves. Few made it through the shrewd and bloody skill of Morbin's warring work. But some did, and Picket winced to see them break steel on his impenetrable breastplate, then die by his cunning strikes. Picket watched the young Fowlers fall, torn and sundered,

victims of Morbin's scything swipes of death. Still, the brave defenders flew at him, falling away in fragments, divided remainders of heroic souls.

Picket gazed at the standing stones in front of Morbin. A small white rabbit in a golden breastplate was leaping ahead with a flashing black sword.

Smalls? Smalls!

Against all hope, it *was* the prince. *Alive.* More than merely alive, fighting! Aiming now for their forbidding foe, bravely racing toward the ancient enemy.

Picket could hardly believe it, but he focused all the more on going straight at the monster just above the seventh standing stone.

Smalls leapt from the first standing stone to the second, stumbling as he went. Picket's heart swelled to see him, the prince in action, advancing towards impossible combat with their evil adversary. Picket willed the wind to carry him faster. The R.F.A. was shattered, breaking on Morbin like water on an ancient rock. The last airborne Fowler fell as Picket neared. Smalls leapt from the third to fourth stone with a cry.

Morbin brooded on the seventh standing stone, his eyes finding Smalls as the prince paused before him on the fourth. Morbin recognized Smalls and cackled loudly, a rattling laughter bursting forth from deep within his battle-poised frame. Picket sped on, aiming at the blackhawk's heart, hoping his foe remained distracted by Smalls.

Nearer. *Nearer*. And Smalls cried out, "Now your dominion is ended, Morbin! I am the son of Jupiter Great, descendant by blood and heir of Flint Firstking! I am Smalden Ender Preybane, and your doom has come."

Morbin laughed again, but his mirth was tinged with indignant rage. "You puny princeling! You'll join your fathers in death, and such a death as dwarfs all theirs. Your end is an end to all rabbitkind. Well done, Small Prince. You mean to win for a mending, but you die in its ending."

Then Morbin, his face still set in a scornful smile, turned suddenly, seeing Picket sail in. But too late. Picket soared straight for Morbin's heart, and the Preylord quickly clawed across his middle to defend against the speeding buck. But Picket bent his approach at the last moment, shooting up at Morbin's face. Talon slashed, meeting air. Beak snapped, just missing Picket's fleet form. The buck barely evaded these deadly perils and reached the iron helm. Picket plunged his blade into an unprotected eye, driving it inside with a ferocious cry, to finally extinguish its light.

Morbin screeched, and Picket was thrown off by a violent convulsion from the stunned raptor. Picket spun, then sent out his arms, regained control, and glided back around. There was a raucous shout from the rabbits around the center of the city, from building tops to ships below. Picket banked and aimed again at Morbin's shimmering breastplate. At the last moment, he broke again to Morbin's face, aiming for the second eye.

Morbin saw and knew. The raptor flapped his wings and rose, twisting away from Picket's strike. The blackhawk swung his scythe, and, as Picket turned desperately, the weapon found the outstretched sword arm of the defiant buck who had blinded him. Picket's right arm, with glider-wing and sword, fell spinning toward the flood below. Picket reeled and spiraled into a diving crash that ended on hard stone.

He lay bleeding on the far lip of the sixth standing stone.

Sudden pain and shock. Gasping. He blinked, eyes wide, then gazed up at the huge looming monster ahead. Behind him, he heard Smalls rushing to leap and land.

"Hold on, Picket!"

But Picket stood and looked up at Morbin, defiant here at the end. Hearing Smalls, he knew his duty.

"My blood for yours . . ." he whispered.

Swordless, Picket Longtreader ran and leapt at Morbin.

He heard a cry from behind: "No!"

Morbin's talons shot out, raking Picket in an upward thrust that at once sliced and tossed aside his feeble foe.

The claws cut deep trenches in Picket's fur and skin, and he cried out in pain. The force of the blow flung Picket up and away. He flipped, then leveled off in midair, looking back in agony at the scene behind. The raking gesture had exposed Morbin's middle. Morbin cackled, his surviving eye following the cast-off rabbit who had dared to blind him, as he readied his scythe to slice Picket in two.

But Smalls leapt then, from sixth to seventh stone now. He seemed to veer right, then correct—somehow, midair—as the starsword shined black in the sunlight. Morbin, blinded on that side, saw too late the leaping form of Jupiter's son.

Picket fell, lower and lower, descending toward a watery end. But he watched on, looking up while his last strength held, to see the prince's final stand. Smalls sailed through the sky, glowing gold in the brilliant sun, as the Green Ember glimmered at his neck. The starsword bit into that—until now—unbreaking breastplate, cleaving it open and exposing the blackhawk's heart. Smalls drove the old blade in as Morbin's scream echoed in the air above the city.

Picket's vision clouded, but he saw the old sword break inside the final foe. He saw Smalls land on the seventh stone as Morbin reeled back and spun down, descending toward the pit. Through a spray of black feathers, Picket saw Smalls standing, holding aloft the hilt and shard of the starsword.

Picket's vision went black then, its last sight the ultimate fight in all Natalia. The death of the final foe. The war's definitive end, and the beginning of the mending.

Chapter Fifty-Four

The Beginning

One Year Later

Heather had made the bread with help from hundreds. Gort came, with his army of cooks, and all the old citadels' cooks helped. This was to be a feast for the ages, and all ages were here. She gazed out over the tables and marveled to see among the endless sea of rabbits thousands of happy children. Babies strapped happily to mothers' backs and toddlers tripping in the grass. The world was alive with life, and sunlight shone on a happy host, all clad in white.

"Pardon me, Your... uh, Your, uh..." Gort said, fretting in front of Heather.

"I'm not 'Your Anything' yet, Gort," she said through laughter. "I'm Heather, and we're old friends."

"Beg your pardon, Heather," he said, smiling, "but I think the last of the loaves is out."

"Good."

Smalls had made the wine, new and dark blue with infusions of those flowers growing all around the surrounding country. These blooms grew from seeds of those flowers found in the ancient glade. Firstflower. True Blue. The

Pilgrim had brought them as a gift for the prince, and they had been planted in the days after the battle. Aunt Jone and Emma, with help from the Pilgrim, assisted the prince in its making.

"It's too soon to be as good as it could be," the Pilgrim said, "but it will be sweet for the feast."

"We've waited long enough," Smalls replied, smiling. "And sweet will suit the younglings."

They had waited long, putting things as much to rights as they could. They could not revive the fallen, nor even completely redeem the ruined city of First Warren, but they did all they could.

And the prince led them.

First Warren, its river restored to its prior banks, was the headquarters of the renewal, but a section was left in ruins around the Chasm of Death, where fell Morbin Lastfoe and many others.

The feast was being held beneath what they were calling Newcity. Newcity was designed by Heyward and Emerson and half-built by the time of the feast. It was set in an old glen of the Great Wood, halfway between First Warren and what had been Harbone. It was unlike any place ever before seen in the long history of rabbitkind, for no part of it touched the ground. Its life was among and above the trees, with interconnecting spans of rope and wood. It was to be a palace and a haven, a place for pilgrims and the royal household.

"Friends!" Smalls cried, red gem gleaming on his chest

as he stood atop one of the many tables set out in the glen. "We feast today, at the end of our long wars but the beginning of our true work. Now comes the end and aim of all our endeavors—the Mended Wood!"

"The Mended Wood!" the crowd echoed.

"This is the Feast of the Mending and shall be marked always on this day, every year, until the end of time, or forever. We will honor the blessed fallen on the anniversary of our victory over Morbin, and it is right and good to look back, with gratitude, upon that day. But this day is also for looking forward. This day will be about more than our fight, but what we fought for. We fought for the mending, and the mending has come!" Cheers, shouts, and glad tears. The children danced, hand in hand, and the grownups smiled and embraced one another. "Now, friends," Smalls said, "I want to share with you the good news of my betrothal to Heather Longtreader. We will marry on my coronation day!"

The crowd cheered loud and long, and the prince motioned for Heather to stand beside him. She stepped up on the table, smiling at him and waving to the crowd.

Smalls kissed her and took her hand in his, then raised his other hand for silence. "Now, before we feast together, I want to welcome our guest of honor." A hush fell over the crowd. They grew reverent and thoughtful. "Lord Captain Helmer, the Last Lord Captain and an unmatched champion of our kind, once said that long speeches before meals are crimes of war." Laughter. "So, I will be brief.

Picket Longtreader, come forth!"

Picket emerged from behind the first rows as deafening cheers poured from the host of rabbits. Weezie Longtreader held Picket's one hand with her right, while her left hand rested on the gentle swell of her belly. Picket limped, and his face and remaining arm were lined with scars, but he smiled as he came forward and embraced the prince. Weezie hugged Heather, and the four of them stood together. The cheers finally quieted when the prince stood up once again on the long table. "This table is for Picket and his family, so come and sit, Longtreaders and those whom I have appointed."

Smalls made Picket sit with Weezie beside him. Then came Father and Mother, along with Jacks, to join them at their table. Uncle Wilfred and Airen came, and Mr. and Mrs. Weaver. Emma, Harmony, Cole, Heyna, and Jo Shanks rounded out the company. Finally, one place was left vacant for Helmer.

Then the whole host sat at tables. Smalls came and stood by Picket. "Are you all comfortable?" he asked.

"Yes, Your Highness," Picket said, bowing his head. "Won't you join us?"

"I would be honored," Smalls said, his arm around Heather, "as I will be joining your family soon, but I have some work to do today. Enjoy the feast!"

He hurried away, and Picket looked on, puzzled. Then he saw the prince put on an apron, tie it behind his back, and begin to serve.

Chapter Fifty-Five

The Scholar

I saw him fall," the king said. "He opened the way for me to finish the fight. As he fell, I leapt and sent the starsword home in Morbin's heart."

"I see." The scholar nodded, rubbing his chin. "The ancient blade broke, and you landed on the seventh standing stone, correct?"

"I did. And that's when Picket hit the water."

"What happened next?" the scholar asked, looking up from his paper with pen poised. "What did you see?"

"You were there," the king said, but at a frown from the scholar, he nodded and continued. "Forgive me, I forgot that you need my unbiased perspective for your research. I shall do my very best for you, sir."

"Your Majesty is kind."

"I saw him go under, and my heart sank as he did."

"Then?"

"Then she was there. The queen—forgive me, she was Heather Longtreader then—leapt into the flood, diving deep as a battered ship sailed alongside the base of the standing stone."

"What happened to Morbin at this time?" the scholar asked, dipping his pen into the inkwell on his desk.

"Morbin had lurched back, beating his wings a few times as he died, and he spiraled into the sinkhole. The Brute's Gorge. He spun and sank down. But I wasn't watching him closely. I was running down the stairs, toward Picket and Heather."

"Were you scared you might lose Heather?"

"Of course! I was ready to dive from that height to save her, but the ship was in the way, so I scrambled down as fast as I could."

"And what did you see next?"

"She came up, broke the surface of the water. And she had him."

"Heather Longtreader had her brother. What happened then?"

"He was dragged onto the ship. You were there—I'm sorry, Whittle and Sween Longtreader were there. Heather climbed back on board the ship, and I met them there. She went to work on Picket, and, after a while, he coughed up the water he'd swallowed, and she... she saved him."

"Did you stay on the ship long?"

"No. We sailed back toward the palace, and Emma helped get Picket to a room. She and Heather did all they could for him. He was in terrible shape."

The scholar looked down, closing his eyes a moment. "You were not able to stay at Picket's bedside, correct?"

"I was not. Duties of state called me away. There was so much to do, and I could do nothing for Picket. I took my leave—reluctantly—and had many urgent tasks to see to."

"When did you next see Picket Longtreader?"

The king sighed. "It was weeks later. Things were just beginning to settle down when I received a note from Heather. I was scouting Newcity with Heyward and Lord Blackstar that day. In the note she asked me to come back to the palace. There weren't any details, but I knew it was about Picket. I was afraid the worst had happened, so I rushed back at once."

"And what did you see there?" The scholar dipped his pen and scribbled on.

"I came to his room, but I stopped in the doorway when I saw your family—sorry, Picket Longtreader's family—in the room, gathered around his bed."

"What happened?"

"Picket opened his eyes and," the king rose and paced the room, "he seemed so surprised to be alive. He saw Heather, and... he couldn't say anything. He just stared at her. She hugged him close and told him everything would be okay. Then the rest of the family came closer, Jacks and Mrs. Longtreader, and Picket's eyes grew wide and filled with tears. I think he was afraid he might be dreaming and that he might at any moment wake up."

"How did this make you feel?" the scholar asked, smiling wide.

"It felt like the end of the bad days. It felt—" he broke

off, wiping his eyes. "I can still remember Heather's face, so lovely and glad. The whole family was there, together again after so many woes. Picket wanted to get out of bed, but they pressed in around him, smothering him in hugs. And he stayed, smiling and crying like a child. Here is the hero of the cause—a living legend of our kind, and he's weeping and I can barely even see it through my own tears. It was a fine day. The best of days."

The scholar put down his pen. "It was then that the mending began for us."

"The world was new," the king said, "and Picket lived to see it."

Chapter Fifty-Six

The Queen

The queen left her pen and ink and rose, stretching. Crossing the book-lined room, she opened the outer door on a sunrise shattering a thick morning mist.

The queen watched the rising blaze as it displaced the fading fog, and the dew-wet morning shone out in glistening emerald. A servant brought her a mug of tea, which she received with thanks, and she gazed on at the growing glory of the illuminated morning. She sipped and savored her blue-tinted tea as the sun's ever-spreading line of light reached the high palace and banished every shadow.

An easel featuring a half-painted canvas stood propped near the far rail of the porch.

"Your Majesty," came a familiar voice from behind.

"Slipped past Heyna, somehow? Come and sit, sister," the queen said, without turning around. She smiled as she sipped again, feeling the warm rays spread over the elegant deck on which she stood.

A red and white doe, steaming cup of her own tea in hand, sat in a chair near the queen.

"Yes. My cousin Heyna is growing positively lax in this perpetual peacetime," she said, out of breath. "I think she's still asleep. Still, it's difficult to get to you. This high palace is some climb, Your Royal Majesty."

"I hope," the queen replied, "it was not too much hiking this height, Your Royal Highness."

"I feel amazingly well, as I dare say you do too. Still, the climb is some work. It was worth it, though, for this view."

"Emma," the queen said, turning to her dearest friend, "how are things coming along? We are so grateful for your work."

"You grew used to that royal *we* so quickly, Heather," Emma said, feigning a lofty tone.

"I meant Smalls and myself, Emma," the queen said. "I would never play the majestic exalted one with you."

Emma laughed. "I know it. But, as Mrs. Weaver once told me, when she thought I would be queen, 'you must be who you are, and let us be who we are. We rise as you rise.' It was something like that. It's possible she's slightly more eloquent than myself."

"Possible, but I've done some research on what you were doing while I was away on holiday in Akolan and the Dragon Tomb. I've unearthed some surprisingly eloquent speeches before battles. You would have been a grand queen, my sister."

"I was never more relieved than when I saw you again. You beside my brother, a new Flint and Fay for a reborn world. How we all cheered! I knew then that not only did I have my very best friend back, but I also wouldn't have to be queen. I'm of far better use where I serve." Emma smiled wide. "Heather, it is the best thing. Firstflower is not only making our tea a truly spectacular treat this fine morning; it has also yielded such cures as we dared not even imagine. My hospital is coming along so well, and the veterans are responding to their healing in ways that astonish me."

"I am so pleased to hear it! If only we could get you married, my happiness would be complete. Lord Morgan is still pining for you, I believe. And Jo Shanks, as I've often said, is quite a gallant captain."

"As I've told you, Heather, I don't need to be married to have meaning. Jo works for me, and he's as good a buck as can be imagined, serving the older votary does with such generosity. But I am happy in my calling. We're doing real good for the veterans and the children, and the cures are astonishing."

"Oh, forgive me, Emma," the queen said, extending a hand. Emma took it in hers. Heather went on. "I am seeing more and more that the mending has meant each one of us flourishing together in such a way that we each are more ourselves than we ever were before. I respect your calling so much, my dear. I will, if you'll allow it, come and serve my shifts at the hospital again this week."

"The veterans love to see you there," Emma said. "It makes the whole place cheerful. And, of course, you are such a help. But I'm afraid the hospital—our old palace—will have to be fully converted to ordinary quarters."

"Really?"

"Yes, Heather. There is no more sickness."

Heather gazed at the sunrise, a misty view despite the burned-off fog.

"Did you see Cole when you came up?" the queen asked.

"I did," Emma replied. "He was with the king, Whit, and Winslow. They were heading off to scout a location for the Votive Sanctuary. Prester Kell and Sage Kins had narrowed down the sites, along with help from the Pilgrim."

"You don't have to call him that," the queen said, smiling. "I know who he is."

"He's the Pilgrim to me. What a gift that he came when he did. If someone were to ever tell of his journey, now that would make for some amazing tales."

Heather nodded. "It's remarkable. And I haven't heard the half of it, I'm sure."

"But he will always be the blessed bringer of Firstflower seeds."

"Indeed. True Blue has changed everything," the queen said, sipping her tea.

"I suppose Jo will be joining the Pilgrim's—as you insist on calling him—next expedition," Heather said. "I am so eager to hear what they discover."

"It is an age of discoveries," Emma replied, smiling wide. "It's as if everything old has meanings now we hadn't ever known, and everything new is like an old thing we are only just now finding."

"Our Pilgrim once told me, 'The world is like a wise old child,' in this mending."

"It's like being inside a perfect poem, I think. Better than even you could write, Your Majesty."

"That's it. Words fail. Even the best-threaded and most ornate adornment cannot clothe this age enough in praise. It is beyond the cloth, and beyond the page."

Emma sipped her tea, considering. "I thought of going along with them on the next expedition, but I want to see my projects through. I think Cole and Heyna are going."

"The aim suits them well," the queen said.

A patter of small feet sounded from the house behind them.

"Mother!"

The queen spun to see a sleepy-eyed young doe, grey-furred and dragging a soft doll along. "Aunt Emma! I need to tell you that I haved seven dreams."

"Oh, that's a lot of dreaming," Emma said, snagging her niece and spinning her around. "Did you dream of being a mighty queen some day?"

"Aunty, no. I've tolded you already. I'm gonna be a doctor, like you."

"My dear Maggie," Emma said, "I don't think there will be any illness anywhere at all to cure by the time you're old enough. It's wonderful, really."

"You help them anyway, even sick or not. When you

comed over yesterweek, I had a good day but then you maded it better."

"She does that, for sure," the queen said, taking her daughter from Emma, easing into a chair, and snuggling her close. "I would be proud for you to be like your aunt. She's a treasure to me and to our community and to all of rabbitkind."

Maggie nodded, then squeezed her mother tight and rested her head in the crook of her neck.

"Heather, have you heard from Kylen recently?" Emma asked.

"Kylen? No, I suppose not. I haven't seen him since Prince Naylen's wedding."

"I got a letter from him," Emma said, settling back into her chair and taking a sip. "He's coming to the Feast of the Mending this year."

"I'm glad. Terralain is so far away and seems less his home than here in many ways."

"He's bringing their tribute this year, traveling with a vast team of those hulking bucks to help construct more of our homes for the war orphans and families who will adopt."

"You mean Uncle Wilfred and Airen haven't adopted them all?" the queen said, smiling.

"No, Mother," Maggie said, head shooting up, "Uncle Airen and Aunt Wilfred haved only fifteen childrens, but Aunt Emma still has more to find families for."

"Yes, Maggie," Emma said. "They almost all have

families now, but we're still working on homes for them all."

"A new colony group is leaving in a fortnight," the queen said. "Nick Hollow, I'm happy to say, is fully settled. The Red Valley is next."

"Did you ever think of going back to Nick Hollow?"

"Not really. I was born *here*," Heather said, "like you. This is home. The Great Wood is the place for me. We see everyone at the feast each year, and I feel like I don't have to go out into the world. It comes here."

"What about Picket?" Emma asked.

"Will he ever go back to Nick Hollow with Weezie and the kids? I don't think so. He's put down roots, in every way, and he has so much to do."

Emma nodded. "I think Weezie can heal him in a way I never could have. I hope he is very happy."

"He is, Emma dear."

The queen heard a cough from behind, and she turned slowly, trying not to wake Maggie, who had fallen back asleep. An older doe with a messy smock appeared, alongside a young black doe in an elegant dress. Both does bowed.

"Your Majesty," Heyna Blackstar said. "Your mother is here."

"Mother," the queen said, extending a hand.

Mother took and squeezed it, then gently patted the sleeping child. "My dear girls, I am glad to see you all."

"Mrs. Longtreader," Emma said, smiling. "I hope I see you well."

"Blooming, Your Highness," Mother said, bowing quickly to Emma. "I thank you."

"I have been admiring your painting, Mother," the queen said. "Are you come to complete it?"

"It is a long job, capturing the impossible beauty of this new world. But I come to continue, if I may, dear."

"You are very welcome, always. And I'm eager to see the painting grow more glorious with time. It is already unbelievably lovely."

Chapter Fifty-Seven

The Farmer

The farmer with the black scarf cut free a head of cabbage and, laying aside his knife, picked up the head and tossed it into a basket. Taking up his knife again, he cut the next cabbage free and added it to the heap. One row over, another buck did the same. Scooting down, the one-legged helper pivoted on his one good knee and pushed himself further down the row.

"You know," the helper said, "you're already a legend. Everyone knows that. But if only you could have managed to die, then Picket Packslayer would have been immortal."

"Picket Packslayer *is* dead, Lallo," the farmer replied. "Now the only slightly less famous *Picket Seedreaper* stands before you . . . or stoops before you."

"Picket Packslayer, see, he used to fly and fight, wielding his flashing blade on high in unthinkable bouts of glorious battle," the helper said, "but your pal Picket Weedeater—"

"Seedreaper."

"Okay, Seedeater," the helper went on, "he kneels and

cuts cabbage free on a little farm with his family and pays unreasonably high wages to other banged-up veterans."

The farmer grunted and added a last head of cabbage to the now full basket. He sheathed his knife and reached for his helper's crutch, extending it to him with a smile. "Sounds like a good life."

"If you say so, sir," the helper said, as together they filled several sacks from the basket.

The farmer snagged a large sack and, twisting to grip another smaller one in the same hand, headed down the road.

Soon he reached the edge of his land, where a small newly built cottage nestled amid a modest garden that overflowed with flowers.

"Hello, the house!" he called.

"Hello, the road," came the reply of a sprightly old doe as she walked out to meet the farmer. "My dear buck, you certainly haven't brought us more cabbage?"

"More cabbage it is, Mrs. Weaver," he said. "Where would you like it?"

"Back in your fields, I think," she said. "I can't let Edward eat another pot of cabbage soup. There's a limit to my mercy."

The farmer smiled and handed over the sack, setting down the larger one. "You're in luck, Mrs. Weaver. Weezie begs you and Mr. Weaver to come for supper."

"Tell Mrs. Longtreader we would be very happy."

"I already have," the farmer said, "Don't wait for me. I

may be a little late. But I'll be there by dark."

"Oh, Picket, may I bring anything?"

"You can bring that new shirt you're making for me."

"That was supposed to be a surprise!"

"I'll act surprised," the farmer said, smiling as he kissed her cheek. She hugged him and rested her head on his chest.

"You're so very good to us, son," she said. "I'm not sure why you do so much."

"Because you loved me. Before I was anything. Before I was at all lovable, you loved me. I won't forget."

"Love you," Mrs. Weaver amended. "We *love* all of you. Even the two who keep taking my barrel hoops for their volley-hoopity ball game."

"I'm sorry about that," he answered. "I'll see that they replace them by tomorrow."

She smiled at him. "I'm proud of you, son."

"Thank you, Mrs. Weaver. Give my best to Mr. Weaver, and tell him to try some chamomile tea. It settles the belly amazingly well."

An hour later, the farmer limped to the edge of New Bridge, adjusting the large sack slung over his shoulder to take pressure off his aching arm. He still sometimes felt as though he might only just reach out with his right hand and grab the sack, shifting the burden. But that hand, along with its arm, was gone.

Two bucks pulling one overloaded cart met him halfway across New Bridge, and he scampered aside, easing his burden onto the stone rail while they passed.

"Thank you, my lord," the larger rabbit said, huffing as they continued.

"My pleasure," he replied, then hollered as the carters hurried on, "but I told you to stop calling me 'lord,' Ray!"

"Sorry, my lord!" came the faint and gasping answer.

The farmer shook his head, then gazed down at the swift river, high after yesterday's rains. *We needed it.* He heaved the sack and continued on his way.

Not long after, he hobbled up some steps, pushed open the door, and entered a cozy establishment half full of happy-looking rabbits. Children played cards in one corner, while laughing does lingered over tea in another. Several bucks leaned on the counter and exchanged conversation with the one-eyed buck behind it.

"Hello, Farmer," the proprietor said, nodding to one of the young bucks to relieve the newcomer of his sack. "Finally brought my cabbage order, have you? I asked for it last week."

"You're lucky to get it this fast," the farmer said, taking a seat at the edge of the leaners. "I know agriculture isn't your trade, but it usually takes me months to grow cabbage."

"Next time put your order in earlier, Cap," one of the leaners said. The bucks all laughed, including the proprietor. A silence followed while they sipped and stared at their cups, until the farmer spoke up.

"How's things in Old Town, Jair?" he asked.

"Oh, about like they were last week," Jair replied. "Most of the best work is over at Newcity, but they're only taking the top crafters there. So, we make do. The old palace annexes are coming along. The princess is intent on getting them done quick like."

"That doesn't surprise me," the proprietor said. "When she gets intent, things get done."

"A lot of veterans owe their lives to her getting intent about it," another buck said. They all nodded and sipped their drinks.

"Well, she says it'll be a shame if the places ain't ready to receive every veteran and every adopting family who needs a home," Jair went on, "so we are hustling to do it."

"I don't know how you can be hustling when you're here every time I come!" another buck said. They all laughed.

"I'm supervising from a distance," Jair said. "You won't tell the princess, will ya?"

The farmer smiled and shook his head. "I'm not a tattler, Jair. And I haven't seen Princess Emma in weeks."

Another silence lingered, and each examined his cup or a section of the wall. Finally, Jair spoke up.

"Will ya tell us about what it felt like when you killed King Farlock the way you did?"

The farmer's head went down. He didn't say anything for a long moment, then only one word. "Scary."

"I'm sorry, sir," one of the bucks said, sensing something change. "I only want to say thanks and to tell you we won't forget what you've done for us."

"Thanks, Gabe," the farmer said. "I appreciate it."

"Stay for supper?" the proprietor asked.

"Sorry, Cap," the farmer replied, rising. "I need to go. I gotta be somewhere for my supper." He drained his cup, left his coin, and made for the door. "Do good work, bucks," he said, adding over his shoulder, "if you ever get around to doing any." Laughter faded behind him as he descended the stone steps.

"Hey, Farmer," he heard called from behind. He stopped and turned to see the one-eyed proprietor hobbling up behind him with the help of a cane. "Don't leave so soon. Stay awhile."

The farmer shook his head. "Those bucks only want to hear about the old days. I don't want to talk about them. Not yet. Maybe never will."

"Well, talk to me, then. Not them. I'll listen to your horrible stories of crops and kids," the proprietor said. "I even like some of them."

"And some of my kids like you," the farmer replied.

"Stay awhile, and let's you and me talk."

"I'd like that, Cap," the farmer said. "But today, I really do have to be somewhere."

"Is there a shortage of vegetables at some country hamlet that only you can supply?"

"There aren't shortages anywhere," the farmer said, smiling wide.

"Ain't that something?" the proprietor replied, returning the smile.

"It is that."

"In the old days, if you'll forgive me," the proprietor said, holding up his hand for pardon, "they used to come to our place for solace when times were hard. Sometimes I wonder why they still come, even in these days of abundance."

"I don't know, Cap," the farmer said, staring up at the warm, welcoming place. It fit in perfectly in this rebuilt neighborhood on the outskirts of Old City. He sighed and smiled. "It's probably the cabbage."

"That may be," the proprietor replied with a laugh.

"I'll send the rest of your shipment by cart in a few days," the farmer said. "And maybe I'll bring it myself, and we'll talk. Maybe even about the old days."

"Please do, Pick," the proprietor replied.

"I don't know why they come here, Cap. I only know why I do. In the Citadel of Dreams you find . . . a welcome that never ends." The farmer turned and headed for the road.

Rounding the corner, he stopped and gazed up at the massive mural painted on the tall building wall across from the palace. It featured a strong black buck haloed in an alcove, one hand holding high a torch, the other clenched in a fist over his heart. The farmer gazed at the icon awhile, then walked over to the wall, reaching out a hand to touch the image. He leaned against the wall. Soon, after touching the painting's base once more, he turned and made for the road.

After some time, as he reached the edge of his land, the farmer paused and watched the sunset slip behind the old home he and his wife had been given as a wedding gift. As the dusk deepened, the farmer watched the stars appear to dot the sky. He watched awhile, waiting for the warrior. Gazing high, he saw the sickle moon stand out against the brightening warrior constellation.

It looks like he's farming now.

The farmer crossed his fields toward the old house. As he neared, he heard the sound of laughing children.

Chapter Fifty-Eight

The Queen and the Farmer Catch a Star

Sween Longtreader was singing. She sang so often now, happy and lighthearted amid the mending. Her grandchildren gathered around her, and she blessed them with her songs. Whittle watched, happier than he ever thought possible, with tears in his eyes.

"Father Tunneler," a young buck asked, "will you be needing me any more today?"

"No thank you, Dote," Whittle replied. "Get along home to your wife and younglings. Young Stretch Doteson is a year old today, if I don't miss my day?"

"You have it, Father," Dote said, bowing. "Frannie is making such a feast!"

"Bless her, and him," Whittle said, "and you, dear Dote."

"And here's a token from us, Master Dote," Smalls said, handing over a small pouch, "with our best wishes."

Dote turned, surprised to see that the king had walked up behind him. "Your Majesty," he said, dipping down onto one knee, "thank you ever so much. My lad will be amazed!" He rose, bowed again to Whittle and Smalls, and hurried off, grinning.

"Your Majesty," Whittle said, bowing low.

"Father," Smalls replied, wrapping the older buck in a warm embrace as he rose.

"Brother Jacks," the king said, as Jacks hurried over from the direction of the house, smiling wide. They shook hands, then hugged. "How goes the school?"

"It is succeeding beyond all my hopes," Jacks said. "And since Father is done writing his history—his history of your father, bless his memory—he has been a tremendous headmaster."

"Thank you for what you're doing, Jacks," Smalls said. "I constantly hear happy reports from grateful parents."

"I'm proud of you, son," Whittle said. Jacks beamed.

They turned back to Sween, whose singing mesmerized the grandchildren. Smalls gazed at his own children, smiling as he held an emerald gem in his hand. Sween was teaching them an old song she had learned from her grandmother, and they all sang along. All but Hanna, who had her younger cousin Jo by the hand and was leading him away toward the edge of a tremendous field bursting with blue blooms. There, on the edge of the flowering field, Picket and Heather stood gazing past the blooming tract and the farmhouse on its right, to the river beyond.

* * *

"Will you grow nothing but True Blue in the future?" Heather asked, her gaze sweeping over Picket's fruitful land.

"No," Picket replied. "All the farmers have agreed to maintain some Firstflower, but I'll stick with my cabbages and carrots, and whatever else I care to cultivate."

"You are the master here, Farmer Longtreader, and what you say goes?" she asked.

"I'm no master. I plant and harvest," Picket replied with a smile, "and rely on sun and rain and help to grow anything. You're the one, Your Majesty, Queen Joveson, who is in charge of things. As in, all the things. You could, you know, order me to cultivate only Firstflower, and I would humbly bow and happily obey."

"The power to command you," Heather said, clasping her hands dramatically and widening her eyes, "it's what every older sister has always wanted. And now that I have it," she said, laughing, "I'm sadly lacking in ambition to use it."

"That is a tragedy," Picket said. "Were I so powerful, I would certainly be far more self-indulgent. I'd stop you writing more stories of my heroics, for one. Aren't you tired of that job yet?"

"You should be happy I don't have as much time to devote to my writing as I wished," she answered, "what with being a mother and, as you so eloquently said, being in charge of everything. And anyway, the volume isn't all about you."

"Well," Picket answered, "now that my glory is to be diminished in your writings, I find I'm suddenly less interested in literature. Farming's the life for me, I think."

"Your heroics certainly feature, but the story is about my husband, of course, King Smalden Joveson."

"I do feel like I've heard that name somewhere before."

"Well, now everyone will hear it for all time."

"You seem to have grown somewhat more confident as an author. Have you considered that your powers may have waned since motherhood and ruling the world have so consumed you?"

"It might have sapped my faculties, but I do it so well, you see, that it actually enhances my powers as a writer. You should try it, Pick."

"Motherhood? Ruling the world?"

"No. Being an excellent parent."

"Ah. Is that your Hanna there?" Picket asked, looking over his shoulder back to where the rest of the family gathered beneath an enormous elm. "She seems to be leading my Jo away from the rest, abandoning his grandmother's generous attentions, in contrast with your specific instructions."

"I am found out," Heather said, sighing. "Hanna is always testing the limits of my instructions."

"Is that ordinary disobedience, my queen," Picket asked, "or is it treason?"

"It feels like treason, to me."

"That might be slightly harsh, Heather."

They watched as Hanna bent to pluck an old dandelion's pale puffball.

"Now she's about to spread weed seeds across my fields," Picket said. "I'm coming around to your view on treason." Hanna blew hard on the puffball. It burst and sent tiny white plumes sailing out in all directions. Jo squealed with delight, so Hanna plucked one for him and carefully instructed him in the art. Picket groaned. "And now the plot has blossomed. It's a conspiracy now. The jury finds the offending niece guilty of treason."

"And we of the royal household confirm the decision," Heather said, "and sentence the malefactor to one hundred tickles, laid on thick."

"I will certainly do my best to carry out the sentence," Picket said, "though it must be understood that I have only one arm and one hand on that arm."

"It would be strange if you had two hands on your arm."

"It depends where these hands sprouted," Picket said. "I might like it."

"You really have become a farmer," she said, "with hands sprouting here and there. The old warrior has actually faded into the past."

"I'm armless as a babe, now," Picket said.

She smirked. "But the warrior lives on, in my histories. And I remember him well, and all the good he did."

"You have worked hard on these histories, I know," Picket said, putting his arm around her neck. "What will you call them?"

"Father's histories were published last year, as you know," she said. "He's been helping me with interviews since."

"Yes, I've read them all," he said, as they turned back to watch Hanna and Jo, hand in hand, wander off into a row of red-leafed bushes on the edge of the forest. "They were excellent. I thoroughly enjoyed each volume of *The Rise and Fall of King Jupiter the Great*."

"So, mine," Heather said, looking over at Smalls, who laughed alongside Father and Jacks on the edge of the elm's shade, "will be called *The Fall and Rise of King Smalden Joveson*."

"It's perfect, Heather," he said, squeezing her neck. "Well done. I'm so proud of you. You are flourishing, my dear."

"Who isn't, Picket?" she asked, smiling wide. "Who isn't thriving in this mending? Weezie and I aren't the only ones having babies. The Great Wood teems with children! Life is everywhere . . . alive! More alive than ever. Do you know, Picket, that Emerson and Heyward came to Smalls a week ago and said their team had found applications for the True Blue—your Firstflower—that seem not only to repair and enliven but to thwart death altogether. They are flabbergasted, and their lab is alive with an elated energy you wouldn't believe. Aunt Jone is with them! Smalls took me to see them at work. He has the highest hopes."

Picket shook his head, tears starting in his eyes. "Will this mending have no limit? Will even death finally die?"

"May it be so," Heather said reverently, touching her

ears, eyes, and mouth, "in this Mended Wood."

"In this Mended Wood," Picket echoed in a whisper.

After a moment, Heather spoke up again. "Picket, would you listen to the ending of my book?"

"I would be delighted to, dear sister."

"It's the epilogue," she said, and she drew a folded paper from a dress pocket. "'So the king ruled, with the queen by his side. Newcity, lit and suspended as it was, became a guiding star for all the world. Rabbits came to it, to pay homage to the king, to honor the war heroes, and to savor the center of the mending. Some stayed, but many more went home again to remake their own places with the light they carried with them after such an encounter with beauty. Every year, on the anniversary of their victory, they celebrated the end of the War for All Natalia and the advent of the Mended Wood. And the Great Wood did mend; brighter and brighter it shined, with more and more light to share. Mending begat mending, and the healing grew, like a disease in reverse, until the wholeness spread to the edge of every map. The rabbits were glad, good, and unafraid. They were free.'"

Picket gazed at her with shining eyes, then reached his arm around her once again. "And the queen was called Starkeeper and Scribe, legendary lightbringer of the greatest age," he whispered. "Oh, Heather. It's too good to not be true."

They were silent for a while, turning back to watch the river roll on past Picket and Weezie's home. Then they heard footsteps and turned to see Hanna and Jo.

"Jo found this in the bushes," Hanna said, holding up a six-sided cluster of sticks, bound by a blue ribbon in its center.

Heather gasped, then laughed as Picket took the starstick from Hanna.

"Now this," Picket said, dropping to one knee, "is a special thing that goes along with a special game."

"Will you teach us, Daddy?" Jo asked.

"I will, Jo," he answered. "This is a starstick, and the game is called Starseek. Aunt Heather and I will teach you and Hanna, and then you will teach the others. How does that sound?"

"Good," Jo said, smiling wide to reveal several gaps of lost teeth.

"Good," Hanna agreed, a protective arm around Jo.

"The rules are simple," Picket said. "One player throws the starstick as hard as ever she can; then when the starstick lands, both players rush to see who can find it first."

"And that's the winner?" Hanna asked.

"Yes, my dear," Heather said. "And the winner throws first in the next round. Now, why don't you let Jo throw it first?"

Hanna nodded, and Picket handed the starstick to Jo.

Jo smiled, then offered it to Hanna. "I want her to. She's always letting me go first."

Hanna accepted the starstick with a giggle and turned back to face the field of blue flowers. "Won't we hurt the pretty flowers if we romp over them like wildsters?"

"We have so much, Hanna," Picket said, "that a little romping won't do any harm at all."

She smiled, and Jo stood poised. "Ready, Jo?" He nodded. She bent back and twisted, then swiftly uncoiled, sending the starstick sailing into the sky, blue ribbon rippling in its wake. They all four watched it go, and Heather felt a quickening of her heart, a sudden rush of memory and emotion that sent her sailing back to Nick Hollow and the innocence they once knew there. She remembered that time with tenderness, but a deep delight welled up within her as understanding grew that the present joy far outshone the pale light of past happiness. Her ever new and ever renewing delight carried within it every sweet remnant of what it had in the past, but it thrummed within her now and swelled to a perfect pitch.

The starstick landed at a surprising distance, and the younglings sprang away, sending up sweet-smelling fragments of Firstflower as they disappeared, laughing, into the field.

"Were we ever so young?" Picket asked.

Heather laughed happily, then hugged her brother. "I think we are younger now than ever we were before."

* * *

Later, the families ate at long tables laid out beneath the Helmer tree. Together, glad, and glad to be together.

There was plenty of food, and all of it was good. They were all healthy and loved one another deeply. The sun shone bright high above them. The wind blew gently, and the shade beneath their tree was sweet.

None of them had been afraid in a long time.

"Uncle Picket," Hanna asked, tugging on his shirt, "who made up Starseek?"

"Your mother, the queen, invented the game," Picket answered with a smile.

"But," Queen Heather said, "Uncle Picket made it magic."

The End

The Queen and the Farmer Catch a Star

Author's Note

A powerful man once said, "What I have written, I have written." That man was not a good man, but what he wrote was true. More true than he knew, though I think he knows now. I feel that way about my conclusion to The Green Ember Series. I may not be the very best man, but what I have written, I have written. And I believe it's true.

Yes, this is a true story. I believe that. Not that the events happened, but that the story is, please God, faithful to Reality. This is how Tolkien viewed his own stories, and if I have never actively imitated his storytelling (who could succeed at scaling that Olympian summit?), I have learned from him this and more besides. He is, in that sense, my master. Whether or not he would approve of this student, I'm not sure. He was profoundly biased against one particular feature of mine, to be sure. I am an American. Sorry, Master.

Like Tolkien, I view this story (and this series) not as a propagandistic allegory, still less a religious tract, but a true story. A faithful story. It is honest, as best as I can tell. And therefore it is necessarily infused with echoes of that deep Reality. I do not apologize for that. We write from the depths of our inner life. As children we pretend at play, but it is always us pretending, and our make-believe is made up from what we believe. We love to make believe, and we make believe about what we love.

These stories will, I hope, like little children born from love, become something more than I could have imagined and make new ways in the world and have a separate—not wholly known to me—life of their own. But they will always have started here in my heart, in my home. They will always be rooted in deep affection for their first audience, my very real children, and their broader audience, which includes you. So, thank you for reading. And thank you for the generous way you have read and received these stories.

There is a generosity both of host and of guest, and when both act from love, a feeling of being at home prevails for both. In awkward meetings, neither party feels "at home." I have long viewed storytelling in general, and The Green Ember Series in particular, as an opportunity for hospitality. These stories belong to my family, and sharing them has been a joy. That others "feel at home" with our adventures makes us happy, like finding that our guests have been genuinely comfortable, refreshed, and at ease in our house.

We are grateful. I am grateful. Because it's been more than simply me inviting you into our home; it's I (through the books) who have been invited again and again into home after home, and heart after heart. Your homes. Your hearts. What an incomparable honor. That kids (and families) all over the world have cherished these stories is an honor I can barely comprehend. I would deny that it's true, but I have it thousands of times over in their own handwriting.

This book was written mostly during Lent and Easter of 2019. That is fitting in so many ways. Lent begins with Ash

Wednesday, a reminder that we are dust, and to dust we will return. We will die. That's real. Each of us will have a death scene. But Lent is not the end. There is Easter, when resurrection is realized and hope lives again. I can't think of a better season to tell this story, to come to this ending.

A good man (in a sense, the only good man) once scolded his followers for blocking children's access to him. He welcomed them and took them in his arms and blessed them. Since this particular Jewish man is my actual master—with all due respect to Tolkien, who would, I know, say the same—I only aspire to be like him. I have so sincerely wished just to bless you, children. I cannot do it the way my Master, or my master, have (and do). But I can do it the way I can. So here is your blessing.

May the Ancient Author bless and keep you. May the Holy Hero be your rescuer forever. May the Story find you, through every painful passage, at home with him in the end. May you delight in his love and exalt in his victory then. May you always aspire to live as a character you admire. May you know the delight of finding out that the Story isn't mainly about you. May you know and love the truth and be brave to obey it. May you make a hard dart at the darkness with whatever light you bring, reflecting, like the moon, a light far brighter than your own. May God give you joy!

Grandview, West Virginia

THE
GREEN
EMBER